D0997970

Born in Scotland in 1910, Jane Duncan spent her childhood in Glasgow, going for holidays to the Black Isle of Inverness. After taking her degree at Glasgow University she moved to England in 1931, and when war broke out she was commissioned in the WAAF and worked in Photographic Intelligence.

After the war she moved to the West Indies with her husband, who appears as 'Twice' Alexander in her novels. Shortly after her husband's death, she returned to Jemimaville near Cromarty, not far from her grandparents' croft which inspired the beloved 'Reachfar'. Jane Duncan died in 1976.

Also by Jane Duncan

MY FRIENDS THE MISS BOYDS
MY FRIEND MURIEL

and published by Corgi Books

MY FRIEND MONICA

Jane Duncan

CORGI BOOKS

MY FRIEND MONICA

A CORGI BOOK 0 552 12876 7

Originally published in Great Britain by
Macmillan London Limited

Macmillan London edition published 1960
Macmillan London edition reprinted 1983
Corgi edition published 1987

Copyright © Jane Duncan 1960

Conditions of sale

1. This book is sold subject to the condition
 that it shall not, by way of trade *or otherwise*,
be lent, re-sold, hired out or otherwise *circulated*
in any form of binding or cover other than that
in which it is published *and without a similar
condition including this condition being imposed
on the subsequent purchaser.*
2. This book is sold subject to the Standard
Conditions of sale of Net books and may not be
re-sold in the UK below the net price fixed by
the publishers for the book.

This book is set in 10/11 pt Plantin

Corgi Books are published by Transworld Publishers Ltd.,
61-63 Uxbridge Road, Ealing, London W5 5SA, in Australia by
Transworld Publishers (Aust.) Pty. Ltd., 15-23 Helles Avenue,
Moorebank, NSW 2170, and in New Zealand by Transworld
Publishers (N.Z.) Ltd., Cnr. Moselle and Waipareira Avenues,
Henderson, Auckland.

Reproduced, printed and bound in Great Britain by
Hazell Watson & Viney Limited,
Member of the BPCC Group,
Aylesbury, Bucks

Dear A.M.,

As you have always liked the story of *My Friend Monica*, will you please accept this dedication of it from your affectionate friend Jane?

CONTENTS

Part I

Part I

PART I

Monica and I first met in the Operations Room of an Air Force station during the 1939-1945 war, and for posterity, if posterity can stop running for a moment and make a pause to read, I wish to record that around the end of 1940 you could have quite an exciting — not to say hair-raising — time in an Operations Room of the Air Force. The German Air Force had tumbled to the idea that if they could reduce the British Operations Rooms to rubble the British forces in the air might be less efficient, so one grey dawn Monica and I crawled out of a heap of rubble somewhere in Kent, ate some sardines out of a tin, got into a lorry, and after a couple of hours were decanted to report for duty at the next Operations Room on the rubble schedule. By the next faint dawn we were able to spite the German Air Force by walking out of this hole in the ground by the normal tunnel entrance and going to the quarters allotted to us, but by this time I felt and looked like so much rubble myself — one of those nasty, crumbly bits with a few clots of damp, disused cobweb hanging on to it. Monica did not. She had taken off most of her clothes and was washing herself at a scullery sink while I sat on a wooden coal bunker, waiting my turn.

'Monica,' I said, 'you are the most beautiful female I have ever seen.'

She smiled at me, spat out some toothpaste and said:

'Thank you very much. The sink is all yours.'

It was true, what I had said, and after I had washed and we were lying in our cots smoking before going to sleep, Monica said: 'I liked how you said that — beautiful female. One gets so sick of the "most attractive", the "terribly attractive" and the "my *dear*, too *devastatingly* attractive" — it always makes me feel that I am being likened to a mere magnet — you know, two legs joined together by not much else. So dull ... Well, see you when the fun starts again. Sleep well, N.N.'

'Same to you, M.M., Mere Magnet!' I said.

'N.N.' as a name for me at that time stood for 'No Nerves'. I am not a brave or a courageous person in any way, but I do not happen to have the type of nerves that the German Air Force could play tunes on. Indeed, as best I can describe it, I, in relation to the German Air Force, was a fiddle with no strings at all, so that every time they dropped a bomb with a large noise all the response I made was a sort of dull, unimaginative 'bonk' when some rubble fell round me and then I went on with my quiet, inoffensive existence. Now, I lay in my cot and watched Monica fall asleep and I thought of what she had said about the word 'attractive'. It was true. Everyone used it of her, but at this moment in her life, particularly, it had no meaning at all. She was simply beautiful, with a beauty that nothing could soil or even reduce.

Now, before I say any more about Monica I have to tell you a few facts about myself, and after I have told you these facts I am going to leave you to find out about me for yourself as you read about me and Monica. There is no point in my saying to you that I am thus and so, and I shall avoid saying such things unless they slip out by mistake. You do not see me as I see me and all the saying of 'I am' in the world will not make you see me so. So all I am going to say about me is that I was born in 1910, in the Highlands of Scotland, and named Janet Sandison; that in 1939 I joined the Women's Auxiliary Air Force; that during my service in it I met My Friend Monica, and after the end of the war in 1945 did not see her again until late in 1947 — a lapse of two years — when I wrote to her to tell her that I was about to get married.

The man I was about to marry was — and still is, for that matter — named Twice Alexander, because his Christian name is Alexander and his surname is Alexander again, and it is just as well, I feel, that his parents did not feel called upon to give him a middle name. And at the time this story opens he was Works Manager at Slaters' Engineering Works at Ballydendran in south-west Scotland, where I was secretary both to Mr. Slater, the main shareholder, and to the company, and it was nearly lunchtime on a Saturday in early October.

'Telegram for you, Miss Sandison,' a typist said, coming in and laying a fat envelope on my desk.

'That's not a telegram,' Twice told her. 'That's a parcel!'

'Bobbie Murray brought it on his bicycle,' she assured us solemnly, in proof that it must be a telegram.

I went on locking up my desk and safe for the weekend and nodded at the fat envelope. 'That's from My Friend Monica,' I told Twice. 'Open it and let's see what she has to say.'

Five or six sheets burst out of the frail envelope. 'She must be demented!' Twice said.

'I've never thought it out,' I told him. 'You see, she says that letter-writing represents a capital investment in paper, stamps, ink, pens — not to mention a desk or a table or something and a place to put it, while if you use the telegraph you get all the materials for free and don't get ink-stains on your carpets.'

'You mean she does all her correspondence by telegram?'

'Mostly. She actually writes to *me* occasionally, though.'

He spread out the crumpled sheets and started to read. 'Good God! The impudent cow! Listen to this — "Entirely disapprove this contract with person with repetitive name is he not the very Scottish character with the temper query have you no sense query you are no longer seventeen stop go no further repeat no further with this until I arrive stop you have enough temper for two stop meet London plane Prestwick Saturday six evening stop am flabber hyphen gasted stop be at Prestwick Monica" . . . Well, I'll be damned!'

Accustomed as I was to Monica, I must say that I felt a little shattered and wished hard that I had opened her telegram

13

myself, but then I took a pull at myself, telling myself that if Twice and I were going to quarrel about a little thing like the eccentricities of Monica there would not be much point in our getting married at all.

'Twice,' I said, 'if we are going to be at Prestwick by six we had better get going.'

'Prestwick?' He gave me a blank, shuttered-window sort of look.

'If I am not there she is capable of persuading the pilot to land her in Ballydendran High Street or something. She is really very nice, Twice, and I think when —'

'She makes a pretty poor first impression,' he told me. 'But I suppose that if I want you I have to take your friends. All right. Let's have lunch and get off.'

We did not talk very much on the way down to the airport. I had a shivering feeling in the pit of my stomach all the way. Monica had been my friend for some very trying years, Twice was the only man I had ever loved, and desperately did I want them to like one another, that my own relationship with either and both of them might not be tarnished. You cannot write about your friends without writing about yourself. You, yourself, and I, myself, are terribly important to you and to me, and when we think of the people we love we are really thinking of ourselves and of how everything that happens to *them* is actually happening to *us* in that it must affect us in some way. So I had collywobbles all the way to Prestwick and did not talk very much, but I remember that at one point on the way Twice asked me: 'How old is this battle-axe we are going to meet?'

'Monica? Only thirty. She is seven years younger than I am.'
'Oh?'

'But a lot older in some ways, if you see what I mean.'
'I don't.'

'You could if you would, Twice. Some people are born old in some ways. Years of age have nothing to do with it. Monica is years and years older than me in worldly experience and in knowing how to deal with people and so on. It's a sort of race inheritance. Her people have always dealt with people and by instinct they know about it as soon as they're born, I think.

14

She's younger than I am, though, a lot,' I boasted, 'about knowing what crop will grow in what ground and whether a cow is in calf or not!'

'How is she on engineering, which is all *I* know about?'

'She will probably think you a rude mechanic,' I told him, and he even laughed.

'And she'll be about right, if I don't feel different by the time we meet this aeroplane. At the moment I feel like a potentially very rude mechanic indeed.'

My stomach continued to have its fluttering feelings and everything became more and more unreal, so that by the time we entered the terminal building at the airport I was not treading the ground of my own familiar world at all. Mind you, apart altogether from anxiety as to whether two people you love will hate each other on sight it is my opinion that airport terminals are very, very unreal sort of places. By that I mean, I think, that by the time that airport architecture was invented I was too old to accept it, so that in buildings at airports, and in the Royal Festival Hall in London, and in the United Nations Building in New York, I always have a feeling of having outlived my era or of having inadvertently taken a trip to another planet. This feeling was not lessened on this evening by watching the antics of a 'film startlet' who was making the most, for the benefit of the gentlemen of the press, of her departure to the United States, while a bearded and world-famous conductor sat in a corner, quietly eating apples out of a brown-paper bag and reading a book, which the sharp-sighted Twice took pains to identify as Jane Austen's *Sense and Sensibility*. I was filled with admiration for the man who could bring his own leisure and his own truth into this shrine of speed-worship and streamlining, take over a corner of it with his bag of apples and his book, and sit there, an inviolable island of individuality, sure and secure within his own strength. *He* isn't a straw at the mercy of every wind as *you* are, I told myself. *He* doesn't feel that he ought to be eating triangular apples just because he is sitting among all this angular chromium and concrete, as *you* would. What if Twice and Monica *do* loathe each other? I bet you that man has lots of

15

friends who simply hate the sight of one another, but he simply goes on eating apples and paying no attention.

'The truly great has an aura all its own,' Twice broke into my thoughts as we walked up and down. 'Makes you feel good just to get within shouting distance of it. Our recording of Beethoven's Ninth is going to sound better than ever after this. . . . Well, here's the plane. Let's go out to the barrier before I forget my manners and smack that chorus girl's behind.'

We watched the machine come up to the front of the building, beautiful, yet ungainly, like a swan on land — ungraceful and inept, indeed, as is anything that is out of its own element. We watched the gangway wheel alongside and the door open.

'Gosh!' said Twice. 'A *real* glamorous film-star! That will put little Tootsie in her place!'

'Film-star nothing,' I said. 'That's My Friend Monica!'

'Bless my soul! If it were so, you should have told me!'

It is about such things that I find myself extraordinarily slow-witted, unimaginative and stupid. I had always known that Monica was striking in appearance, but the thought of her is so familiar to me that I felt that Twice and all my other friends who had never seen her must know when I spoke of Monica that I meant *Monica*, with the deep voice, the fine-boned good looks and the grace of movement that is her picture in my mind. Monica is not merely beautiful — she is, as the French would so accurately put it, of an elegance. When Monica was created it is as if the Sculptor woke up from a deep sleep one morning and found it was suddenly spring and said to Himself: 'Where is that woman-size lump of elegance that I put away last year to wait for an idea? Aha, here it is!' and, pushing the lump of elegance into the spring light of the window, He took up His mallet and chisel and, inspired by the freshness of dawn in the delicate green of a young birch tree, He carved out Monica.

It was natural to me that she should be the first passenger to come off the plane, the first through the landing formalities, and that she should be followed by the handsome, well-aired-looking young steward of the aircraft, who was carrying her suitcase as if it were the Holy Grail.

'Thank you so much, Pete, darling. Just stick it in that corner. See you again soon ... Well, Jan! You look blooming — and is this the character?'

'Monica! It's good to see you! Yes, this is Twice. Lady Monica Loame, Twice.''

'It's masel' that hopes Ah see ye weel, yer Leddyship,' said Twice, touching his forelock, holding out his hand and smiling at her with his teeth clenched, which is a particularly vicious-looking trick he has.

'Oh, God!' I said. 'I might as well tell you right away, Monica, that Twice happened to open your telegram and that he can be very, very awkward. I always said that that telegram thing would get you into trouble, and why you had to say —'

'That's right,' Twice said. 'Just you two girls have a nice public row right here while I put the suitcase in the car and then we'll go to the bar and have a dram.' He picked up the suitcase.

'You wouldn't be awkward, would you?' Monica asked.

He grinned down at her. 'I *was* going to be, but I've changed my mind. You find that as usual and quite in order?'

'Clever one!' she said, with her sidelong glance out of her long eyes.

'But don't be impertinent again,' he adjured her. 'Come along, both of you.'

He shoo-ed us before him like chickens in the direction of the door to the car-park, and I was so slack with tension released that I would have walked blindly over a precipice had not Monica suddenly stopped in her tracks and said: 'Sir Charles: *Where* are you going?' and fallen upon the famous conductor, who put his empty apple-bag inside his book, rose to his feet and said: 'America, my dear. And what brings you to Scotland?'

'Visiting. Gadding about. Janet, Sir Charles Acton. Miss Sandison, Sir Charles; and this is Mr. Alexander.'

He shook hands with us gravely and with a penetrating glance from his brilliant little eyes. I do not think that either of us spoke a word.

'But you aren't travelling alone?' Monica asked him

'Oh dear me, no. Trudie and Miss G. are in the place over there having coffee. You have been out of London lately?'

'Paris. I'm home now, though. I went over to be with Gerald for a bit . . . I think that's your flight they're calling.'

'Oh.' He picked up his brief-case. 'I'd better find Trudie. Have a nice visit, child. A delightful country, Scotland. Goodbye.'

He moved away towards the restaurant, and Monica and I had reached the door to the car-park before we discovered that Twice was not with us. Looking back, we saw him stock-still in the middle of the hall, the suitcase at his feet.

'Hi, there! *Come* on!' Monica called.

He started as if out of a trance, picked up the suitcase and hurried towards us, put his free arm round Monica, lifted her from her feet, kissed her soundly on the temple and then set her back on the concrete. 'All is forgiven you! Come and have a dram! Two drams!' He plunged, suitcase and all, into the bar. 'Never have I felt so exhilarated! What will you have?'

'Whisky, please, if they have it,' said Monica. 'I take it that you like music and admire Sir Charles? He is an old pet, setting the touch of genius apart. He and Trudie are our next-door neighbours in London. I am not madly musical myself, but, anyway, he's a nice person . . . Well, when and where is this wedding to be? As chief bridesmaid, I am interested.'

'Oh, it's not going to be that sort of wedding!' I said hastily. 'I am too old to leap up an aisle in white satin!'

'Age apart,' said Monica, 'you are not the type, anyway, any more than I'd be a success in pastel chiffon and sweet peas. But I take it that the thing is to be legal, with witnesses?'

'We have planned nothing at all yet,' I said. 'We thought up at home at Reachfar would be the place. My family would like to be at the wedding, but, as you know, it's not a travelling family.'

'Wise people. All this flying round the globe is the death of

18

real family life. My family isn't a family any more — it's a cosmopolitan club and rather a boring one at that . . . Where is *your* home stamping-ground, Twice?'

'Berwickshire, but my family is practically extinct, except for my old cousin Alex in Edinburgh.'

'How old is he?' she asked.

'Too old for *you*, my voracious pretty,' he told her, and she laughed. 'He is really old — lives back in Edinburgh's claret days among his law books.'

'He is not that lovely thing, a Writer to the Signet?'

'He is precisely that. Why?'

'Bless you a thousand times! I have always wanted to meet a Writer to the Signet. Swop you for sir Charles!'

'Done!' said Twice. 'Any time. Have another dram.'

'As for *when* we'll get married,' I said, feeling a little neglected, 'that's another matter. We have to find a place to live and somebody to do my job at Slaters' — which reminds me that *you*'ve still got to find a place to sleep tonight. You might have given us a little notice, Monica!'

'I couldn't. I only got back to London last night and didn't read your letter until this morning. But, anyway, I'm staying with Uncle Andy. The Crook is quite near your Bally-what's-is, isn't it?'

'Sir Andrew Craig of the Crook?' Twice asked.

'Yes. That's the one.'

'I didn't know he was a relation of yours,' I said.

'By marriage he is, only he's a widower now. Besides, how *could* you know? My family is related to half the population of Great Britain, not to mention Ireland and most of the continent of Europe.' She turned to Twice. 'A great-aunt of mine married a Habsburg — you know what that does to a family.'

'Not precisely,' Twice said solemnly, 'but I can imagine.'

'It's their noses that are so awful.'

'Never mind,' he consoled her. 'The nose influence didn't get to *you*. — But are you sure you'll be all right at the Crook?'

'You mean Uncle Andy being dotty? He isn't, you know, when you know him. It's just that there are a lot of things and people that he doesn't want to be bothered with and he escapes into dottiness. In actual fact, he is very clever.'

'I know — the Craig valve and so on,' Twice said. 'But he has a local reputation as a mad genius.'

'He invented it, just like the valve. He is a selfish old brute, really, and doesn't want to do County work or anything, so he hides behind this reputation as a crackpot. You can't have met him or you would have seen it for yourself.'

'But that's the point!' I said. 'He is a local legend — nobody has met him!'

'All part of the act,' said Monica and began to giggle.

'What now?' I asked. 'That's only your second drink!'

'That word legend,' she said. 'When I first began to read I pronounced it "leg end" — The Leg End of Till Eulenspiegel. I still think of it that way. I can't help it.'

'What a fool you are!' I told her, but without rancour, for many a wartime hour had she and I beguiled with discussions about words.

'Tell me,' Twice said, 'Why do you treat flabbergasted as a hyphenated word to the point of paying extra to hyphenate it in a telegram?'

She shook back the satin curtain of her red-gold hair and looked at him gravely. 'Because it so obviously *is*! It can only mean that a person is completely gasted up with flabber — *you* know, stuffed up to the throat with cotton wool or something.'

'Rubbish!' I said. 'It's a nautical sort of thing like keel-hauling or belaying! A person who is flabbergasted is hoist with his own petard when the ship is going round the Horn before the mast!'

'You are quite wrong!' she told me decisively. 'Flabber is obviously a substance like blubber or slobber — a stuffing-up sort of substance. In fact, it should be spelled P-H-labber, like phlegm.'

'Look,' said Twice, 'let's all have another dram as a gargle and have a little more chat about your Uncle Andy.'

'I'll always have another dram,' Monica said, which was no more than the naked truth. Never have I seen a more willing drinker who got less drunk. 'But why chat about Uncle Andy?

I've got lots of other relations.'

'I'll tell you why,' Twice said as the drinks arrived. 'Because he owns, among other things, a row of nice, old, stone cottages called Crookmill, and Mr. Slater and I have written to him three times about them and he won't answer.'

'What do you want with Crookmill?' I asked.

'Be quiet! It was to be a wedding surprise — but if we can't get on with the surprise, there won't be any wedding. We want it for us to *live* in, you dope.'

'But it's a ruin, Twice!' I protested.

'You'd be surprised, but it isn't. I agree that it has no windows and no doors and no floors, but the walls and the roof are sound and it has its own water supply and the electric main goes past within a hundred yards of it.'

'You might have told me before, Twice Alexander!'

'It was to be a *surprise*, I told you! I was going to tell you as soon as we'd got something out of Sir Andrew.'

'You want to buy it?' Monica asked.

'Preferably, but I'd rent it on an agreement about repairs and so on.'

'No,' she said. 'We'd never get him to let it — too much trouble. But I'll make him sell it, though. Is it on the Crook Estate proper?'

'No. At least, it was, but the farms between it and the Crook House were sold off before the war. This place was an old mill, but the mill part has pretty well fallen down. Only the cottages are left.'

'It's a go,' said Monica. 'Let's have one for the road and then make for Bally-what's-is. By letter, you would never get anywhere with Uncle Andy in a thousand years. He won't write to anybody.'

'Maybe he just doesn't want strangers around his property or writing to him either,' I said, which I thought was quite a reasonable point of view. 'After all, if Crookmill were mine I might get peevish if people kept asking to buy it when I had never indicated I wanted to sell it or anything.'

Monica looked at me. 'One of the reasons I came up here to examine *him*,' she said, nodding at Twice, 'is that you are far too apt to study what everybody else wants. You want a house, don't you? So that you can get married? All right. Never mind what Uncle Andy wants. Just concentrate on what *you* want. Do you want this Crookmill place, by the way?'

'Of course!'

'And do you want this man here? Remember that time you were going to marry that type who got into the R.N.V.R. by mistake, and was always seasick, just because he told you how unhappy he was? You are sure you really *want* to get married?'

'Of course I am! Really, Monica, I don't think you realise how impossible you can be half the time —'

'Never mind that! As long as you're sure ... Where's this car of yours?'

Late at night we dropped Monica at the door of the big stone house that was known as 'The Crook', where she was met by an aged manservant who told her that the 'Maister' was attending a dinner in Glasgow and would not be back until after midnight but that a room had been prepared for her.

'Come for me in the morning,' she told us, 'and we'll look into things.'

'Well,' Twice said as we drove away, 'you two as members of the Air Intelligence must have been a riot. You didn't think to tell me that we were making an excursion into Debrett — who are her parents?'

'I just forgot about her title — one doesn't notice it much. Her parents are the Marquis and Marchioness of Beechwood, if you are interested. They are very nice. The mother gardens all the time and the father is one of these people who have been useful round embassies and the Foreign Office all his life, but he's retired now. There's a huge family of them — eight or nine. Monica has five brothers and three sisters or the other way on or one more or less. I've never sorted them out. You see, it was in the war I met her and they were all over the place and coming and going. I've been to Beechwood, but we used to go more often to her eldest sister's house in London because it was handy and there seemed to be such a mass of them and their friends in and out of there that one got muddled. Especially as Laura — that's the sister — was married to

22

Dmitri who was some sort of middle-European royalty and they had a lot of refugees coming and going and Laura had to act Her Serene Highness a lot of the time.'

'Great Heaven!' said Twice.

'It's the truth I'm telling you. That was her title. Serene Highness. It was rather trying, for, as Monica will tell you, she is neither very serene nor very high but very excitable on gin and addicted to betting on horses. It's odd, Twice. I had sort of forgotten a lot of these factual things I am telling you about Monica until now. They are so sort of — foreign to my own world. I suppose she is an odd sort of friend for somebody like me to have. It was the war, I suppose. Maybe wartime friendships are like shipboard ones — temporary and unlikely in their very nature. Yet, I don't know. It isn't really like that, for here she is, two years after.'

'It wouldn't occur to you that she might just plain *like* you?' Twice enquired.

'Do *you* like *her*, Twice?' I asked.

'I don't know. I don't know her. But one can't help being interested in and fascinated by the strange and new — wrapping her arms around Sir Charles Acton when one is so overawed that one can hardly *look* at him — especially when the strange and new is so good to look at as she is. Are they *all* good-looking?'

'I think Monica is the most beautiful of the girls — that is my opinion of those I have seen, anyway. But, in general, it is a good-looking family.'

'Money?'

'Pretty well rotten with it, I think,' I told him. 'They are in steel and ships and cotton and Lord knows what else. They seem to have *all* the gifts, including long ancestry as well as wealth and good looks. Of course, I don't know how the war and the post-war has affected them — not much, I think.'

'Monica doesn't look as if they had just sold off the spare tiara,' Twice agreed, 'but there's no telling. You and I are the sort of people who'd show it in our faces if the family pig died, but people like your friend Monica are different. A lot of claptrap gets talked about people being all God's chillun and all men being equal and only human and bilge like that. I don't hold with it. There is quality in people just as there is in anything else. Your Monica has the look and the feel of the Quality — or the Gentry, as we have it in Scotland. She wouldn't react as you or I might in any given situation.'

'She often doesn't react quite as one would expect,' I agreed.

'I am in favour of the gentry, myself.' Twice stared over the moonlit countryside. 'I was brought up in the country of the Border Dukes, surrounded by the "Big Hooses" of the local gentry — a lot of these houses are hospitals and schools and asylums now. As I see it, the hospitals, schools and asylums nip a fair bit off my salary cheque and give me no dividend of glamour in return. Hospitals are all very fine, but when I had pneumonia as a nipper I had a duchess to bring me peaches. I suppose it is a choice between peaches and penicillin — I have a certain faith in the peaches delivered by Grace, myself.'

'So have I — as long as Grace delivers them and doesn't keep them all for the ducal table.'

'That's the snag, of course. But say that only fifty per cent of people got the odd peach delivered by Grace. At least fifty per cent would have contact with and proof of the said Grace. I feel that that may be even better than the full hundred per cent who have had no contact with anything other then the impersonal hypodermic of penicillin ... The truth is that I am a reactionary, but I do believe in a system that allows of the development of an aristocracy. There ought to be Rolls-Royces among people, just as there are among cars, and the only way to develop them is by time, leisure, the expenditure of wealth and the application of selectivity.'

'The correct plural, I have always felt,' I said, 'should be Rolls-Ryce.'

'Why?'

'Because of mouse-mice.'

'Fallacious. It isn't grouse-grice. You might as well say Rolls-Rouse.'

'No, I mightn't. Rolls-Ryce *sounds* more the thing than Rolls-Royces or Rolls-Rouse when you say: "I knew a man once who had seven Rolls-Ryce".'

'Is that the sort of thing that one is likely to have to say?'

'Maybe not. But it would be nice if one *could* say Rolls-Ryce.'

'And in a trice all the nice little people that she knew would say Yice, but it couldn't have been Twice that she knew that had seven Rolls-Ryce!' Twice recited, tapping out the rhythm with his hands on the steering-wheel. 'But listen, my pet. I feel that we are a day's march nearer home. If Monica can persuade that old man into letting us have Crookmill —'

'She is very good at getting what she wants,' I said.

'Yes. That is written all over her,' Twice agreed.

The next morning, when we drove up to the Crook, Monica was sitting on top of a wooden stile that bridged the fence between the lawn and some woodland in a russet and green sweater and skirt and hand-made brown brogues, looking like a well-posed, well-taken picture of that autumn's best country wear in an expensive magazine. Her uncle was standing beside her with his back against a fence post, in a baggy, hairy, tweed suit, looking like an old sheep farmer and not in the least like an inventor of complicated valves. When Monica introduced us he glared at me in a hostile way, or so it seemed, muttered a greeting and then said to Twice: 'I've seen you before. Long time ago. Where was it?'

'I don't think so, sir. I would have remembered if we had met.'

'Well, you *haven't*! But *I* remember. Can tell you where and when it was too — in the engine-room of a ship at Clydebank in 1922 and you swore at me about some gearing and, by God, you turned out to be quite right. And you called the chief draughtsman a half-witted bastard — you were quite right about that too!' He smiled suddenly and held out his hand. 'Fine to see you again. Just come over to my workshop here — I've a little thing that will interest you. It's a little —'

'Uncle Andy, stop doddering!' said Monica. 'This man couldn't have been out of the nursery in 1922. 1922 is a quarter of a century ago.'

Sir Andrew frowned at Twice and then turned fiercely to

Monica. 'You said this fellow was an engineer —'

'It would be my father you met, sir,' Twice said. 'It sounds just like him, and I am told I resemble him very strongly.'

'There you are!' Sir Andrew told Monica triumphantly. 'It was his father! Same thing! I *knew* I had met an engineer called Alexander who was about as broad as he was long. Nurseries! Quarter-centuries! Quibbling! You women are all the same — accurate about all the wrong things.' He swung round on me. '*You* don't belong to this part of the country!' he said accusingly.

'No, Sir Andrew. My home is in Ross-shire,' I told him.

'Pretty county. Fine-looking people. Well, nice to see you — get Monica to show you the place ... Come, my boy.'

He walked away with Twice across the lawn and into the house, talking, with many gestures in the way of engineers, as he went.

'Hell!' Monica said. 'This isn't going to plan at all and we haven't much time. He's leaving for London tomorrow. He'll dodder on in that workshop until the cows come home. We'll have to take a good hard pull at him at lunch ... Feel like a walk up that hill?'

'How old is Sir Andrew?' I asked as we began to walk.

'Not so old. All that stuff about meeting Twice in 1922 is part of the act — he knew darn fine that Twice was a schoolboy in 1922 and probably guessed that it was his father he had met. He has a phenomenal memory — that's why this doddering act is so irritating. Let me see. Aunt Constance — that's Uncle Andy's wife — was three years older than Mama. Mama will be sixty-five this December. So if Aunt Constance had been alive she would have been sixty-eight, and Uncle Andy was seven years younger than Aunt Constance — it was quite a thing in the family — Aunt Constance and her "young man" from Scotland. He's not a day more than sixty-one, the old devil, although you would think, to hear him, that he had been alive and could remember the day when James Watt invented his engine.'

One of the many differences I had noticed between Monica and myself was her dispassionate attitude to her family, coupled with her intimate knowledge of the age and ancestry of every sprig of her enormous family tree and all the relations by marriage. All the family that I had ever known consisted of my paternal grandparents, my father, my mother (who died when I was ten), my uncle, my aunt, and our old handyman Tom, and I had never thought of them as individuals until I met Monica. To me these seven people had a composite entity, known in my mind — and with capital letters as 'My Family', a sure background that could be depended on always, and to react in a certain way towards myself. In the early days of the war, when I — camouflaged for the emergency, like many people and things of greater importance, as Aircraftwoman Sandison — found myself billeted in a small, requisitioned, jerry-built, damp, depressing house in company with some thirty other aircraftwomen, including a red-haired one called Aircraftwoman Loame, I found her forthright attitude to everything amusing, and it was only after we had polished many brass buttons, talked a lot of nonsense and drunk a deal of watery beer together that I saw a letter to her which had been addressed: 'No. —— Acw/I the Lady Monica Loame'. War, like death, they say, is a great leveller, but that is a statement that has the appearance of truth but not the substance. I had been attracted to Monica because she was 'different', and in spite of having a six-digit number and a set of brass buttons like all the rest of us she *was* different.

It took me a little time to reach the point where I could ask her the questions that I wanted to ask, but in the end the opportunity arose of itself when, one Saturday night, two of our colleagues in the jerry-built house came in very drunk and had a fight about an Army corporal friend of theirs, a fight with all the feline savagery that two powerful young women of Liverpool-Irish blood can bring to battle. I am a much taller and more strongly built woman than Monica, but by the time we had them separated and locked into two different rooms of the house and were picking up the torn clothing and the handfuls of hair from the floor my hands were shaking and I had a humiliating desire to vomit.

'Sit down!' Monica said. 'You are too finely bred for this sort of thing. Bitches!'

'Don't be silly,' I said, pushing a newspaper full of torn, soiled underwear into the stove in the scullery. 'Have you a match?'

'My lighter's in the pocket of my tunic. Can I borrow your soap? Mine is in the bathroom along with that cow Haggerty.' She began to wash at the scullery sink, incongruously beautiful, as usual, in nothing but a pale-pink brassière. I began to laugh.

'What the hell is there to laugh at?' she snapped.

'You, in the brassière.' There was a loud crash. 'Oh, damn! Now the black-out's fallen down!'

Monica collapsed, naked and shivering, on to the cold stone floor to be out of sight while I struggled with and pushed at the ill-fitting black-out frame for the window until it was restored to position.

'My God!' she said as she pulled on striped flannel pyjamas, 'this is the end! Barracks or no barracks, I'm going to have a drink and so are you.' She hauled her kitbag out of the cupboard, delved into its depths and came up with a pair of dark-blue 'issue' knickers and unwrapped from their folds a large, heavy, monogrammed, silver flask. 'Whisky, for great emergency,' she said. 'Provided by my mama. And this is my opinion of great emergency. Where did you put our mugs?'

'Here they are. But, Monica, what a magnificent flask!'

She unscrewed the cap and held the flask up for a moment, looking at it. 'It *is* rather Imperial Train,' she said. 'It is one of a set of six that live in a leather case, the whole presented to Mama's great-uncle by a Tsar of Russia. Here you are. Get some water from the scullery.'

'I should think the Tsar is turning in his grave,' I said, coming back with the water in an old condensed-milk tin. 'This is no place for that flask — or for you either.'

'Cheers!' said Monica, tucking herself into her cot with her mug of whisky and water and lighting herself a cigarette. 'You are quite wrong, you know. I am better at this sort of thing — the coping with the bitches, I mean — than you are. I didn't feel like fainting as you did. Basically you and I are the same sort of people. In plain words, we are thorough-bred, in the literal sense, in that we are both of unmixed blood as to class or of a mixture so far back that it no longer counts. The only difference is that in your case it was an accident of nature, and in mine it has been planned and contrived. There were Loames at Beechwood before the Conquest and they were determined to hold what they had and they did it by fighting and by breeding more Loames to maintain the fighting and the holding on. It is as simple as that, if you are interested.'

'That may all be true,' I said, 'but this —' I waved my mug at the shabby plaster and raised my eyes towards a loud bang followed by a stream of oaths from Haggerty in the bathroom. 'It's a far, far cry from Beechwood, Aircraftwoman Class One Lady Monica Loame.'

'No further than from that farm called Reachfar in Ross-shire that I saw pictures of, Janet Sandison, lady. In fact, not so far. I bet I have seen more people like Haggerty at Beechwood than you have seen at Reachfar. You see, the thing about planned breeding is that the plans don't always work out. There have been a lot of very unpleasant sports among the Loames down the centuries. Nature makes a much better job, left to herself, only there are very few pockets of the world left now where nature gets a free hand. You fascinate me, Janet, for you and your kind — the few there are — are about the last of a race. The wag of the world is against you. I bet all the girls up in your village are walking out with Poles or something. Damn this war!'

'It's Czechs they have up there and some Indians with mule transport,' I said in an automatic way, for my mind was engaged with what she had been saying of my race.

'Oh, well, let's have another tot. There's a dance in the officers' mess tonight so there's no chance of old Frisky coming round Girl-Guiding.'

'Monica, what was your life like — before the war, I mean?'

'Nursery, schoolroom, a convent in Paris, a little travel — France, Switzerland, Italy — all very dull and disciplined — but how exactly did you mean?'

29

'You'll probably think this very naïve, but I cannot imagine being a little girl who is the Lady Monica from the day of her birth!'

'The old handle?' She laughed. 'It's just one's name, like your Janet. The important part of my name is Loame, like your Sandison. The title is newish — only about three hundred years old. Not that I would scorn it and go around calling myself Miss Loame in a loud voice for no reason like some of these affected asses. Isn't it odd that people seem to think that you can only be affected in an aspiring direction? You can be affected in a down-spiring — is that a word? — direction just the same. The title is something I was born with, and — well, it is part of what I am, I suppose. I say, I've never talked to anyone like you before. What is it in you that makes one know what one thinks in a clear way that one never knew before?'

'Probably the great white light of my ignorance,' I said, and she laughed.

'That's worth another tot on the Tsar! Here's to him, poor old blighter, and to Mama's great-uncle too, the amoral old goat! Thank God Mama didn't inherit the promiscuity of that side of her family!'

'Monica!' I protested.

'What? Some of that family were satyrs — nothing was safe from them! It's the truth! Oh, I see what you mean. But that's part of the difference between you and me, Janet. You don't think of your people as *people* — your family is an entity of which you are a part. You are somehow much more *intimate* with your people than I am with mine.'

'I should think that's because of the upbringing,' I said. 'You see, until I was about seventeen I think I had almost every meal with my family, worked with one or another of them when I wasn't at school, sat with them in the evenings when I wasn't doing my lessons. You didn't do any of these things. You went from the nursery to the schoolroom, from the schoolroom to the convent — I see yours as a system of training which has evolved almost accidentally to produce a ruling class, to produce leaders. The system puts you on your own feet at an early age, teaches you to stand alone without personal influence from your parents, so that later on you will be able to administer your inheritance or what-have-you.'

'That's a fine theory, but the system doesn't always work. And, anyway, look at us here now. If your theory worked *I'd* be the leader of the bunch of hooligans in this dump.' She glanced upwards in the direction of Haggerty. 'But I'm not. *You* are the Big White Chief!'

'Oh, rot!'

'It isn't. *I* can't make Porter wash her underwear!'

'Oh, that's partly age — I'm a lot older than you and Porter — and partly because you are too polite to her. It is merely my specialised knowledge of the right insults to hurl at her. No. Your system of training tends to produce stronger and more original people than mine. People with my sort of background tend often to be a sort of copy or reflection of their parents — in thought, morality and everything else — a stunted growth that has been mentally cramped from birth.'

'I'd rather have that, I think, than some of our originals like the cousin who went off and married an illiterate mulatto. Oh, well.' She stared at the cracked ceiling. 'I wonder why it is that that word mulatto always makes me think of extremly large, floppy breasts shaped like rugby footballs?'

'Association, I should think,' I said.

'No, rugby — the long sort of ball.'

'Association of ideas, I meant — although when I hear the word mulatto I always visualise a long, snaky whip of some kind for driving a team of mules.'

'What an absurd notion! Why?'

'No more absurd than rugby football breasts,' I said.

Looking back on it, Monica and I talked our way through the war. Late in 1940 we were both commissioned into the Intelligence branch and sent to what was known in the current slang of the time as a 'hush-hush' unit, where leaves were few and widely spaced in time, and in the off-duty hours there was little to do except walk, talk, smoke and drink, although the last, by a probably providential condition of wartime shortage, was limited.

31

Historians of the future might, I think, reasonably take the view that war was a normal condition of life for the people who lived through the first half of the twentieth century, but my own experience convinces me that, in fact, peace is still our accepted norm, because the years from 1939 until 1945 were regarded by most of us as an interlude, a departure from the ordinary conditions of life to which in the fullness of time we would return. Monica had the effect of intensifying this feeling for me, for her presence as an intimate friend in my life was as unlikely, as exotic and as certainly episodic as would be the perching of a bird of paradise in the old rowan tree in our back garden at Reachfar.

In the autumn of 1945, when we were both demobilised, I said goodbye to her with sadness and went up to my home for a month's holiday before taking up my appointment at Ballydendran, but just after I left my home Monica called there, on her way south from Skye, stayed for a weekend, enslaved my father and my uncle, made allies of my aunt and old Tom, and left for London the firmly established friend of my family. If you knew my family, you would recognise this for the tour de force that it was. My family has very firm ideas about the stations in life to which people have been called, and firmer ideas still about the duty of people to remain in those stations, but the gap was bridged without loss of integrity or dignity on either side. My father even went so far as to say that 'that Monica was just as nice a lassie as he had ever come across'. When my father called Monica a nice lassie I was amazed that he should apply such a phrase to what he thinks of as 'the gentry', for his normal attitude to the gentry is that he does not know enough about them to express opinions on them, so that thereafter my own view of Monica was coloured by the fact that my father had said that she was 'a nice lassie', for I have a great respect for some of the opinions of my father.

Life would be much simpler if it were not so interwoven, if one were less susceptible to influence, if my relationship with Monica were just a simple 'me-and-Monica', but to achieve a state like this I would have to live my life in a cell like the Venerable Bede, in which case I would never have met Monica, anyway.

Well, here were Monica and I walking up this hill, and I was thinking back to the time I met her and thinking further back than that, too, for as soon as I am walking in the open, or indeed when I am in any place I like or when I am in serious trouble, I tend to find myself thinking of my home and my childhood. Maybe everyone does this and it is nothing new, but I have read of many people who were unhappy in their childhood, and it seems to have had the effect of making them much more mature and grown-up people than I am. They seem to have got away from their childhood and to have put it behind them, while mine is always with me still, ready to come to the forefront at sight of a dandelion with its white wig of seeds, a little girl in woollen gloves, or the rain slanting like steel knitting-needles against a background of evergreens. This 'having put away childish things' was a major difference between me and Monica. She seemed to have done it. I had not. And even now, I think, some of my childish things are with me still.

'Monica,' I said now as we climbed the hill, 'it was nice of you to call at Reachfar that time in 1945. My family were thrilled and simply loved it, and they still talk about it.'

'And I was thrilled and simply loved it and still think about it,' she said.

'You must go up again when you have nothing better to do,' I said.

'I will. I long to go. But there are always so many *things*. I'd like to go when *you* were there, though. I found some of your places for myself. I found the Thinking Place quite easily, and the Picnic Pond, of course, and the Stalwart Tree, but I wasn't sure about the Waving Tree.'

'It's older now and not so slender and wavy-in-the-wind as it used to be about thirty years ago when I named it,' I said.

'And George and Tom laughed like anything when the clock wound itself up and started to strike and I said: "Ippi-*tee*! Ippi-*tee*!" . . . And Tom told me another of your sound-words.'

'Oh? What?' My 'sound-words', like the Ippi-*tee* of the

33

whirr-and-silver chime of the kitchen clock at Reachfar, were so early in my life that I had forgotten many of them. 'Was it *Yaw*-aw-took?'

'No. Pet-*oh*-nya!'

'Throwing a stone down the well! . . . Did you throw one down and hear it?'

'Yes. Tom let me throw two down . . . What was *Yaw*-aw-took?'

'The door of the kitchen cupboard closing. It sticks on the floor at the bottom a little — "Yaw — aw" — and then clicks shut with a sharp "took!" . . . I can remember a lot more of the sound-words when I am actually at Reachfar, though.'

'That's part of why I'd like to go there when you are there . . . Of course, it will be different, now.'

'Different? Why?' I asked.

She glanced sidewise at me. 'Be your age, my sweet! Your husband is not going to want *me* hanging about going Ippi-*tee* and *Yaw*-aw-took all the time!'

'What a fool you are!' I said, and we laughed and climbed on up the hill.

'Your Twice is a most prepossessing character,' she said suddenly when we were sitting on the summit.

'I'm glad you think so,' I said awkwardly. I *felt* awkward, for I had never discussed Twice with anyone before — in my mind he was the most private of thoughts and emotions, a part of myself so sensitive and delicate of fibre, balance and construction that it must be cherished inwardly, not bandied about in the market of discussion.

'I should think, though,' she continued, as if she were discussing a piece of furniture or a length of tweed, 'he'd be most frightfully cussed.'

'He is,' I said, 'but then I am fairly cussed myself.' I thought it absurd and impertinent that *she* should, on a few hours' acquaintance, be attempting to describe Twice to *me*.

'No one could call him handsome,' she went on thoughtfully, looking away into the distance and talking as if to herself. 'Although the eyes are beautiful —'

'I rather go for the teeth, myself,' I broke in with an edge of

34

sarcasm on her reverie. 'I'm not marrying a pair of eyes or a set of teeth!'

She turned to look at me, her face empty of expression. 'You don't have to tune in the old temper,' she told me with a blank look. 'This marriage idea of yours is something of a surprise to one and one has to adjust to it.'

It was something of a surprise to me, myself, that at the age of thirty-seven I had found a man that I wanted to marry, and still more of a surprise that he should want to marry *me*, but what woman is going to admit to a thing like that? After all, one has one's pride. 'What's so surprising about it?' I asked belligerently; and then, because I was afraid she might haul off and tell me in a few plain words, I went on hastily: 'Anyway, there it is. I'm getting married. Shall we go back?'

She rose and began to walk beside me down the hill. 'As long as you know what you're doing,' she said. 'Anyway, don't say you haven't been warned!' Her tone was only quarter-serious.

'Old Gypsy Loame!' I said. 'I'll cross your palm with silver when we get back to the Crook!'

But I did not, for when we reached the house Twice had the promise of the cottages at Crookmill from Sir Andrew, and Sir Andrew had Twice firmly enmeshed in plans for their rehabilitation; and during lunch Monica and I felt like a quantity of flotsam or jetsam or something equally unamusing and unwanted.

Now, I was brought up to the idea that when 'the men' were talking, 'the women' sat quietly and did not interfere, but Monica came of a different tradition, and when Sir Andrew said: '. . . and this end would be the kitchen —' she said: 'Oh no it wouldn't!'

'What d'you mean, no?' he barked.

'Just what anyone else would mean. NO. In the negative. And to develop a little further, I think it is time you boys came out of the realm of theory. Why don't we all go and *see* this place?'

After a few looks of wild surmise on the faces of Sir Andrew and Twice and some discussion, this was decided to be a reasonable idea, so we drove about four miles in the sharp autumn sunshine, and I saw, for the first time, my new home.

Of course, I had seen Crookmill before. I had seen it as a row of low, grey-stone, broken-down cottages at the end of a short rough road by the course of a stream, showing nothing to the main road but a blank, defiant gable wall, but there are many ways of seeing things and one of the most extraordinary of these ways is suddenly to see something as your own, something that hitherto had no personal significance. When we had bumped up the steep rough road beside the little burn that gurgled over its rocky course, we left the car where the road ended in an irregular patch of grass and crossed a rotting little wooden bridge to go through the gateless gap in the wall that enclosed the cottage gardens. These were rank with nettles, docks and run-out gooseberry bushes; the roughly boarded windows of the building looked like a row of blind eyes. Nothing, had it been the possession of someone else, could have had less appeal, but suddenly, taking it for my own, I had both love and pride for it.

'Monica!' I said. 'We've got four front doors! I bet that even at Beechwood you haven't got *four* front doors!'

Suddenly we all — even Sir Andrew — burst out laughing, a joyous peal in which the hill burn seemed to join as it chuckled on its way and it became a moment of pure happiness in every sense — sound and sight, the smell of frost-bitten bracken, the feel of Twice's tweed sleeve, the taste of joy on the tongue amid the laughter of friends.

'Have you thought,' Twice asked when we had fallen to silence, 'of coming out of one front door into a snowdrift and in through another to get to the bathroom?'

'*Il faut arranger tout ça!*' said Monica, who tends to revert to her French convent youth in moments of enthusiasm. 'Let's break our way in and have a look!'

'There are ways in round the back,' said Twice. 'I've been here before. Come on.'

The row of cottages consisted of eight rooms in all, with four front doors, four small front halls, four back doors and four little lean-to sculleries at intervals along the back wall.

'All fearfully *parti-carré!*' said Monica. 'And I suppose that once there were four dear little inconveniences at the bottoms of these four back gardens? Tell me, what in the world are all these great wooden boxes built into every room?'

'Beds,' said Sir Andrew.

'Beds? You mean for horses?'

'Don't be a fool, woman! Have you never heard of a box bed?'

'No,' said Monica.

'God above us!' Sir Andrew stepped between a pair of the wooden walls that went from floor to ceiling at right angles to the stone walls of the room. 'This had a platform about four feet from the floor, the mattress lay on that — feathers, as a rule — and when you went to bed you climbed in and shut the big doors that were in front here — very secure and warm.'

'And then somebody cleared out the asphyxiated corpses in the morning?' Monica enquired.

'Asphyxiated rubbish!' said Sir Andrew. 'Over two hundred and fifty cubic feet in here! People in these days went for comfort, not fads!' He turned to Twice. 'Well, my boy, I must say I wouldn't have thought of trying to convert it, but once these scullery passages are joined together in a continuous passage you are well on the way. It's a fine old building — I'd like to see it in use again.'

'Well, you might have answered the man's letters!' said Monica.

'I thought he was a rambling club or a hostelling youth or something. I don't hold with them. If he had told me he was thinking of getting married — well, what do you think, my boy?'

'I want it, sir. Eh, Flash?'

'Yes, please,' I said.

'All right. I'll get my lawyer fellow to come down from Glasgow and we'll come to a bargain. Something reasonable, if you will agree to make these drawings I mentioned for me. My eyes are not what they were. That's settled ... Now, what about this man Slater you were telling me about? I'd like to meet him.'

'We could go there now, Twice,' I said. 'Mrs. Slater loves to have people for tea on Sundays — that is, if they're at home,' I added in a tone that is private to Twice and myself.

'No point in driving to the other side of Ballydendran to find an empty house,' said Twice, catching on at once. 'I tell you what — you can telephone from the cross-roads and see.'

Sir Andrew and Twice got into the front of Twice's old Bentley and Monica and I got into the back.

Mr. Slater, whose employees Twice and I were, and his wife were delightful people and very good friends of ours, but I knew that our visit would be spoiled for Mrs. Slater if we suddenly arrived at her house and presented two titled people without warning, especially when one of them was the locally legendary 'daft' Sir Andrew Craig of the Crook. Mrs. Slater was a pretty woman of about sixty who looked as if she were about forty-five, and I have never known a woman who was more completely the hospitable housewife. She was a miraculously efficient housekeeper who never seemed to be in either a hurry or a muddle. Her house, a small modern one and the pride of her soul, seemed always to have been newly lifted out of an Ideal Homes exhibition and set down in its prim, immature garden on the outskirts of Ballydendran, and she loved to meet new people in her own home where she could ply them with endless food and drink. She would never forgive me if I did not bring My Friend Monica to Glendale, but, equally, she would never forgive me if I brought Lady Monica Loame as if she were just any ordinary Miss Loame. From the kiosk at the cross-roads I made the call.

'Hello, Mrs. Slater — it's Janet!'

'Lo and behold!' she said.

This being her customary opening gambit and her frequent use of the phrase 'wonderful to relate' and her Christian name being Mirabel had long ago caused her to be known privately between Twice and myself as 'Mirabile Dictu'.

'Well, now,' her pretty voice went on, 'what are you two up to today?'

'Mrs. Slater, Sir Andrew Craig is going to sell us Crookmill!'

'Wonderful to relate! My goodness, I *am* pleased!'

'And listen. We've got Sir Andrew with us now and he wants to meet Mr. Slater; and his niece Lady Monica Loame is here too. Can we bring them to Glendale?'

'My goodness gracious! Oh, Janet, I've only got the one fresh cake and the sponge is cut into already. I *knew* I should have made these tarts yesterday — but, just a minute, I've still got that tin of biscuits that Lizzie sent from America. My goodness! What did you say the niece's name was?'

'Lady Monica Loame.'

'Oh!'

'I knew her when I was in the Air Force. She was in it too.'

'My goodness! Well, why I am standing here talking, I don't know! Daddy and I will be pleased to see you all. I was just saying what a dull Sunday it was and it such a nice day. Well, just you come on over as soon as you like.'

It took less than half an hour to reach Glendale, but by the time we arrived and went into the bright, lavishly ornamented, brilliantly clean sitting-room, the dining-room table on the other side of the hall was groaning with food on the splendour of a lace cloth and the silver teapot was glittering in the evening light.

'Lo and behold!' Mrs. Slater greeted us in her front porch as if we were the last people in the world that she expected to see. 'Isn't this just splendid! I *do* enjoy it when people come in on a Sunday. And this is your friend, Janet?'

'Yes, Lady Monica Loame, Mrs. Slater, and Sir Andrew Craig. Mr. Slater, Sir Andrew.'

'Come away in! Come away in!' Mr. Slater, white-haired, pink-cheeked and beaming, added to the welcome. 'Mother was fussing about not having enough tea, but we never died a winter yet in this house ... And so you've got your house, lassie?' he said to me as we went into the sitting-room.

'She's got *four* houses!' said Monica. 'And with eight box beds in them!'

'Lady Monica had never seen a box bed before,' I explained.

'Oh, but there's queerer than that this side o' the Border, Lady Monica,' Mr. Slater told her. 'Have you ever seen a jawbox?'

39

'Oh, but I know that one!'

'Daddy!' said Mrs. Slater, shocked. 'What words to be teaching to Lady Monica!'

'It's Glasgow for the kitchen sink,' said Monica.

'Well! And how did *you* come to know that?'

'Our head gardener at Beechwood — that's my home — is from Ayrshire and he knows a lot of words from all over Scotland and he used to teach them to my sisters and me.'

Monica's out-turned charm had the Slaters enthralled. The visit was a tremendous success, and my feeling of happiness swelled and deepened until it seemed to fill the universe, and my stupid Highland heart, which is always aware of the twilight at the edges of the world, was afraid and defiant by turns until I felt breathless.

After tea Sir Andrew, Mr. Slater and Twice got into a happy engineering huddle, and Mrs. Slater, Monica and I talked about Crookmill — or at least Mrs. Slater and Monica did most of the talking while I sat back and thought that, after all the tumult and the shouting of their planning had died away, Twice and I would get together and do exactly what we pleased with Crookmill.

And that is what happened. Twice and I planned to get married at the beginning of December, by which time we hoped to have at least a good part of Crookmill in a habitable condition; and although as part of the aftermath of war essential materials such as timber and piping were in short supply, goodwill and enthusiasm can accomplish miracles. Twice is nothing if not an enthusiast and a potent begetter of goodwill into the bargain. At times, it seemed to me, especially on Saturday afternoons and Sundays, the entire craftsman potential of Slaters' Works was concentrated on Crookmill, some laying flooring, some jointing water pipes, some glazing windows, while the father-in-law of the Assembly Shop foreman, who was the best amateur gardener in Ballydendran, bossed a squad of labourers who were clearing the garden, and old Willie, the accountant from the works, bullied his son-in-law, who was a master carpenter at the local timber yard, into faster and faster production of window-frames and doors.

All this good-natured activity was managed and controlled by Twice as Master of Works, although he concentrated most of his energy and attention on the main structural section, which consisted of an old stonemason who lived with his spinster daughter in a cottage on Sir Andrew's estate in idle luxury, on the lavish allowance made to him by a son who had gone to America thirty years before and had done very well for himself — and, by his generosity, for his family. This old man was very bent, very wizened and very, very bad-tempered and despised the three labourers provided for his assistance in the work of joining the four sculleries into a continuous passage along the back of the house.

The first Saturday that Sir Andrew brought him along in his car, took him to the back of the building and explained to him what we wanted to do with the sculleries, he smoked his short pipe and spat and said nothing at all for a long time, while we all waited as for the words of the Delphic Oracle, and when he did give tongue it might as well have been the Delphic Oracle at that.

'Whin Ah wis a laddie,' he said in a rumbling grumble, 'it wis a gidd stane brig.'

I intend to record his speech phonetically, not only because it was part of his character, but because he spoke a graphic language which ought to be recorded.

Sir Andrew glared at the row of sculleries and then glared at old Matthew and said: '*What* was?'

'Tha' oo' there.' He had a fascinating glottal stop which, when I knew him better, made me lead him into saying words like 'glo''al and 'bo''le' just to hear him do it. 'A gidd stane brig. It wis ma gran'faither tha' bigged it.'

'Where?'

'Oo' there.'

'Out *where*?'

'Whaur we cam' in. It wis they yins fae the agriculturrral tha' broke it doon, gaun ower it wi' they big tractors. A gidd stane brig it wis.'

41

'Forget about that now, Mattha,' said Sir Andrew. 'What about *this*?' and he pointed with his stick at the row of sculleries. 'You understand what we want to do?'

Mattha' spat again. 'Aye, forget this an' forget that! It wis a gidd stane brig, Ah'm tellin' yees ... Them there? Them oothooses?' He cast a jaundiced eye at the sculleries. 'Ye cud jine them thegither wi' a bit brick wa'.'

'All right, then,' said Twice.

Mattha spat again, struck a match in his cupped hands and glared at Twice over it until the flame went out. 'An' a bonnie hash it wid be when ye wis done wi' it!' he said spitefully. 'Them oothooses is gidd wa's — it wis ma faither that pit them up fur Sir Andra's faither, the thrawn auld devil that he wis!'

'Your father or Sir Andrew's?' I asked, throwing care to the winds.

'There wisnae a hair ye cud split atween them for thrawnness, naw, nor dourness aither,' he informed me, and then he gave an eldritch cackle of laughter. 'Folk wis *folk* in they days — no' like noo ... Ye thowless lump ye!' he bawled suddenly at a labourer who came round the building with a wheelbarrow full of rubbish and failed to clear the corner-stone with his wheel. 'That Ah shud live tae see the day when a man cannae hurl a barry! ... If it wis me that wis jinin' they oothooses, Ah wid jine them wi' a gidd stane wa'.'

'But it is *not* you who is going to join them, Mattha,' said Sir Andrew.

'Whae says it's no'?' the old man asked belligerently. 'If onybuddy's gaun tae jine they oothooses that ma faither pit up fur *your* faither —'

'The thrawn auld devil that he wis!' I had to interpolate.

'Aye.' He narrowed his little eyes and leered at me like an old, wizened hobgoblin. 'An' mebbe Ah'm kinna thrawn masel' whiles, bu' Ah widnae like tae see a bricklayer's wa' at Crookmill.' He turned to Sir Andrew. 'Gie me twa-three o' they thowless dreeps ye ca' labourers tae haun'le the heavy stanes fur me and Ah'll start come Monday.'

Sir Andrew exchanged an intense glance with Twice as old Mattha hobbled away to poke here and there at the walls with his stick and make acid comments on the other men's work, and it was a glance that held the pride of victory.

Several people have written several books, some of which have been best-sellers, about the frolicsome fun of rehabilitating a ruined house and garden. Twice and I found it quite a lot of fun and quite a frolic, but I would not write a book about it. It was not *that* funny or frolicsome, for old Mattha constituted himself Master of Works in Twice's absence and, indeed, yielded his place in Twice's presence with an ever-increasing grudge. He interfered with everyone, quarrelled with the man who came to inspect our drainage system, threatened to brain Mr. Slater's foreman electrician with a mallet and 'warmed the lug' of the master carpenter's apprentice in such a fashion that the boy's parents threatened to bring suit for assault. But he built the wall joining all the sculleries, and Twice, who is not by nature patient, had endless patience with old Mattha. On Saturdays and Sundays, to give the sorely tried labourers a rest, he used to 'labour' for Mattha himself, fetching and carrying stones and mixing mortar. On these days the work went forward at a great pace, and on the third Saturday at mid-afternoon Mattha, Twice and I were able to stand back and look at the completed wall, all ready for the corrugated iron roof to be put into place.

'Pity we can't get slates, but we can't,' said Twice.

'Ye'll get yer slates come time,' said Mattha and spat. 'Jist you wait ere Ah go tae me brither fur what they ca' ma holidays come the summer and Ah'll get ye a wheen slates. It widnae be worth a damn tae write to ma brither — he wadnae spen' a stamp tae write back — he's that mean he wad skin a loose fur its tallay — but if Ah get speakin' tae him Ah'll get the slates he took affa his auld byre when he turnt it intae a milkin' paurlor. Milkin' paurlor! Sic a contrivance!' He spat again with vehemence and glared at the house. 'Ah'm no' hearin' like as if ony o' they workmen o' yours is pittin' their backsides ooty j'int in there wi' hard work,' he said malevolently. 'There's no' been twa nails driven this last hauf 'oor!' And with remarkable jerky agility he betook himself into the house, spoiling for a fight, so that, perforce, we had to follow him. We headed him

43

into an end room which was complete as to windows, doors, floor and fireplace and ready for painting.

'Iphm,' he said, his attention caught by the wrought-iron fire-basket which stood on the hearth. 'A nice enough wee parlour. Whit blacksmith wrocht that fur yees?'

'Twice made it,' I told him.

I think it was the first time that I really saw his rheumy old eyes as the frowning, wizened lids were raised to show their hazel gleam. 'Aye?' he said. 'Iphm. Ah've been thinkin' whiles that ye had the haun's o' a craftsman, lad, although they ca' ye an ingineer. Iphm. Some nicht, when ye hae the time, ye maun come doon tae the Royal an' we'll hae a bit dram o' the Article thegither.'

I saw Twice give a convulsive swallow and the only other thing that I could imagine that would cause such a movement or bring such a look to his face was something like the feeling of the sword on his shoulder at the moment of the accolade. Twice and I were trapped in a taut silence while the old man puffed at his pipe and examined the ironwork in detail, so that I was eventually forced into speech as I so often seem to be.

'The comical thing about this house,' I said in a high, false sort of voice, 'is that the bathroom is the same size as the parlour!'

'Whit's that ye said?' Mattha asked, straightening up from his inspection of the wrought iron, and I repeated the remark, hating and regretting, now, every word of it.

'Och,' he said disgustedly, 'when ye think on it, so it is! That'll no' dae at a'!'

'It'll *have* to!' I said. 'Because that's how it is.' He glared at me. 'Besides, I *like* a big bathroom.'

'Ah dinnae care a damn *whit* ye like!' he said fiercely. 'It's no' the thing at a' an' it'll no' *dae!*'

A strange gleam came into the eyes of Twice. 'It would be grand,' he said, 'if we could knock this room and the next one and the passage at the front into one, but I'm not going to interfere with those inside walls. I don't want the bloody roof down on my head.'

'Whae says the bliddy riff'll come doon?' bawled Mattha,

44

sticking his scrawny old neck out of its carapace of muffler like a wicked old tortoise. 'Riffs that ma faither wi' auld Sandy Mitchell as his j'iner pit up *dinnae* fa' doon! No' if they're treatit richt!'

'Well, these walls are not coming out!' bawled Twice just as angrily as Mattha.

Mattha snorted. 'A fine wey that is tae treat a bonnie wumman aboot her first hoose!' he said nastily. 'If ye'll no' let an auld man knock doon a wee bit wa' jist as an obligement tae gie her a richt paurlor, Ah widnae gie much fur her chances as yer mairrit wife!'

'What about the chimneys?' said Twice.

'Them lums? Weel, *whit* aboot them? It's a' the yae gidd big lum an' the twa wee fire-en's can mak' yin big yin. So ye maun awa' an' mak' a bigger iron basket an' pit that nice wee yin ben the hoose in wan o' the wee-er rooms an' dinnae gie me ony mair o' yer impidence aboot the riff o' Crookmill fa'in' in!' and he marched angrily out, bawling for his unfortunate labourers.

'Come on!' said Twice. 'We're winning! You're a genius. I was beat to think of a way to broach the subject of these inside walls — let's get out of here!'

There was a road out of Ballydendran that led up and over the moors and wandered away across country to emerge near the town of Jedburgh. It had been, long ago, a drove road for the movement of cattle and sheep but was now little used except in the picturesque idiom of Mattha's speech, who, one day when cursing at his labourer who handed him a blunt chisel, said: 'Awa' tae hell wi' that, man! Ah could ride ower the hill fae here tae Jeddart on the face o' it!' On a high part of this unfenced road Twice and I pulled the car on to the grass verge and got out our flasks of tea and packets of sandwiches.

'What a thrawn old stick he is, though!' said Twice, harking back to Mattha.

'Twice,' I asked, '*why* were you so pleased because he liked the fire-basket?'

I am as silly as most women, and sillier than many, probably, but Twice had made the fire-basket for *me*, because I had said

45

once that I liked wrought iron, and I was pleased with it and it irked me that a cross old man's admiration should seem to be more important than mine.

Twice flushed a little. 'So you noticed that? Oh, well, you're right. *His* praise gave me far more pleasure than any recommendation I have ever had and was a far bigger thrill than getting my degree.'

'But why?'

He stared at me. 'Because he is a *craftsman*, of course! Any fool that can read and remember what he reads can take a degree, but fewer and fewer men can use their own hands to work a material. Men like Mattha are the last of a race. My father was another of them.'

'The last of a race?'

'Yes — the race of independent craftsmen — independent in every sense of the word — men who will brook no opinion about any of their doings unless it is the opinion of a craftsman that they reckon to be better than they are themselves — only they don't, as a rule, reckon that there *are* many of those. Equals, yes, they will admit, but not betters. Mattha is in the tradition of the old free-masons, who when they heard that the old monks at York were going to put up another bit of their Minster went to York and set up their lodge near the Minster and offered themselves as craftsmen for the new work. They were men who stood absolutely by themselves, with no capital to invest, no wares to sell except their ability in their craft. The Border phrase for them, in my father's day, was "men who worked tae their ain haun". In other words, no hand but theirs did the work, and no hand but theirs took the payment for it — but the hand had to be good. Do you wonder that I am pleased when a man of that kind says to *me*, a poor poop of a works manager or production engineer — or in the bastardised language of today, Technologist, B.Sc. — when a man like that says to *me*: "I've been thinking whiles you have the hands of a craftsman!" . . . Do you *wonder* that I'm pleased?'

He was breathless when he had finished, for the words had tumbled out of him like a triumphant Niagara, and his eyes were glittering and his hands, gripping mine, were tense and springy with the upsurge of pride through his blood. I felt small and humble. 'I see,' I said.

'And Mattha likes *you*, you extraordinary creature, you! Monicas and Matthas! We are very lucky. Have you heard from Monica since she went back south?'

'No. Why?'

'No reason, really. I just wondered.'

'She's not much of a correspondent, as I told you,' I said.

Monica, having introduced us to her Uncle Andy, by which means we became the owners of Crookmill, had gone back to London and was not scheduled to reappear in our lives again at any time in the immediate future, but Monica is not much of a one for schedules, so I was not unduly surprised when, one morning, she arrived without warning in my office at Slaters' Works.

'Well,' she said brightly, 'is this your office?'

'No,' I said, 'it's the Throne Room at Buckingham Palace. Where have you come from?'

'London via Glasgow.'

'Why?'

She sat down. 'I remember,' she said in reminiscing tones, 'my sister Sybbie was just the same before she got married. We could do nothing with her and not a civil word in her head . . . Mr. Slater got anyone to take your place yet?'

'No,' I said, putting down my pen. 'If he had, I'd be a lot more civil. I don't *want* to be a career wife.'

'My dear, where *do* you pick up the bad language? Never have I heard such an expression!'

'Oh, shut up, Monica! It isn't funny at all.'

'You can't just say to Mr. Slater: "Excuse me, chum, I'm getting married so I'm off"?'

'Would you, in the circumstances?'

'I don't know. They are not my circumstances.'

'A hell of a help *you* are!'

We were sitting glaring at one another when Twice and Mr. Slater came in, full of enthusiasm at sight of Monica. I felt jaundiced. Getting married was about the most exhausting thing I had undertaken in my life until this time, and if you don't believe me *you* have a try at applying for Slaters' steel quota in the morning, running to Glasgow to your tailor for a fitting in the afternoon, coming back to the office for a production and progress meeting and then going out to Crookmill to find that old Mattha has insulted the plumber who is connecting the water so that he has downed tools and gone home in a huff.

'Well, well, so you couldn't stay away from Ballydendran, Lady Monica?' said Mr. Slater in his genial way.

'I found it difficult,' she said. 'Besides, I gave birth to an idea.'

'I bet it was hydra-headed,' said Twice. 'Well?'

She looked at him out of her long-shaped, long-lashed eyes in the way she looks when she is about to deliver one of her *coups de grâce*, and then she seemed to change her mind. She transferred her glance to Mr. Slater and said, 'I think it is quite a skintillating idea myself.'

'Most people say it with the "sc" as in hiss,' said Twice. 'Well?'

'*I* say *skin*tillating,' she said with a sort of exaggerated calm. 'It is a skin titillator of an idea.'

I still felt jaundiced. 'Don't you think this build-up is getting overripe?' I asked. 'Let's have the idea before it rots!'

'We-ell.' She looked back at Mr. Slater. 'It occurred to me that I could take Jan's place here until you could find a new person.'

'*You?*' squeaked Mr. Slater, and Twice threw back his head and had himself one of his big laughs.

'Come in, Mr. Ikey Moses,' he said. 'Meet our office dogsbody, the Lady Monica Loame! Don't be a fool, Monica!'

After his startled squeak of the word 'you' Mr. Slater did not speak again, Twice sat looking at Monica with his eyes narrow with amusement and his glittering teeth clenched in a mischievous smile, and Monica sat, wearing her 'dead-pan' look, her right leg crossed over her left and the narrow, high-arched right foot in its tan court shoe was wag-wag-wagging like the upright tail of an angry cat. I had an awareness that both Twice and Mr. Slater were wrong in their attitude to

48

Monica, but I am slow to find words when there is tension among people. I got up from my flat-topped desk and began to pace to the other end of the room. There was no doubt that Monica could do my job here at Slaters', but better than that, she would do it in the way that I had done it, in the way to which old Mr. Slater was used, and that put her in front of any of the many people we had interviewed. And what a relief it would be to me to get married, knowing that Mr. Slater had someone I could really trust in my place. I turned round to pace my way back to my place at the desk and saw Monica sitting there, pen in hand, the other hand picking up the telephone.

'Miss Loame speaking,' she said. 'I'm so sorry — Mr. Slater is in Edinburgh this morning. Can I ask someone else to help you, sir? Mr. Alexander? Certainly, I'll send for him.' She put down the receiver. 'Janet, what can you do that I can't? I can take fast shorthand, type, spell, and I am an authority on the use of the semicolon. I can carry a set of accounts to the balance-sheet stage.' She looked at Twice. 'As an idea, what's wrong with it?'

'Nothing, Miss Loame,' said Twice and looked at Mr. Slater.

'Well, Miss Janet,' the old man said to me, '*you* should know. You know the job and you know Lady Monica. What do you think?'

'She can do it,' I said, 'and better than most.'

'Thank you so much, dear,' said Monica.

'And it's not for ever,' I continued, 'but it will give us all a breathing space.'

'That was the idea,' said Monica.

We all talked about it a little more, to and fro, but in half an hour it was settled and I rose, full of gratitude to Monica and feeling as if I had been given an injection of new life. 'God bless you all!' I said then. 'I'm going out to Crookmill to see about the kitchen sink.'

You will have noticed that I am not a very 'romantic' person. The decision of two people to spend the rest of their lives together is not one, in my opinion, to be taken with eyes that are blinded by 'romance', and thoughts of things like the kitchen sink are an excellent antidote. The fact that there may be a considerable amount of the kitchen sink in this story does not, however, mean that Twice and I, even at our ages, were strictly down-to-earth and utilitarian about everything. Once we were in the car to go away to spend a week wandering about in Caithness, we were people who belonged only to one another and whom only one another could know, and true union of that sort is a relationship so intimate that it is pointless to attempt to describe it, for it cannot be shared. We were very, very happy. Looking back on the little day of my life, that week was the point of high, midsummer noon, when the sun was overhead and the clock was striking twelve on the summit of the hill of the day.

Part II

Part II

Twice and I sneaked back from our honeymoon to Crookmill a day ahead of our announced date in order to be there ahead of the welcoming committee, and that worked very well. The house was habitable, and now that Mattha had finished his major operation on it, the original eight rooms, four sculleries and four front passages had been turned into, reading from left to right: a large living-room, a kitchen, two bathrooms, two bedrooms and two rooms full of packing-cases, bags of nails and a lot of presents that had been sent to us and that had not even been opened, much less acknowledged. And all this was connected by the continuous passage along one side which had been made out of the joined-up sculleries. We still appeared, from the outside, to have four front doors, but, actually and on the inside, we had only one which led into our main large room, while the second front door and passage had been made into a large larder, and the third and fourth had provided cupboard space for the other two rooms which had not yet been allotted a function.

'It is the nicest house I have ever been in!' I told Twice that day we sneaked back to it.

'It will be, I hope, by the time we're done with it,' he said. 'Tell me, what *is* in all those packages?'

'That big tin trunk is my mother's tea and dinner services — Dad said that we were to send back the trunk. The long thing

is the standard lamp that Bruce's the electric shop gave us . . .
We'll have to write some Thank-you letters.'

'*You*'ll have to! It's the bride that gets the doings.'

'Not in this family! Look at that!' and I pointed to a box
addressed on a typewritten label to Twice.

'There's a similar-looking one for you,' he said. 'Let's open
them and have a look. Yours is bigger than mine, but mine is
far heavier. You open mine and I'll open yours!'

One can be childish when one is happy, probably because
happiness is mostly a childish gift.

Twice is much more deft with his hands than I am, and
before I had taken the first covering from my allotted package
he said: 'Good God!' and set on the floor beside us the most
hideous vase that I have ever seen. It was made of what is
called, I believe, oxydised metal, in a virulent acid green, was
about two feet tall and had an angular handle at each side of its
bulbous body. Scrawled, very artily, in gold across its belly,
were the words: 'Home, Sweet Home'.

'And to think that somebody must have *made* it!' said Twice.

'The operative thing is that somebody must have *sent* it!' I
said. 'Isn't there a card?'

He rootled among the packing and then peered into the
depths of the vase itself. 'No — open your one!'

'I'm frightened.'

'Bah! My strength is as the strength of ten! Flash, I really do
love you. Give it here!'

From the second package there emerged what I can only
fairly describe in engineering terms as a pretty rough casting,
in poor quality bronze, of a man's head, with the word
'Beethoven' written across the part where the neck died away
into a squarish lump of rather jagged metal.

'By golly!' said Twice with pride. 'Weighs a stone if it's an
ounce!'

And then we saw the envelope on the floor and both
pounced on it at once. I got it and read the message aloud:

'Dear Mr. Alexander, This is from us all at the hotel. We
thought when you were always playing Beethoven's records

54

you would like this statue and we are sending a vase for Miss Sandison. We hope you will be very happy. And we will miss you, so come and see us sometimes. Yours sincerely, Mary, Ida, Chrissie, Lena, Willie, Hughie at the Royal Hotel.'

I looked at Twice. 'I feel like crying,' I said.

'Then don't. Although it's very civil of them. But then, look at the beers I've bought *them* all the time I was staying at the Royal' He put the vase and the 'statue' side by side and sat back on his heels. 'Well, Mrs. Alexander, you are the first bride I have met who has both a Storied Urn and an Animated Bust!'

'Don't be coarse!' I told him, but I was laughing again. 'Let's just go ahead and have an orgy and open the lot!'

By Christmas-time our household was in order. We had everything that we needed, in spite of curious shortages in the shops of the most unlikely articles such as dusters and dishcloths. Slaters' Works was going full ahead under the guidance of Mr. Slater, Twice and that open secret 'Miss Loame', but Lady Monica had quarrelled with her Uncle Andy. This was inevitable, I suppose. For many years Sir Andrew, not to mention his ancient servants, had been accustomed to a bachelor establishment at the Crook, and the even tenor of their way was being severely disrupted by Monica roaring in and out, with her red hair flying, in a second-hand Jaguar which she had acquired from some overseas friend who had been home on leave. I do not mean that Sir Andrew and Monica sat at opposite ends of the dining-table and did not speak to one another, but Monica was tired of staying at the Crook and Sir Andrew was tired of having her there, and they were thoroughly on one another's nerves, for the strain of not quarrelling is far worse than the rush of blood to the head and the explosion of a good-going row.

'Monica,' I said on a Saturday afternoon between Christmas and the New Year, when she and I were having tea and toast in front of a big fire while Twice was out coaching the works' newly-formed rugby team: 'Wouldn't it be easier if you had a place of your own to live?'

'Easier? It would be heaven! But since that carpet factory got going there isn't a place for miles around — not even a room.'

'There are two rooms through there,' I said, nodding towards the far end of Crookmill. 'With a small cooker and a little arrangement you could live through there and use the spare bathroom and we need never see each other except by arrangement.'

She gave me her sidelong glance and her long smile. 'I have been waiting to see how long it would take you to get to the obvious solution!' she said.

I was conscious of slight irritation, for, like most people, I imagine, I do not like to be openly accused of being slow-witted although I am acutely conscious that it is one of my failings.

'I don't see that it is so obvious a solution!' I said. 'It is not easy to visualise you in two rooms, cooking your own sausages. You can't boil a kettle!'

'I won't have to,' she told me blandly. 'Lucy will do all the kettle-boiling.'

'Who the devil is Lucy?'

'A family hanger-on. She was a by-blow baby belonging to a lady's maid who died and she was more or less brought up by Mama's people. She keeps on getting married and getting widowed and coming back on the family. Stephanie has her just now, but Steff and John's place is near Birmingham and she keeps going to the skating rink and spraining her ankles and bumping her bottom and things and it's all very inconvenient. She is supposed to cook for them and they are carrying trays to *her* all the time. I can't remember whether this is the third or fourth husband she has buried, and, as Steff says, one would think she was giving them arsenic or something except that this last one ran away two years ago and died in Australia. She is an excellent housekeeper when she keeps her mind on it, and there's no skating rink in Ballydendran. Let's go and look at the rooms!'

As I may have remarked earlier in this chronicle, I waited until I was thirty-seven before I married, and in the course of these thirty-seven years I had gathered from various literary and unliterary works and from general observation that many people have difficulty in making the transition from the single to the married state and go through a 'shaking-down' period which often shakes them up to such a degree that they are never the same again, and frequently, even, instead of settling down, they come to a settling up in the Court of Admiralty, Probate and Divorce, these extraordinary three, which always make me think of Faith, Hope and Non-Charity.

Having had no feelings of having been shaken up, down or sideways, I tended to the self-satisfied view that maybe the fact that I was thirty-seven and no longer young and flighty was a good thing after all. It did not occur to me that I was thirty-seven, had been in executive posts for some years and was perhaps a little too accustomed to taking decisions on my own, so that I was very shaken indeed when I told Twice of the arrangements for Monica and he said: 'Oh, Flash! You shouldn't have done that!'

'Why ever not?' I asked. 'The rooms are there. We're not using them. It seemed like sense to me.'

'But this is *our* place, Flash!'

'Of course it is! I haven't *sold* the rooms, dammit!'

'I know ... Oh, well, I suppose it's all right.'

'*I* can't see anything wrong with it!'

'I just wish you had spoken to me about it first, Flash.'

That touched me. Twice can always touch me and hit home.

'I am very sorry, Twice. I just didn't think of it,' I said. 'She looked so darn fed-up when she was here this afternoon and I just thought of it and offered her the rooms ... Look, though, it needn't be final. I can make some sort of excuse. I can say —'

'No!' he said. 'No, don't do that! Let it stand. It would be awkward, and it won't be for long, anyway, now that the Old Man has made up his mind to take this amalgamation with Allied Plant.'

'But I don't want you to be —'

'I won't be anything, my pet. Don't you worry. Actually, as you say, it's a very sensible arrangement.'

I was a little uncomfortable for a day or two at this first faint difference of opinion between Twice and myself, but there was no further discussion of the subject between us, and Monica moved in so smoothly and with so little fuss that my first vague discomfort disappeared. The Loame family rallied to the standard with contributions of essential furniture, and in less than a week Monica was installed.

Lucy — or Mrs. Wilton — arrived forthwith, and, indeed, rather earlier than forthwith, for she was supposed to be met at Glasgow on a certain morning and arrived from Edinburgh the evening before. It was early January, very wet and dark, and Monica was alone in her rooms at the other end of the house when Twice and I were startled to hear a voice calling from the road beyond the bridge: 'Is anybody there? Is anybody there?' Before we could get out, we heard Monica's window go up with a bang and her voice yelling: 'What the hell are you doing out there, you old fool?'

'Trying to get in!' the voice yelled back. 'It's Lucy!'

'As if I didn't know! Wait a minute.'

'God, what a family!' said Twice, seizing his electric torch and disappearing into the wind and rain.

'You're not supposed to be here until tomorrow morning!' said Monica sourly when we had got the little stout creature inside the house.

'I know. But I seem to have come away a day early and I *know* I got into the wrong train,' she said with satisfaction, 'but I'm a very determined woman and here I am.'

'Oh, all right. Where's your luggage?'

'Down there!' said Lucy, jerking her head in a direction that was approximately south-by-east.

'Down where?'

'At the station.'

'Oh. Well, let's have some supper — I've got a tin of soup and some sausages and beans and things, and then I'll run down to Ballydendran and get it.'

'Oh, it isn't at Ballydendran!' said Lucy with a gay laugh.
'I didn't see the Ballydendran station nameplate until the
train was moving again and I jumped out and it was *moving*,
my dear, but a man caught me — a very nice large man with
—'

'Never mind that! Where is your blasted luggage?'

'At the next place. Something — doon. The stationmaster
said —'

'I *knew* I shouldn't have done this!' said Monica to nobody
in particular and seized Lucy by the upper arm. 'Come on!'

But politeness — or something — had to be served.
Dragged by Monica to a dangerous angle of forty-five degrees
to the floor and looking like one of these little lead-weighted
dolls that cannot fall down, Lucy waggled her eyelashes at
Twice and gave him a roguish smile. '*So* nice to have met
you!' she said and was hauled bodily from the room.

'Well,' said Twice, closing the door to the back passage
behind them, 'I am very glad we have a remote-control sort
of house and don't have to see them unless we want to. Flash,
you really do have impossible friends — very helpful and a
fascinating study, in a way, but impossible, if you see what
I mean.'

'I know,' I said humbly, wondering if letting Monica have
the rooms was such a sensible arrangement after all.

You would think that with Twice, me, Monica and Lucy,
Crookmill now had as much as it could hold, but not at all.
Monica managed to suborn Mattha and a carpenter he had in
his thrall and caused to be thrown up a wooden partition
which divided one of her two rooms into two bedrooms,
which meant that she and Lucy were able to have a place
each for themselves and had a room left over to entertain in.
With this, and a small electric cooker and a sink in the
blocked-off end of the sculleries-turned-into-passage, the
amount of entertaining they contrived to do was prodigious.
They became the social hub of Ballydendran, not to mention
Glasgow, Edinburgh and various satellite towns; and when
Twice and I wanted an evening out, which was seldom, all
we had to do was to walk along our part of the passage and

take what we found on the other side of the communicating door. This was in the nature of that obscure dish *hors d'oeuvres variés*. Sometimes there was a theatrical sprinkling in the form of the cast of some play that was trying out in Glasgow; sometimes some Loame had recommended friends of his or hers to call at Crookmill for a drink; sometimes Monica and Lucy were entertaining the town, which meant the butcher, the baker, and would have meant the candlestick-maker if we had not been on the electric main. For two years in Ballydendran I had lived in lodgings and had got on to visiting terms with perhaps half a dozen people, and for the same length of time Twice had lived at the Royal Hotel, which had culminated in the Storied Urn and the Animated Bust; in two weeks, as I have said, Monica was the social hub of the district and a far wider province besides — all of which only goes to show how different people can be.

And, too, people can be very astonishing. Lucy, who made hay of the railway system, arrived on the wrong day and let her luggage go to the wrong place, was a fantastically efficient housekeeper and cook. She always remembered to buy extra bread before a Trade Holiday, she seemed to know by instinct when the electric power was going to be cut off, and, of course, how she kept their household supplied with alcoholic drink I will never know.

After Monica and Lucy had been installed for about a month a particularly uproarious party took place in their end of Crookmill, and, although we had a standing invitation for any and every evening, Twice and I had chosen not to be present. After a bout of confused conversation and a resounding crash of glass and metal, Twice looked at me across our fireplace and said: 'Plenty of fun tonight, ben the hoose!' From then on Monica's part of Crookmill came to be known, not only to Twice and me but to the world at large, as the 'Ben the Hoose'.

Very soon she had some very stylish notepaper supplied to her which was headed: 'The Ben the Hoose, Crookmill, Ballydendran, Scotland. Telephone Ballydendran 70', and one of her London friends wrote to say that Monica had learned to use writing paper at last but that the 'Scotland' in the address was mere tautology and swank.

I remember that one evening we did attend one of Monica's parties — the occasion for it was a visit from Monica's brother Gerald who was something in the Foreign Office but who since the war had been working in the planning of the United Nations Organisation. He was to fly from Prestwick to New York the following day and was spending the night in our spare bedroom. He was obviously one of the 'clever' Loames, and it was impossible to be in the room with him without being aware of his keenness of mind. He and Twice found immediate interest in one another, and as I watched them and listened to them — it was one of the smaller, less rowdy parties — I saw Twice, as it were, through other eyes and heard him with other ears. Gerald Loame had that curious detachment of the diplomat who sees all round a person or a situation, with a sight uncoloured by emotion, and it was as if, temporarily, he had imbued me with something of this gift of his.

I realised then that a complete, round relationship which embraces and merges every facet of two natures, as is the relationship between Twice and myself, constructs round itself its own round world, which protects it, as the larvae of some insects are protected by a cocoon. Everything and everyone is seen in the light of this world, which is filtered and coloured, as it were, by the protecting surrounding filaments. I had not been aware of this until that evening and I became aware of it through the realisation that Monica and Gerald, too, had a world of their own and that it was a world that had no real communication with the world that Twice and I inhabited. During the war years I had felt that I was intimately in touch with Monica, that we breathed the same spiritual air and fed on the same mental food, but now, when two Loames were gathered together at Crookmill, which was my own place, part of my own world, I came to know that I was in touch with Monica only as the earth can be said to be in touch with the other planets of the universe. I was aware of her existence; of her nature I knew little or nothing, and between us there was no real communication.

I had, of course, been in the presence of more than one Loame at several times in the past when during the war I had spent short leaves at Beechwood or in London. I had seen then that the Loames had a closely knit family world, but I had felt at that time that that was a bond between Monica and me — a bond of similarity — for did not we Sandisons have a closely knit family world at Reachfar, although ours was of a different pattern? It was only now, however, that I realised that the Loame world was actuated by influences different from ours, that it was composed of different elements and responded to different laws. In the sphere of the physical universe we — and especially I — know very little about the planet Saturn, but we know that our own earth is subject to the influences of the sun and the moon. Looking suddenly, on this evening, at the Loame world which had swum into my ken, I did not feel like the poet with the translation of Homer or stout Cortez on his peak in Darien. I felt that right there in front of me was something like Saturn, complete with nebula, and that it was possible — for all I knew — that when the rings tightened around it like a rubber girdle its whole population might breathe out anything from fire and brimstone to a strong distillation of attar of roses. I did not *know*. I felt a strange fear. I wanted to go home — back to my own part of Crookmill.

'Ready, Twice?' I asked at the first decent opportunity. 'Don't worry about how late you are in coming through, Gerald. You can't wake anybody — the walls are too thick.'

Twice and I went out into the passage, through the dividing door, and were safe in our own end of the house.

'What an interesting chap Gerald is!' Twice said as I was putting our soup on the table. 'The decadent aristocracy, my foot! I wish that some of the half-baked intelligentsia had a tenth of his brains!'

'The Loames are always at one extreme or the other, it seems,' I said as we sat down to supper. 'This generation is pretty well all right, except for Laura, who has a feather brain and the sex-instincts of a she-cat, but I believe two of

Lord Beechwood's brothers are pretty dotty ... I *like* Monica and Gerald and the rest of them, but I couldn't live among them in their own world. They breathe — both in and out — a different air from the kind I live by.'

'I see what you mean,' Twice agreed.

'Theirs is literally a world apart from ours — or mine, anyway. I don't mean that they are more highly developed, or of a finer fibre or anything to be envious of and wish to attain to,' I went on. 'I don't even mean that they are bloodstock to my carthorse, although that may be true. It is difficult to say what I mean. Listen. During the war, did you ever have any experience of gas-proof buildings?'

'No. Why?'

'Being in the East all the time, you wouldn't. But here in Britain, we used to have buildings that were supposed to be gas-proof and sometimes they let tear gas off outside in order to test them. They never *were* proof — at least, not the ones *I* met. Well, when I find myself surrounded by a bunch of Loames I feel as if I were in one of those buildings during a test. I am all right for a bit, and then gradually I feel myself starting to cough, mentally, and my mental eyes begin to water and my sight to blur — as if the gas were getting the upper hand ... I hope this bird isn't tough — it's a cock that Mattha's daughter killed because, she said, "it was bein' ower sair on the hens". I don't think she approves of males in general.'

'I must say,' said Twice, sharpening the carving-knife, 'that you move out of the Loame world and back to your own uncomplicated and robust one with remarkable speed and ease ... No. He doesn't seem to be tough ... But you've never mentioned this rarefied atmosphere of the Loames before. Why?'

'I hadn't noticed it in such a pronounced form before, but I got a bad attack of it with Monica and Gerald tonight. Twice, I wonder if they are ever aware of *our* world being different? I wonder if Monica, when she is with you and me, for instance, ever feels as much at sea as I felt through there for a bit tonight?'

Twice chuckled. 'That young woman is *never* at sea, my love. Don't you worry. Monica is as old as sin and you are still among the innocents — that is why you are so sensitive to atmospheres, but don't let them worry you. There will be no leakage of Loame gas into *your* world ... Have some more of this immoral bird. I think he's jolly good.'

'Not for me, thank you. You go ahead, but leave room for a little Stilton.'

'That's the kind of joke I don't appreciate. Stilton is a sad, sad memory that shouldn't be awakened.'

'It isn't a joke. Gerald brought it and I have to give part of it to Monica, but she has to come in here to eat it because Lucy won't stay in the same house as Stilton cheese.'

'If it's that easy to get rid of Lucy I think Monica is crazy. Bring the Stilton forth. That old woman would drive me mad.'

'She's not that bad,' I said. 'Why?'

'I feel I may be blushing ... Seriously, though, she is a bit frightening — almost a nymphomaniac.'

'At *her* age? Twice, don't be an ass!'

'Fact,' he said. 'Did you see her with the doctor tonight? I thought she was going to have at him in the middle of the floor and, in the words of Mrs. Pat Campbell, frighten the horses!'

'You exaggerate!'

'If you were a male you wouldn't think so ... But thank heaven you are a female. And thank you for my nice dinner. And thank you for loving me and coming to live with me and for everything. If you wait till I light my pipe I'll come and dry the dishes for you.'

'This is love indeed,' I said, 'but you needn't. This is not my night for being a good housewife. I am going to hurl the dishes into the sink, run the tap on them and leave them. I've got all day tomorrow to wash dishes and all tonight to talk to you.'

'Hurray! Rule One for successful people — there is only one time to do anything and that is the *right* time. Sit ye doon, Mistress Alexander, an' tak' a bit smoke! *I* will hurl the dishes into the sink.'

It was a flawless happiness that Twice and I had in those days, fresh, new-minted and unscarred by time, and with daily use it became more and more warm in its soft, bright polish, like silver that is handled with love and care.

Spring at Ballydendran is a lovely season, as spring tends to be in places that are subject to a harsh winter, and by early March, when my birthday comes, the spring was invading the garden of Crookmill. Very little had been planted in the garden — nothing, indeed, but a dozen bushes of climbing roses along the wall of the house in the autumn, just after we had cleared the worst of the jungle that had prevailed, but it was a wonderfully exciting garden none the less, because so many unexpected things happened in it. A length of dead-looking fibre that trailed about like a frayed old rope on one wall suddenly burst out all over with yellow stars and declared itself to be a jasmine of some sort, and all over the black earth and rough grass, where odd lots of rubble, old nails, scraps of corrugated iron and pieces of rotten wood still lay about, little green sword-points poked up and were identified, with wonder, as snowdrops, crocuses and daffodils.

On the morning of my birthday Twice came in carrying in his cupped hand two infinitesimally small violets and a heart-shaped leaf. 'Flowers for your birthday, my lady. And from your own garden. Excuse me for a little. I'll be back for breakfast.'

He backed the car out and went off down the road, but was back in about ten minutes and came into the kitchen where I was frying bacon.

'Hi, Missis,' he said, 'here's us!'

In his arms he held a small pup — it would be more correct to say a 'young' pup, for he was not exactly small. He was about fifteen inches long, with gangling legs and enormous feet, and had a buff-gold coat, with a black muzzle, black rims round his eyes, black edges on his ears and a golden tail that shaded to a black tip.

'What a *craitur*!' I said. 'Put him down! What *is* he?'

I squatted on the floor. The pup came cavorting towards me, lost control of his gangling legs on the polished floor and slid into my arms on his bottom.

'What *is* he, she says! What a thing to say to a well-bred fellow! And him only six weeks old. He's a mastiff!'

'Oh, Twice! He's beautiful!'

And he was. His coat was the colour of whisky and as smooth and satiny as a very good blend at that.

'And his name is Drambuie of Kilcarron.'

'Gurr!' concurred Drambuie and leapt at Twice's shoe-laces.

'He'll make an awful mess, Flash, and probably take the house apart,' said Twice apologetically.

'He will *not*!'

'You are pleased, Flash?'

'Oh, Twice! I'm so pleased I'm tongue-tied!' I seized the pup and kissed his silky head. 'Sorry! Wrong person!' So then I kissed Twice, of which Drambuie did not approve for he snatched the dish-towel from the rail and made off down the passage with it, shaking it violently as he went.

'Come back here, you brute!' bawled Twice.

'Don't *bawl* at him like that!'

'Expect me to stand here shouting Drambuie of Kilcarron? We'll have to get a calling name for him. What about Sandy? After all, he's sand-coloured and he's an Alexander now.'

'God, the bacon!' I snatched the pan from the fire and stood looking at Twice over the smoking fat. 'No. Not Sandy.'

'Why not?'

'It's a name I'm saving up.'

'Saving up?'

'We — we can't have two people called Twice in the house.'

'Flash, what do you mean? Do you mean to tell — Oh, damn and blast it!' He shook the hand that had got into the hot bacon fat and began to suck it. 'Do you mean to —'

'Oh, Twice, I'm sorry — about your hand, I mean. Yes. Yes. It's nearly three months —'

'Put down that cursed pan! Honestly, the times you pick to tell a fellow —'

'Let me see that hand —' I put the pan back on the stove.

'My hand's all right. Flash, you are the most wonderful —'

There was a hideous crash from the living-room. 'God Almighty! What's that?'

Drambuie came scuttling, terrified, into the kitchen and leapt straight up into my arms. Fearfully, we went and looked into the living-room. Drambuie had discovered the corner of the breakfast cloth and the floor was a litter of broken plates, cups, saucers, spilt sugar, milk and marmalade.

'Oh, Dram! You wicked dog!' I said and gave him a resounding slap on his fat bottom. He yelped, sprang from my arms and disappeared under the sofa, all except the black tip of his tail.

'Well, Dram Alexander, you certainly bought it, name and all!' said Twice. 'Gosh, I'm having a wonderful your-birthday!'

The bacon was well and truly burned by now, but by the time we sat down to eggs without bacon the baby was part of the family.

'Mind you,' said Twice, 'if she's a girl I won't have her called Sandra or anything silly like that.'

'Certainly not,' I agreed. 'I thought Elizabeth, if you like it. But she's a boy.'

'Now, Flash! Don't you start any funny ideas! I don't mind what IT is and neither do you!'

'Of course I don't. But I just have a sort of feeling.'

I had all sorts of feelings and all of them good and pleasant to have. I felt extremely well and full of energy, and at the same time full of content — a strange combination, for one did things about the house and made plans and used the energy in such a satisfactory way. It was not the energy that strives after something. It was energy moving forward to a foreordained conclusion, so that there was no haunting sense of effort being perhaps misdirected. There was no uncertainty. It is a most strange thing, to feel so much alive, to be so much a part of life and yet be completely free from uncertainty.

I was now living in a world within a world, living inside a sphere within a sphere, like these amazing sphere-enclosing spheres that the Chinese can carve out of jade. In this innermost world of mine I was protected on all sides, insulated against the normal wear and tear of the events of every day, so that of this time I remember only a blur of happy contentment and very few of the actual details of what happened. I remember that one night Twice came home with a guilty look about him and eventually confessed that he had written to my aunt at Reachfar.

'I know that you don't like to be fussed around and have people always about you, Flash, but don't be angry,' he said. 'I don't mean to be insulting or ungallant or anything, but you *are* a little old to be trying this baby-having thing for the first time, so I've asked Kate to try to find some woman, just to *be* here and help around the house and so on.'

'Why should I be angry, my pet?' I said. 'It's a very good idea, and if it eases your mind in any way let's have a dozen women here if you like.'

I think that it was about then that Dram came in, stepping very proudly, carrying a large, half-dead water rat from the burn which he laid like an oblation — if that's the word — at Twice's feet.

'Dram, it's beautiful,' Twice said. 'Take it away, for pity's sake, and kill it.'

Dram sat back on his bottom, put a large forepaw on the rat and looked solemnly at Twice.

'He won't kill anything,' I said. 'I think his mouth is too soft or something.'

'Well, so is mine!' said Twice. 'Dram, take it outside, there's a good dog. Thank you very much.'

At these words Dram lifted his rat on to the arm of Twice's chair, struck it a stupefying blow with his paw, left it and went to lie in the middle of the floor with a pleased expression.

'My God!' Twice burst out. 'Has the brute no sense?'

'Dram!' I said. 'Take that beastly rat and GO RIGHT OUTSIDE!'

Dram, hurt and insulted now, picked up his rat, carried it with dignity to the passage door, which he butted open with his square head, and disappeared, rat and all, into Monica's quarters.

'Holy cow!' said Twice.

'Lucy's cat will kill it and put Dram out,' I said comfortably. 'Of course, the day will come when *he* will kill the cat, but at the moment this baby and I are not worried about that ... And Dram has a *lot* of sense. He hasn't widdled in the house for over three weeks.'

'That's wonderful. But what is he going to do with that hole he has dug in the front garden? Bury a horse?'

Before I could say anything in extenuation of Dram's weakness for excavation there was a hideous shriek from the passage and Lucy hurtled through the doorway and threw herself at Twice.

'It's enormous!' she yelled. 'And it's *alive*!'

'You are a liar, you know,' said Monica calmly as she appeared carrying the dead rat by the tail. She bent a wicked eye on Lucy, who was clawing at Twice's shoulder. 'But I suppose one excuse is as good as another.' She picked the lid off the hot-water stove in the scullery and dropped the dead rat in and then went to wash her hands at our sink. 'Come through and have a drink before supper,' she called over her shoulder. 'You have to collect your dog, anyway.'

'Where is he?' I asked.

'Under my bed. You should have got a bitch. Nothing is safe around here. He is afraid of Lucy.'

'One bitch around the place is enough,' said Twice, disengaging Lucy, but quite kindly, although with a dirty look at Monica.

She turned her back on Twice in a deliberate way and looked at me. 'Well, how is the child?'

'Very well, thank you,' I told her.

She looked at my waistline. 'I must say it's developing quite a personality. Come on.'

We went along the passage and into the different world that was Ben-the-Hoose.

'Twice and my aunt are trying to find a wet-nurse for me,' I said.

'What? Already?'

'You know what I mean — somebody to be around the house and lend a hand.'

'A very sound idea. That old trollop' — she jerked her head in the direction of her passage-kitchen and Lucy — 'wouldn't have the *nous* to lift the telephone if anything went wrong. I hope they get somebody with some sense. If Lucy couldn't cook I'd poison her!'

Out of my serenity and contentment at this time I had liking and toleration brimming over and to spare for all the world, and I thought Monica was a little hard in her attitude to Lucy, and blamed it on the fact that Monica was under a fair amount of stress all day at Slaters' Works and probably found a scene about a half-dead rat (being herself neither afraid of nor revolted by rodents) a silly and unnecessary irritation during her evening. I apologised for Dram's misdemeanour, but I was little affected by Monica's whiplash comments not only on Lucy but on everything. Nothing outside of myself seemed to affect me as formerly, as if I were encased in some elemental and invisible armour.

When my aunt wrote to say that we were 'in luck and Daisy Mackintosh would come', and Daisy Mackintosh was due to arrive at Crookmill the day after the letter, I was unaffected by that too. I got the spare bedroom ready to receive her, but in my mind she had no reality as a person. My world was growing smaller and smaller, closing in and shutting out everything except the baby, Twice and myself.

When I was a child of five and went to the village school up at my home for the first time Daisy Mackintosh had been one of the 'big girls' in the 'Big Room', which meant that she was fourteen and would leave school altogether that summer. Since that time I had never seen Daisy Mackintosh, for she had worked at home on her people's croft for a few years and then went away to Edinburgh to train as a nurse. As I was making up the bed in her room I remembered that I had heard once, when home on vacation from my university, that Daisy Mackintosh had never completed her nursing training, but instead had married some man who had given her two children and then got himself run over by a bus. It was typical of my aunt and my family in general, I thought, to ignore this occurrence which had taken place in far-off Edinburgh and not in their own countryside, and be sending me 'Daisy Mackintosh', who was really Mrs. So-and-So in spite of all their ignoring.

When Twice and I met her at the station she turned out to be a tall, dignified-looking woman with an authoritative look, as she got out of the train, as if the entire British railway system were under her personal control. Her first words, therefore, were most unexpected when she came to me and clutched at my hand and said: 'You're Janet! Mrs. Alexander, I should say! I'd know you anywhere by your Granny! Goodness, I'm in a perfect daze! I'm so nervous, travelling by myself!'

'You must be tired, Mrs. — I'm sorry, my aunt wrote nothing but Daisy Mackintosh.'

'And what *would* she write? It's Ramsay, but Daisy will do fine. And this is *Mr.* Alexander?'

She had a coy way of saying it that made me want to say: 'No, he is Napoleon Bonaparte', but Twice held out his hand and said: 'I am very glad to see you here, Mrs. Ramsay.'

She clung to his hand with both of hers and gazed earnestly into his face. 'And I'm so pleased to *be* here! I'm not the kind of woman that likes to be all on her own.'

'Let's get your luggage,' said Twice hastily and strode away up the platform.

When we got back to Crookmill, of course, we had Monica and Lucy in for a drink and to meet Daisy, and at once she and Lucy went off into some conversational world of their own in which we three had no part.

'And you have no children?' Daisy asked at one point.

'No.' Lucy sheered away from this question. 'My second husband was in the Army and —'

'I have the two boys, Hugh and David —'

'And my third husband was —'

'People have said to me I should marry again, but —'

'This is a classic!' Monica hissed at Twice and me in a corner of the kitchen. '*Two* of them! God help the males of Ballydendran now!'

I think, but I am not sure, that it was Twice who coined the phrase or composite name for them, 'Loose-and-Daze', but it came into our vocabulary that evening and came to stay.

I would not wish to mislead anyone or give any wrong impressions. Loose and Daze were, in most ways, very nice women, both extremely gifted in the housewifely arts; both attractive to look at and both of quite pleasing personality, but both had tried marriage, had enjoyed it and were determined to have another go at it at the earliest opportunity. Twice, remembering moments of embarrassment in tranquillity, would accuse them of near-nymphomania, and Monica, in her frequent moments of irritation, would apostrophise them as 'trollops' and 'tartes manquées', but neither person was making a fair judgment. Neither Loose nor Daze would have recognised nymphomania if they had met it in Ballydendran High Street, and Monica's lapses into the French language when at a loss for a suitable word in English merely sent them off into a gale of giggles. When Loose and Daze smoothed the sleeve of Twice's coat and gazed into his eyes; when they clung to Mr. Slater's arm when they welcomed him to the house; when they lingered to exchange coy confidences with the bank manager, they had no designs on my husband, Mrs. Slater's or the bank manager's wife's — it was all merely a manifestation of their instinct to keep their hands and eyes in, as Twice would put it in his calmer moments.

Loose and Daze, had a casual observer seen them walking down the street or sitting in a train, would have looked like what they were, two not ill-looking, well-dressed, respectable widows, with pretty, not over-intelligent faces, going contentedly about their small daily business, but when I look

72

back to this time at Crookmill I see that they brought into the house and kept alive there what I can only describe as a consciousness of sex. The windborne seed has no future without the soil that it finds fertile, the flying spark is on its way to extinction unless it strikes dry tinder, so Loose and Daze might have gone together to a million other places without this influence of theirs exerting itself, but Crookmill at this time was the soil for the seed, the tinder for the spark. There was the further accident of old Mattha, who, largely out of his liking for Twice, I think, coupled with that loneliness to which old people in retirement are prone, had attached himself to the household and who, in his very nature, was the force of polar opposition to the motivating force behind Loose and Daze.

And, of course, the spring, that notorious season, was now in full cry round the green hills and among the little woods of Ballydendran. I remember the evenings, when, as long as it was light, Twice and I — and often Monica — would grub about in the garden, 'helped' by old Mattha, who sat on the wall and spat and made acid comments on the efforts of two of his many grandsons whom he coerced into working for us and whom we had to pay in secret because he did not approve of 'folk gettin' peyd tae get learnt'. Loose and Daze were taking a strong part in the social life of the town and were in a frenzy of sewing-meetings and whist drives and bazaars connected with the church; and although Twice pointed out that if they stayed at home and simply gave the church the money they spent to hire a hall and have tickets printed for whist drives, not to mention what they paid for cloth for sewing-meetings and bus fares to get to the meetings themselves, the church would do much better, they merely smiled archly at him and said: 'You old stick-in-the-mud, you!' and went on their way a-whoring, as Monica put it. At least, their church and charitable activities mostly saved us in the evenings from the embarrassment of having them and Mattha in the garden at the same time. Mattha, on the whole, had a low opinion of women, coupled with a keen eye for the foibles of humanity in general. He also had an overweening belief in the right and freedom of the individual to express any opinion about anyone, either in that person's hearing or out of it.

Loose referred, privately, to Mattha as 'that dirty, spitting, ill-natured old man', and Daze, in her own idiom, called him 'that thrawn, cantankerous, ould craitur', but, of course, Mattha too had his opinions and was less private about them. He watched Loose and Daze one evening, from his seat on the wall, go down the road to catch the bus, and when they were no more than out of earshot, he spat and said: 'Ye can see by the waggle o' their backsides whit thur efter. God help the pare sowl o' a man that gets catched atween they twae mill-stanes!'

For the rest of us at this time it was all very amusing, this push-pull of sex comment, and for me the crowded, kindly household was ideal. I could be alone if I wanted to be, but there was always somebody about and within call, and they were all people I liked and some of whom I loved. It went on like that until one evening at the end of May, when Loose and Daze had a whist drive and at six o'clock Monica rang up to say that she and Twice would be late because some people who should have arrived at the works for a meeting that morning had not come until the late afternoon. This caused one of these wordy exchanges between Loose and Daze that they so much enjoyed but which were so tedious for everyone else.

'I'll stay with Janet — you go. You can manage my table for tea as well as your own.'

'No, *you* go. All you have to do is pick up Mrs. Fisher to play in my place and she'll look after *my* table as well.'

'But *I'm* here to look after —'

'Nonsense, my dear! Besides, you missed the last one, remember, with your toothache.'

'I know, but —'

'You'll *both* go!' I said. 'Good heavens, you'd think I was half-witted!' and I pushed them out of the house.

Mattha did not come along that evening, but I had a happy time, playing gramophone records and sewing nightgowns for the baby and finding myself some supper; but about nine o'clock I discovered that it seemed to be very cold and went out into the front garden to look at the weather. It *was* cold, with all the indications of one of these late May frosts which can do so much damage to a garden. There was nothing I could do and what I had already done was silly, for I had let Dram out and he went galloping across the burn in the dim light and in a few seconds had all the sheep and lambs in the adjoining field running for their lives, while he cavorted behind them, having the time of *his* life. In sheep country, the worry of the dog-owner is that word 'worry'. A young dog chases sheep for fun, but he can so easily get his teeth into the wool and start to shake it as he would an old rag, and then he gets the taste of blood and the degeneration is complete. I have never known a sheep-worrier to be cured except by destruction.

I ran down the path to the bridge, calling the pup's name, and I saw him check in mid-caper and turn to come back to me, so I stopped on the bridge to wait for him. I remember the slip of my foot as I stopped, I remember the clutching slither I made as the wooden parapet cracked, and I remember the boulders under my back and the coldness of the water as I struck the bed of the shallow stream only a few feet below. Twice and Monica found me about half an hour later, Dram shivering in the water beside me. I had lost my baby, I had precluded all possibility of having another baby and I had broken something in my back so that I could not move my legs. It was as simple and as complete as that . . .

Part III

Part III

A merciful mental anaesthesia comes to the very ill. I do not mean coma or complete unconsciousness, for I was, within the medical meaning of the word, conscious from the fourth day after my fall when I came out of the anaesthetic that had been given me for the full examination of my back and the encasing of my body from waist to hips in plaster. I could see, hear, speak, swallow, smile at Twice, and even put out my hand and touch him, but it was not until about four weeks had elapsed and the doctors were extremely pleased with my progress and everybody was looking less anxious that I realised how damnable I felt all their good cheer to be and became conscious of the full enormity of my situation. I was alive, I had no pain of any kind — but I might never walk again.

Some fine and some great books have been written by fine and great men and women about their incredible conquests of all kinds of physical disabilities, but I think that I can say of myself with conviction and with truth that I am neither fine nor great. I am of poor metal and of small spiritual stature. And this was my first failure in life. As a small person, of small ability and small ambitions, I had never tried to do anything very big and I had succeeded in all the little things I had tried to do. Now I had tried to do the most ordinary thing that any normal female animal can do, and my attempt had ended like this. And all my life I had enjoyed, consciously, my ability to move. I had loved the acts of walking, running, dancing — I had enjoyed them and had studied my enjoyment of them as a gourmet watches himself enjoying some carefully chosen dish. And never in my life had I been ill at all. I had never spent a day in bed, never been unable to attend to my own toilet, never had been dependent on anyone to help me with the normal functions of my body . . .

Do not be alarmed. This is a story of My Friend Monica, and it is not going to turn into an opus on my operation, but it is against the background of my illness, my irritability, the anxiety that I caused and the distortions of my sick mind that the story of My Friend Monica developed.

I am a fortunate person. Many people like me and several love me deeply, and the large living-room of Crookmill, in a corner of which, near a window, I lay on my surgical bed, should have been a happy place. Nothing came in there but kindness to me and the desire to help me and — oh, how my mind and nerves were frayed by it all.

'Thank you for the flowers. They are beautiful!'

'Thank you, Monica — it's just the right colour and *real* linen!'

'Thank you, Twice. I love it.'

'Thank you, Daze, for the bedpan.'

'Thank you, Twice; I didn't know it was published yet.'

Thank you. Thank you. Thank you. Damn you! Damn you all! And Twice and his endless, cheerful patience — the cursed and damned patience that was clamped down over all the bubbling volcanic fire and passion — my heart was sick to death when I looked at him.

The atmosphere of the house in the midsummer sun was bright and gay; the visitors came and went all day and every day; Dram daily became more intelligent and amusing. The gaiety became a little forced on the days when the doctor came, accompanied by the consultant from Edinburgh, and there would be a silence when they drove away, which one of us would eventually manage to break with some lightsome quip. Crookmill, people said, was the happiest place in the world; it did them good to come there, they said; they had never seen, they said, an invalid who was so patient and cheerful and contented — and *such* a sense of humour, too, they said.

Towards the end of August we had some sullen thundery weather when the air was leaden with weight and the sky was leaden in colour. The doctors came and went one day, and I was having what, in theory, was my afternoon quiet spell. This was the worst part of the day, just as three o'clock to four was the worst hour of the long night. During the last week I had arrived at a certain acceptance of hopelessness, and as I lay on the tilted bed in the dim light behind the drawn curtains I thought of my mind drifting, a frail craft, on this lonely, grey sea of hopelessness, lost and wandering, rudderless, under a sky that had no stars. It became clear to me that there was only one thing to do in such a case. The wretched little ship must be made to sink, to disappear for ever into the depths of this uncharted sea which would not mark the event by so much as a ripple. Yes. That was it. Pull out the peg and let the sullen grey waters flow in. It would be quite simple. Just wait for the next evening when Loose was on duty, get her flustered to the extent where she would leave the sleeping stuff within reach, and then, when she had gone away and you were alone on the grey sea, you could sink into it for good and it would be better for everybody.

I felt quite pleased and cheerful, now that I had solved the problem of the grey sea. I had looked so long and so carefully for land, a harbour or even a sandbar that might betoken a shore. It was good to have solved the problem of that limitless sea — you did not try to sail across it, looking for land. There *was* no land, only the deep nothingness that lay beneath its grey surface, and that was where you had to go. Just wait for a night when Loose . . .

I do not mean to convey the impression that from the moment I knew that I might not walk again I went steadily downhill into this slough of depression that took on in my mind the character of a grey, shoreless sea. Indeed, it would be more accurate to say that I did not move at all mentally, but that the grey sea was a thing of which I gradually became aware and that slowly but steadily it seemed to come nearer to

81

me, like the process of erosion on some coastlines. Like most coastlines, the coastline of my essential self was of varied character, with soft unresisting sand-banks at some points, where the sea made an easy encroachment; and at other points I found in myself rocky promontories, against which the sullen water sucked towards and sighed towards its ebb and pushed towards and rumbled towards its flow without making much progress.

The first soft sandy barrier to be overrun, for instance, was any sort of pride in my own outward person. I came to hate the kindly daily toilet that was performed for me — the sponging of my skin, the brushing of my hair, the trimming of my fingernails. I did not want any of it — I wanted to be left alone. In a similar way I lost my pride and interest in my house and garden, although I had been brought up in the tradition of meticulous housekeeping and had applied this training at Crookmill as a natural part of my character. What did I care about the polish on the silver or the growth in the garden? These things mean nothing if you are not a part of them — they owe, for you, their very existence to your ability to pour out tea from the polished pot or your sense of the tilled earth under your feet, or the tenderness of the green shoot that brings the gentleness to your fingers. Little by little I was thus overtaken by the grey waters. The books, the poetry, the beautiful words of all the poets were swept away, reduced to a sodden grey mass of meaningless pulp where no beauty remained. And last of all, the people were engulfed — all the visitors, Loose, Daze, Mattha, Monica, my family and, last of all, Twice — until I found myself alone on a bleak, rocky headland, against which the sea lapped and bit and sucked and swept, persistent and insidious, towards greedy destruction.

I held my place on the headland for a long time, for the time of thought is not days and hours but a far swifter thing. For three months of ordinary days and hours of time I had tried to outmanoeuvre the encroaching sea, and that is a long time in the thought world. And for another long time of thought I had tried to defy the sea from the rocky headland of my lone self. Force me to destruction, would it? *Me?* Nothing could do that!

I could not be destroyed. I had seen things, felt things, touched things, smelled things, thought of things in a way that no other person had or could. I was unique. I was the only one of my kind, I, this person, known to the world as Janet Sandison Alexander. I was immortal, beyond destruction. I was the one who had seen the purple spikes of the orchis rise between their spotty leaves and who had looked up into the bells of the fritillaries, seeing there something that only I and no other person could see ... But the sound of the grey waters overcame the inner voice which was growing steadily more faint.

It was this loss of the value of memory and experience — this disintegration of the main girders of the structure of the 'I' — that drove me to thoughts of suicide. Almost invariably after a case of suicide has been considered by a court the verdict brought in has the rider 'while of unsound mind' or 'while the balance of the mind was disturbed', which implies that the suicide destroyed himself because he was unaware of what he was doing. Or does it imply that only a madman's mind could run so counter to the life force as to contemplate self-destruction?

If I had committed suicide in 1947 the probable verdict of 'while the balance of the mind was disturbed' would have been just enough, but either of those two implications which I have quoted would have been completely unjust, for I was contemplating suicide because I was fully aware that my mental balance had been upset by my physical condition and I did not wish to continue to live in that state of mental disintegration which was anathema to me. As that grey sea encroached, eating away tenet after tenet, standard after standard, emotion after emotion, until no memory, no thought, no encounter, no experience had any value, to go on living — in the sense that breathing in and out is to be alive — became pointless. If I could have escaped into cantankerous ill-temper and have become a 'difficult invalid' I would have done it. If I could have convinced myself that I was a martyr to my past sins and could have taken to hysterical religion, I would have done it. If I could have become a professional invalid, interested in my ailment and trying new doctors, pills and treatments every week, I would have done it. But I could do none of these things. I simply was not interested in being or doing anything. My mind was paralysed as surely as were my legs; I was aware of it and could do no more to mend it than I could to mend my legs. The legs, will as I might, would not move, and the mind, too, seemed to be inert, watching itself die from the edges inwards, as a green leaf withers and desiccates at the onset of winter.

In every island there is some hard core of rock that will be the last to erode away; in every leaf there is some main vein of sap that will be the last to desiccate; and in every mind there is some resistance that will be the final bastion to fall. After Twice had receded into the grey meaningless unreality, I found that by remembering back to my childhood at my home at Reachfar and thinking forward in time I could make Twice become real again by remembering him there, in that place, when I had taken him home to meet my family for the first time, but quite soon even that began to fail. Reachfar began to draw away into the mist of time and space as if it were a story I had heard long ago; a picture I had seen through dusty glass or a dream that I could only vaguely remember. The grey sea, featureless, horizonless, limitless, no longer stormy and cruel now, for it had me beaten and it knew it, stretched away on every side and lapped, lapped at the unresisting shores.

One day, when the clock struck four and it was time for me to become the bright, cheerful invalid again, the sea had insidiously made a big gap in the headland and was sucking and slithering about in the darksome cave it had found in my mind, so that I could hardly bother to open my eyes, when Twice's voice said: 'Hello, there! A nice private evening — Monica is off somewhere in a temper in her car and I've told Loose and Daze to go to the movies. Are you ready for tea?'

I pushed my eyelids up and saw him in the doorway. 'Yes, please,' I said.

He went round the room, drawing back curtains so that the full light came flooding in, striking all the familiar things which had only one shape for me now that I always saw them from the same angle. Some of them were beautiful things, some ugly, like the Animated Bust which sat on top of a bookcase in a darkish corner, but a few months ago I had loved them all. Now I hated them. They were not themselves any more, but mere flat shapes and forms that always looked the same, a jumble of lines and angles and curves against a flat wall. The grey sea was better, the sullen grey sea. Anything was better than this flattened, distorted, unreal world.

With his large yet neat efficiency Twice came in with the tea-tray and began to sort plates and knives on to my bed-table and on to a small table for himself. This was what I had done to him — turned him into a cross between a sick nurse and a butler, the shocking indignity of it!

'There!' he said, giving me a cup of tea and handing the bread and butter. 'And what's your news?'

I whipped up my nearly dead horses of simulated interest. 'Dram found a wasps' nest this morning and got his nose all stung up, and Daze had to sponge him with ammonia to get the swelling down. It made his eyes water —' I hoped that my laughter sounded convincing and it seemed to be. 'I've never seen a dog crying before!'

'I thought he seemed a bit subdued when I came home. By the way, I wrote to the kennels the other day.'

'Oh? Why?'

'I've ordered a bitch to be a missis for Dram. I think it would be fun to breed some pups, don't you? I'd love to see Dram doing the proud papa.'

Oh. Here we were. We could not breed children, but we could be ever so clever. We could breed dogs.

'That's a wonderful idea,' I said.

'We could make a run out there by the wall and you could see everything that went on. A litter of pups can be very funny —'

'Twice, you think of everything! I'll love it. Thank you.'

So now the carefully planned carnation bed, specially made because Twice loved carnations, was to be turned into a wired-in run for pups to amuse the invalid. All this damnable self-sacrifice in small things and in great — it must be brought to an end.

'Twice, I thought you were going to Sir Andrew's tonight?'

'No. Tomorrow night.'

'Oh.'

It was not true. He had altered the day of that visit. More and more, he was altering, postponing, cancelling altogether appointments of that sort to meet the exigencies, as he saw them, of my condition. He was going out less and less, seeing increasingly little of his friends in the engineering and business worlds, asking them more and more seldom to come to Crookmill. It was as if I held a life between my useless hands and were wringing all the colour and substance out of it.

'You are dispirited tonight, darling,' he said suddenly.

He had never accused me of low spirits before. 'Nonsense!' I said, smiling at him. 'Why should I be? It would be wicked if I were when I appreciate everybody and everything around me so much! I always feel that I can never thank you all enough —'

'Oh, rubbish!' He rose and stood looking down at me for a moment.

'Oh, I forgot! I've got a great dollop of flowers in the car for you — absolute fizzers! I've never seen marigolds such a size!'

He dashed out of the room. Marigolds. I like nearly all kinds of flowers, but I have a loathing for marigolds. The kind called 'African' I find only bearable at some yards' distance; the flat-faced, many petalled, orange ones I dislike even at a greater distance; and the yellow ones, that look like rubber sponges on green wires, I loathe with a deadly loathing at any distance. And as if loathing by sight were not enough, their rank, pungent, chemical smell nauseates me. Surely, I thought, Twice must know all this? Surely Twice, who would not allow a door or gate-hinge anywhere around the house to creak because it is a sound I hate, must know — You miserable, puling egotist, I told myself. How should he know? In spite of his apparently highly developed instinct for your tastes, why should he know that you like all flowers but marigolds? You don't wear a label with 'I loathe marigolds' written on it! A label? To indicate something about me to Twice? No. Twice and I don't need labels. Or — wait. We, now, are not Twice and I as we were. Since I have been adrift on this shoreless sea I have lost contact with Twice and he must be adrift too. No. No. Twice is never lost and adrift. Yes. Twice, now, could easily have forgotten your dislike of marigolds even if once you told him of it. He could have forgotten. You are no longer the person he knew. You are no longer the person called Flash who hated marigolds. You are a hulk of a cripple, with no small rights of love or hatred. The only right you have is to express gratitude for all the love and care and thought and kindness that surrounds you — that is your right and your duty . . .

Twice was back in the room, smiling jauntily, carrying nothing other than the poison-green metal vase, full of stinking, canary-coloured marigolds, rubber sponges almost three inches in diameter on wiry stems about three feet high — the most monstrous, obscene and repulsive vegetable growth I have ever seen in my life.

'I had to put them in the Storied Urn,' he said. 'We've got nothing else big enough. Aren't they enormous?'

He set the vase on the bed-table, right in front of my face. The smell caught at my throat, nausea clutched my stomach.

'They are beautiful. Thank you —'

I looked up at him, and suddenly a grey glint of steel came into his blue eyes. He snatched the vase and hurled it with all his force across the room, where it crashed on to the Animated Bust, whereupon both fell to the floor, breaking to smithereens a crystal bowl and a china cigarette-box on their way.

'Thank you! Thank you! Thank you!' Twice shouted before the noise of breaking crystal and china had died away and Dram, terrified, crawled out from under my high bed. 'Thank you! They are beautiful! You know you hate the bloody sight and stink of them! Have you no guts? No mind of your own? How did you turn into an automaton that can only say Thank you?' He bent over the bed until his convulsed face was only inches away from mine. 'Can't you see what you are doing? I live and breathe and am what I am only through you and *for* you, and you are pulling away behind a screen of Thank you, thank you, thank you!'

He seized my shoulders in a trembling grip, and Dram, in a frenzy of divided loyalty, raised his black nose to the ceiling and gave vent to a dreadful howl. Suddenly Monica was in the room, behind Twice, her hands on his shoulders, dragging at him, her face greenish-white, her eyes blazing.

'You damned savage!' she spat like some creature of the cat tribe. 'Let go! Come away!'

Twice's grip on me relaxed, Monica's grip on him tightened and his face was beginning to draw away from mine when I heard my own voice say: 'Let go of Twice! Monica, let go!' The green-white lids dropped over the blaze in her eyes. 'Let go of Twice!' I repeated, and then: 'Good God! What's the world coming to if he and I can't have a private row in our own house?' Monica's hands fell to her sides. 'As for *you* —' I looked at Twice and with horror I felt rage boiling in me and heard my voice rising — 'you made that damned mess over there, you clean it up! And so help me when I get out of this accursed bed and back on my feet I'll break the pair of that crystal bowl over your bad-tempered skull! Get out of here, Monica! This is no place for you — this row isn't nearly over yet! Get out!'

Monica backed away out of the room and closed the door. I was only dimly aware that she had gone and now my brain was black with rage. I had not felt so alive since the evening of the accident and I did not know what had made me so angry, but I did not care. I let myself go in a debauch of blind rage, with the marigolds as a peg to hang it on and Twice as the rock against which to throw my pent-up fury.

'Bringing me those stinking weeds! Get them out of here! Get them *out*, I say!' I yelled, and Dram, deciding now that the whole performance was some new kind of game, jumped around the room, barking and rushing at Twice who was scrounging about picking up splinters of crystal and broken marigolds. 'You *knew* I loathe them, that the smell of them makes me sick! How dare you bring them here? How *dare* you?'

I was aware that I was raving, clutched in the toils of debauch, as a drunkard must feel when he takes another and another drink, but, like the drunkard, I could not stop. Like the drunkard with his drink when he can no longer smell or taste it, I was not thinking or hearing the words my voice was saying — I was conscious only of poison pouring out of me as the drunkard is conscious of spurious comfort pouring in through his gullet. It must have been a bestial exhibition, but it broke down at long last into exhausted sobs and tears which ran hot down my face and gathered in a pool at my throat because I had not the energy left to raise a hand to wipe them away. I became conscious of the touch of linen on my face and looked up at Twice, silent, absorbed in the plying of his handkerchief. Lying on the bed beside me was the oxydised metal vase, a large dent in its plump green belly. I laid my hand on it.

'It says ha-home sweet ha-home!' I sobbed.

'Aye, so it does, and it is quite right. This is more like the thing. I like to see a little life about the place ... Now I'm going to get some water and we'll have a dram and a nice quiet chat and see if we can remember what it was that we had all that row about. We haven't had such a rowdy one since the day you hit me over the head with the file of papers in the office and I've never even known how that one started either.' He fetched a jug of water, poured out two tots of whisky, diluted them and brought the glasses over to the bedside. 'Why *did* you suddenly hit me over the head that day? I could see no reason for it and it struck me as being most damnably unjust.'

'You made a crack about me being a good housekeeper.'

'What was wrong with that?'

'Wrong with it? I wanted to marry you more than anything in the world and I thought you didn't like me and were being funny at me. God, I was mad!'

'So was I!'

'You called me a Highland vixen and shook me.'

'There was nothing wrong with that either. I like Highland vixens and enjoy shaking them, up to a point.'

'That was the part that you didn't tell me that day — that you like Highland vixens.' I took a sip from my glass. 'That's the

89

trouble with things. Like today — I thought I *had* to say thank you all the time. The half is not told one.'

'No. And to misquote Browning: "That's what all the blessed *faith* is for", Flash.'

'Faith?'

'Yes, faith. Listen, the half is not told you. It is not told to me either, but you did not come out of that night in May alive for no reason at all. I cannot tell you all the reason why you are still alive, but I know part of it.'

'What?'

'I do not think whatever made me so dependent on you could pull all my props away like that and leave me all alone. I need you so much that you *had* to be left alive.'

'But — like this?'

'What is the alternative? The empty bed? The empty room? The empty world? For me — like this will do. And I am eternally grateful for it. But I know more than this — like this will not *have* to do, for always. You are going to dance, walk and run again, Flash.'

I stared at him and shook my head. 'The doctors —'

'They don't know. They admit they don't know. And they don't. But *I* know.'

'Twice, it is no good having pipe dreams. We have always gone for the truth —'

'This *is* the truth. It is the half that has been told to me and not to you or to the doctors or to anyone else. You and the doctors have got to have faith, but I don't. I *know*. And I am secure and happy and I want to share my happiness with you. I want you to be just yourself and cuss when you feel like cussing and be happy with me as you have always been. I know that it is hard for you, for you have only my word for things and the baby will —' It was the first time that the baby had been mentioned. '—the baby will never be again, but try to believe me — you are going to walk again, Flash.'

'I always *have* believed you and believed in you —' I said very hesitantly.

'Yes, but this is more difficult — you must try.'

'All right, Twice. You are sure?'

90

'I am absolutely certain,' Twice said and his voice had the ring of true gold against true gold.

There was no overnight miracle. I did not get up and walk the next morning, and during many ensuing nights often I would still find myself adrift hopelessly on the sullen grey sea, but there was something I could do now. When I found myself adrift with the greyness all around, I could 'cuss' and call out, but often I did not have to go so far as to call out to people, for if I listened very hard I could hear the ring of gold on gold, and if I looked in the direction from which the sound came I would see a pinpoint of light, which was the lighthouse on the rocky island which was Twice in his loneliness, and if I tried with all my force against the push of the grey water I came time and again to the shore.

And, of course, the world did not stand still just because Flash Alexander was unable to walk. The big world and the small world of Ballydendran inside it, and the smaller world of Crookmill inside the latter, kept turning, and in the smallest world my plaster cast was taken off, and in the next smallest world Slaters' Works of Ballydendran turned into a subsidiary of the huge Allied Plant Limited, and in the great big world away outside people got on with organising a pact for world peace and with the making of deadlier weapons for world war. But the events of the outside worlds were not real to me — hardly anything was real to me at that time.

It was as if I were suspended in space-time in a sphere again, but this time a sphere fabricated of some insulating material so that I could see and hear what was happening around me but was powerless to experience events in the sense of taking thought of them, making deductions from them, enjoying them or being saddened by them. Enclosing the sphere that held me, like the atmosphere that enwraps the earth, was the life I had known before I became ill, and beyond that, like the stratosphere, was the life I would have when I could walk again. There was no present, for I was teaching myself not to contemplate it, for thought of the here and now of the present brought the vision of the grey sea to my eyes and the sound of its eternal ebb and flow to my ears.

I lived, to all appearances, in my surgical bed in the gay household of Crookmill all these months, but I was, in actual fact, living largely in the past, re-experiencing happiness that I had enjoyed in the former years of my life. When I thought of Twice, it was not of Twice *now* that I thought, but of Twice when I had first met him, of Twice when I had first taken him to my home at Reachfar, of Twice standing in the assembly shop at Slaters' looking narrow-eyed at something that displeased him and whistling 'Scotland the Brave' while he thought of ways and means of improving things. I do not think that at this time when he came into the room I even saw him as he stood there. There was, as I have said, no present. What came into the room as seen from my insulated sphere was the thought of Twice, a memory, and what I saw with my mind was some picture of him from a deeply experienced moment that was now of the past.

Similarly, I did not see the Monica of the now, of the present moment that was elapsing outside this sphere of mine. When Monica was in the room with me I lived again our days during the war and went over again many of our absurd conversations and looked back with laughter on our many even more absurd love affairs.

I think it is proof that I was not really alive but in a state of suspended animation when I can say with truth that I have few memories of how Twice and Monica looked or of what they said at this time. Normally I have a good memory for conversations, and my mind is full of clear pictures from the past of people dear to me standing or sitting in certain attitudes, the light striking their faces in a certain way, the line of a bookcase or the fold of a curtain framing them in certain angles and colours. There are few such pictures of Twice and Monica from this time and fewer still of Loose, Daze, Mattha and other people. Indeed, the only picture I have of Loose, Daze and Mattha is one of all three of them, united for once to express strong indignation at me to Twice — indignation that was really a cloak for their worry because they thought, I believe, that I was going mad.

Mattha had brought into the house some petrol in a vinegar

bottle, had left it on a shelf in the kitchen, and Daze, thinking the bottle contained vinegar as per the label, tried to pickle some beetroot with it. The composite Loose-and-Daze and Mattha arrived beside my bed to lay complaints against one another.

'That yin there had nae bizniz touchin' ma things on ma shelf in the kitchen, onywey!' said Mattha.

'It might have gone off!' said Daze.

'And set the place on fire!' said Loose.

'In a vinegar bottle!'

'Like an explosion!'

'We had them all piled up in a heap at first,' I said, 'but then we decided that they were a zoo.'

It was probably very fortunate that Twice came in just at this point, for after he had listened to their indignation at me for not taking a serious thing seriously and had chased them out of the room, I was able to explain to him quite reasonably that the word 'explosion' had merely made me think of one of Monica's and my word conversations of long ago and I had spoken the thought aloud.

I once told Monica over some wartime gin that the word 'explosion' always made me think of a prickly bundle of all those terms and signs that we have in the written form of our language — a great jumbled heap of exclamation marks all exclaiming and question marks questioning and cedillas and umlauts and diphthongs and ampersands and asterisks all jangling, with, precariously balanced on top, the two little dots called that word I can never spell, 'daoerisis' or something. Monica, of course, said that this whole idea was quite wrong. She said that all these signs and terms are what is the zoo of the word world, and when I thought of this I tended to agree with her. We then went into detail on the matter of the word-world zoo. We decided that the asterisk is something prickly, like a porcupine; that the umlaut is a snake and that the diphthong is a large, hairy animal like the buffalo, from which biltong might be obtained, we thought. The cedilla, of course, is an insect, and the ampersand one of the burrowing, hibernating, smaller animals, while the exclamation mark is a relative of the llama sheep which stands very erect with a long, disapproving neck and is always saying: 'Ray-a-ly!' It was towards the end of the gin, as I recall, that we got to those two dots that I can never spell, but although I cannot spell them that does not mean that I know nothing about them ... As my friend Tom says: 'I canna play the fiddle myself, but I can tell when a man iss making a proper mess of *trying* to play it!'

'The da-whatsis-two-dots,' I said, 'is one of these low, amoebic forms of life that live in water and propagate themselves by dividing themselves into two.'

'That's quite wrong!' said Monica. '*You* should live on water instead of gin if you are seeing the da-whatsis dividing into two! You are all wrong. It's a small white furry thing, like an ermine, except that it's got two humps on its back like a camel and only migrates into English at Noël.'

'Dromedary,' I said.

'Don't talk rubbish! A dromedary is nothing to do with this that we are talking about zoos. A dromedary is not an animal at all!'

'Then what?'

'It's a place at Aldershot or somewhere where the men with the leopard-skin aprons put their big drums when they're not using them ... We might as well empty this bottle. We are going to have heads like drums in the morning, anyway.'

Yes. My escape from my present was fairly complete. At Crookmill we had little contact with the great big world outside, but the Ballydendran world affected us in that Mr. Slater retired from business except for having a seat on the board of what was now called 'The Slater Subsidiary' of which Twice became the managing director. All sorts of expansion and replanning were going on; all sorts of new people were being drafted in to what was referred to as 'Slatersub' from the parent company's head office in the Midlands, and Monica was preparing to retire in favour of a new young man called Enderby, who was to fill the position that she had taken over from me.

All this change made my will to escape even stronger than

ever, I think. I do not like to see the little individual enterprises being swallowed up by the big battalions — it makes me feel that the time of what George Orwell so hideously and aptly called 'the prole' is at hand. Although at the time that Slatersub was coming into being I did not appreciate all that was happening, I was uncomfortably conscious of the change in the atmosphere about me, a subtle difference in the visitors I saw, a murmuring, subterranean uneasiness in the intimate people about me. In one way I wanted to come out of my escape sphere to investigate it, but I had not quite enough courage. I made little, half-hearted probes at the surface of things.

'You will miss Monica,' was one of the things I said to Twice when her handover to Enderby was almost completed.

'I will,' he agreed, 'but there is so much change going on that one is calloused and does not notice it so much — not nearly as much as one noticed it when Monica took *your* place — that felt like a revolution. In *this* revolution Monica's going is only an incident.'

'Monica would not like to be called an incident.'

'No. Nor is she — but you know what I mean. I am glad that she's going in one way, though. It means the end of Loose too! She and Daze are going to come to blows about Blair if they're both here much longer.'

Mr. Blair was the manager of one of the bank branches in the town.

'What I can't understand about them,' I said, 'is that they are so well organised here in the house. They team up over the cleaning, the laundry and the catering and so on; and they are so well organised in their good works. Why can't they come to some working arrangement about their men? They *always* go after the same one, who always has to run away or marry someone else to escape the "twae millstanes" as Mattha called them. It passes comprehension.'

This was the bare truth. Loose and Daze had chased one of the local doctors until he went away for a short holiday and came back with a wife; they had hounded the postmaster until he had applied for a transfer; they had bedevilled the minister of Daze's church until his sister who kept house for him had practically forbidden them from the manse; and now they were in full cry after this wretched bank manager who suffered from acute bronchitis in the winter and from duodenal ulcers all the year round, and who had enough to worry him, I thought, without Loose and Daze horning in.

'In any well-organised community,' Twice said, 'we'd be forced to keep them tied up, like people who keep jaguars for pets . . . Hello, Monica!'

'What d'you know?' said Monica, coming into the room. 'Loose tells me she is going to supper with old Blair at his house tonight!'

'Keep your voice down!' said Twice. 'Daze is in the kitchen. Is this the old one-two, do you suppose?'

'Looks like it. The tête-à-tête is usually Loose's trump card. She is very good at the homey little woman thing, especially when she is playing on *their* ground. Daze is more of a *social* success, wouldn't you say?'

'I wouldn't say anything about either of them,' I said sourly, 'except that one won't feel comfortable until they are both married.'

'What about the poor man?' Monica asked. 'They are bound to choose the same one!'

'This is where we came in,' Twice said. 'Can I help you ladies to a small drink? Then I have to run over to the Crook for a little.'

After Twice had gone, Monica and I were having another small drink and chatting of this and that, when Daze came in and said: 'The supper's all ready and the table's all laid there. I don't feel very well. I am going to lie down.'

Monica and I looked at each other, and then Monica said: 'I'm sorry, Daze. What about a drink? Some aspirin? Have you a headache?'

'No.'

'Have you caught a chill, do you think?'

'No. No. I think it's my heart,' she said, with a dramatic gesture of hand to side.

I saw Monica bite her lip and turn away, ostensibly to light a cigarette, but when you are in bed and immobilised from the hips down you cannot turn away to hide the giggles that are threatening to bubble out between your lips. I pulled hard at all my muscles as Daze more or less tottered from the room, but when Monica had shut the door and was leaning back against it, shaking with laughter, I found myself saying: 'Monica! Monica! Monica!' in a frightened whisper.

She ran to the bedside, her eyes wide with fear. 'Jan! What is it?'

'Monica!'

'What *is* it? What's the matter?'

I reached down and clutched the covers in my hands and pulled them up to expose my legs. 'Monica! Look!' She looked at where I pointed, to the muscle above my left knee. 'Look, Monica! I can make it *move!*'

'Oh, *Janet!*' she said, whereupon the hard-boiled, hard-drinking, debonair, unshakable woman of the world threw herself across the end of my bed, her red-gold hair like crumpled satin, and burst into a storm of tears. I let her cry for a little while, while I watched myself making my muscle move another time or two and then I said: 'That's a hell of a way to carry on! For Pete's sake get us another drink! I want to celebrate!'

'Sorry,' she said. 'It was a bit dim of me.' She began, still sniffing, to pour the drinks. 'Janet, I wonder?'

'*I* don't,' I said. 'By tomorrow I'll be able to make the other leg do it too! You just wait and see. By next week —'

'No! No! Now, stop it! . . . The first thing we have to do is to report to the doctors about it. And no more of your making other legs do it. It must all be very slow and careful and super-vised —'

'Oh, horsefeathers! Either I can move or I can't, and I'm *going* to!'

We had quite an argument about it and became very heated, and Monica threatened to telephone to Twice at the Crook and to the doctor straight away and went quite a length in general, until in the middle of it all I realised how joyously happy I was and began to laugh like a maniac. Monica, well into the stride of her anxiety, indignation and argument, went rattling on regardless of my laughter, and at last I heard the two words: ' — massage and physiotherapy.'

'It's *not* therapy!' I shouted. 'It's the rappy!'

'Huh?' she said and left her mouth hanging open.

'That word. It's "the rappy".' She sat down and stared at me. 'All right. Get on with your drink,' I told her. 'You are probably quite right in what you say about doctors and treatment and massage and all that. I won't go for that ten-mile walk tomorrow after all.'

'Thank God for that. But I ought to ring Twice.'

'You'll do nothing of the sort. It's *my* muscle and I am going to be the one to tell him about it. He'll soon be back . . . I was telling you about the rappy. You know old Tom up at home?'

'Certainly I know Tom! What's the matter with you?'

'Nothing. That's an idiom, you fool. Well, Tom can read and write — very unusual for his generation and class up there — and he used to be very proud of both, as well he might have been, and every time he went to Dingwall or Dornoch or Inverness to the market or anything he used to buy a copy of the local newspaper and read it in the train coming home.'

'Snob!' said Monica.

'Of course! And more snobbish still, he would come into the house and say to my grandparents: "I see in the newspaper so-and-so and such-and-such", with the paper sticking out of his pocket and he would *not* give it to Grandad, who was dying to read it, until he had told him every mortal thing that was in it.'

'That's exactly how Uncle Egbert is with detective novels. He gets all the new ones, tells you the plot and then offers to lend them to you.'

'I know, and then you wouldn't read them if somebody paid you. Well, Tom did that with the paper. But one day he came in and said: "Ardgruanach Big House has been bought by the government, I am seeing in the paper. Aye. They are going to be bringing what they'll be calling backward bairns there — kind o' eediots, ye know — and be doing what they call 'the rappy' on them, the poor wee craiturs!" '

One of my few accomplishments is my ability to reproduce

the soft accent and gentle idiom of Tom to the life — even my family admits that I can do it — and Monica has always been a great appreciator of stories of Tom. She laughed uproariously and, of course, took to 'the rappy' as an expression right away. This led to another drink and to my telling her of Tom's delvings into French history of a Sunday afternoon, his Sunday reading frequently being an eight-volume encyclopaedia that was the property of my father. I do not know whether on this occasion he had got the volume covering 'B' for Bourbon or that covering 'L' for Louis, for this happened long, long ago, when I was about seven years old, and on summer Sunday evenings Tom used to take me for a walk before supper and bed. On this walk, on this Sunday, he told me of the three kings of France, Lewis Quince, Lewis Seeze and, most picturesque of all, Lewis Quaytors — three very dirty wee mannies who wore 'big white wigs on their heads and the wigs so full of lice that they had to be wearing a wee pottie of honey inside the wigs to be drowning the lice'. Naturally I thought it the most delightful story I had ever heard, and when we came home I told it to my family over the supper-table.

'My grandmother almost went through the roof!' I told Monica now. 'She had Tom severely on the mat for telling wicked lies to the bairn on the Sabbath Day!'

'But it wasn't lies!' said Monica indignantly. 'There's a honey locket at Beechwood that belonged to a French marquis!'

'Well, my grandmother didn't hold with that kind of history. My grandmother had the belief that a deal of history was better forgotten — maybe she was right, at that. Besides my grandmother had a prejudice against the French in general. The Auld Alliance mean nothing to my grandmother!'

'Auld Alliance!' said Monica and began to giggle. 'Ne me dites pas ça! I've told you about old Dowie — she came from Perthshire so a lot of the history we heard in the schoolroom had a certain bias. The Auld Alliance was always coming into it and, I don't know why, I thought of it in private as the Oiled

Alliance — maybe something to do with whisky . . . I say, let's have another.'

'That'll be four.'

'Sure it isn't five? Never mind, I'm pouring them small. Anyway, if we can't have a tot or two on your muscle, when can we?'

'Here!' said Twice, appearing in the doorway. 'Lay off that! Good heavens, that's the whisky ration for a month and *look* at it!'

'We can't,' said Monica; 'most of it's inside us. But calm yourself. I'll present you with a bottle right now.'

'Why?'

'You'll find out.' She went out and shut the door.

'What's got under *her* tail *now*?' Twice asked, staring at the door panels. 'Has Loose married the banker in this short time?'

He went to pour himself a drink. 'No,' I said, savouring my moment to the full. 'I think it's *me*, even if it is unbiblical grammar.'

'You? How?'

'You don't have to sound as if I couldn't get under anybody's tail or even create a modicum of interest. I still just might could, couldn't I?'

'Grammar!' he said and sat down in his own armchair by the fire with his drink.

This was exactly right. That was where I wanted him to be sitting. I was very happy. I had had a lovely few hours. Monica and I had been catty and mischievous about Loose and Daze — all very harmless — and then my muscle had moved and I had begun to look forward to his coming back and telling him about it. Then I had talked to Monica, the sort of nonsense about my old Tom and her old Dowie and about words that she and I had not talked for so long. I felt not only that I had been reborn, but that with my rebirth the whole world had taken on a newer, stronger, sharper, more zestful life.

And there was Twice now, with his pipe in his hand, drinking his drink and looking at the fire — contented, I knew now, to have a wife like me, tied to a bed, unable to move. Very quietly, I pulled the covers away so that my legs were exposed. Nature has been kind to me — I have long, quite shapely legs, and a few months in bed had made their skin soft and cosseted-looking but had not altered their shape.

'Twice,' I said, 'come here. I've got something to show you.'

He rose, glass in hand, and came to the bedside, looking into my face. It crossed my mind that for months now no person had looked at my hands or any part of me except my face, and always with this smiling, well-wishing, indulgent look.

'What is it, darling?'

'Look!' I said and pointed and made the muscle move, such an absurdly small movement, just above the knee.

Twice put his glass down on the bed-table and laid his pipe beside it, moving very slowly and carefully, as if, suddenly, the whole world and its encircling air were made of something brittle and easy to break. For what seemed a long time he stood looking at me, and at last he said in a low trembling voice:

'I knew it. I *knew* it! Oh, Flash — well done!'

He began to walk up and down the room — I think he had a desire to run outside and rush shouting to the top of the furthest hill — and he seemed to exude joy until the room was at bursting point. As if drawn by some magnetic force, Monica appeared at the back-passage door with her bottle of whisky in her hand, Daze appeared out of her bedroom and Loose came in through the front door with Mr. and Mrs. Slater.

'Well, what's going on here?' Mr. Slater asked, feeling the electric atmosphere.

'It's Flash, sir!' Twice exploded. 'She can move a muscle in her leg!'

'Lo and behold!'

'And I'm getting drunk!' Monica shouted, waving her bottle.

There was a general orgy of laughing, hugging and kissing, ending with Twice, quite unable to contain himself now that he had let go, careering round the room embracing the furniture and everything that he bumped into. In the end he bumped into Monica. They were just beside my bed when he caught her in his arms, and, in spite of the surrounding chatter

101

and laughter, the three of us were trapped in a pool of silence. It was all over in a split second. Twice crushed Monica against him, kissed her, released her and hurled himself on top of Dram and kissed him too. Monica swayed on her feet a little, opened her eyes, looked down at Twice rolling on the floor with the dog and began, with unsteady fingers, to unwrap the foil from the neck of the whisky bottle. I was suddenly engulfed in pity for her, and it was a hateful thing, for, badly as I may have described Monica, I hope I have made it clear that I never expected to feel pity for her. It was at the same time, for me, tragic and incongruous, that most shocking of combinations.

'Monica?' I said on a questioning note.

She tilted her head and looked at me sidelong out of her long, veiled eyes, and with my reborn acute awareness of the present I saw, and memory recorded with the speed of photographic film, the beautiful clear line of her jawbone and chin.

'Want a drink?' she asked jauntily. 'So do I!'

She had the corkscrew driven now and, bending down, she put the bottle between her knees and drew the cork with a hollow 'Plop!' By this time the rest of the room had returned to some semblance of sanity and I heard Daze saying sourly to Loose: 'I thought you were *out* for supper?'

'Well, I'm *not*!' said Loose snappily.

I thought for a moment that they were going to quarrel, but basically they were friends and I know now that their liking for one another was stronger than all their rivalries in housekeeping matters as well as in their affairs of the heart.

'*Not* the way people behave where *I* come from,' Loose went on with dignity, conscious now that not only Daze but all of us were listening.

'What happened?' Daze asked, while we all held our breath.

'He sent a message down by that slatternly servant of his to say that he was in bed. It's his stomach,' she said. 'At *least* he could have telephoned!'

'My dear, I don't believe a word of it!' said Daze. You would have thought that she and Loose were alone in the room. 'I saw him in the High Street this very afternoon — there was no trouble with his stomach *then*!'

'Exactly!' Loose said. 'And there was I and no bus back till nine o'clock, so I went up to Mrs. Slater's and —'

'And here you are and isn't that nice! Have a drink, you old fool!' said Monica.

Loose and Daze retired to Daze's room with their whisky-flavoured water, no doubt to write the epitaph in the annals of love of Mr. Blair, and the rest of us sat around my bed talking, first of my muscle and then of the all-prevailing changes at Slaters' Works.

'It won't be long now until the change-over is complete and all the new staff eased in,' Twice said.

'And, lo and behold, Lady Monica will be out of a job!' said Mrs. Slater, to whom the idea of Monica working in any way at anything had always been a tremendous joke.

'A woman without a place to lay her head!' said Monica, with a dangerous curl of her lip and a glint in her eye.

I prayed silently that Mirabile Dictu would not blunder us all into some dreadful humiliation, but it was Twice who said: 'No need to curl your lip like a vicious horse, Toots!'

'I know you prefer dogs!' Monica said. 'No need to make a point of it!'

Twice gave her an ugly, level look out of hard eyes. 'Now then, dearie, don't be quarrelsome. I never could bear a woman who got ugly on her drink!'

'You could never bear, full stop!' said Monica.

'Look here,' I broke in, trying to keep my voice light and free of tremor, 'is this private? Or can we all join in?'

'There is nothing private,' said Monica. 'In fact, there is nothing — if I may repeat myself — full stop. Anyone who wants a share in it can have it. Me, I'm going to collect that old bag Loose and have my supper and go to bed. Good night, everybody.'

I was glad when the others went away too, but when Twice came back into the room I felt uncomfortable. One side of me wanted to tell him to be kinder to Monica, but the other side told me that I had no right to interfere. Whatever quarrel lay between them was private to themselves, and I knew that it did not impinge in any way on the relationship between Twice and myself. That was inviolate, I knew, because it was inviolable. So I pushed away the discomfort, I shut Monica out of my mind and retired into the walled city that was Twice's and my private world. This proved to be possible at all times except when Twice and Monica were together in my room, and then it was impossible, for my senses were now fully alert to the world that *they* shared — and a stormy battleground of a world it was — and I was on the watch all the time to prevent a collision between it and the world that belonged to Twice and me.

I once read a story with the title 'There is No Conversation', and I always think of that phrase when I think of Crookmill at that time. Of speech, talk and what my friend Martha would call 'yackety-yack' there was plenty, but there was no give and take of real exchange between people, no interchange of spiritual coin. I do not know what factor it is that suddenly comes between people and dries up the stream of intercourse between them, leaving them like a series of pools, connected by nothing except the stony water-course, with its few discarded tin cans, broken plates and old boots of speech, talk and yackety-yack. My relationship with Twice — and in a shallower degree with Monica — had been of the sort where nothing is barred. There were between us, at need, the words or the gesture that communicate anything and everything, but that had suddenly ceased to be so. There was suddenly a barrenness, an isolation, as if we were all being drawn apart by some invisible and intangible force.

For some reason that I cannot explain, too, I did not bang my fist on that table, which would have been one of my methods in the past of dealing with such a situation, and say: 'Look here, Twice, something is wrong! What is it?' Nor did I use another of my methods and say: 'Monica, do you feel that I am peculiar these days? Because I *feel* peculiar.' No. I did not say any of those things, partly out of a cowardly but natural tendency not to awaken a sleeping dog which I felt might be an ugly-tempered beast and largely because the days, weeks and months now were being taken up with 'the rappy', and it was

104

all very joyful and exciting, because it was all so continuously progressive. There were no setbacks or relapses, so I did not want to think of setbacks of any kind. Every day the movement became easier, stronger and more complete, and on the last day of November I was able to stand on my own feet, balanced and unsupported. It was to take a little longer to reach the stage of putting one foot in front of the other in the attempt to walk, but that came, too, in time; and as the story of anyone's 'operation' is always a bore I shall leave it at that, except that in its chronological place I shall tell you of the first time I walked without help.

During this period of 'the rappy' my mind ranged round and round the problem of Monica, but still 'there was no conversation'. She was bitterly unhappy, with a deep unhappiness to which she tried to give neither word nor look nor gesture, going ahead in her debonair way — to the eyes of most people — as she had always done. There were times when I would almost manage to convince myself that what I had seen had been a figment of my sick, off-balance brain, but when this conviction was almost complete, some little thing would happen to demonstrate to me again that the unhappiness was real and close to overwhelming her.

I felt responsible, rightly or wrongly, for what had happened to Monica, for I had brought her into this world of mine, but alongside of this I owe, by nature, so much respect to another person's intimate feelings that any form of interference is utterly repugnant to me. So I plodded on, learning to walk again, while my mind, like a mouse on a turning wheel, revolved and revolved round Monica and what I could do to help her and how I could do it.

By mid-December the doctors had conceded that I might now be carried to the car and be driven out, without risk of damage to my spine, which meant that, in general, the world was opening up for me again and, in particular, that we could accept one or two invitations for meals during the Christmas and New Year period. Monica's job at the works was now virtually at an end, her hand-over to young Enderby completed, and I began to hope that she would leave Crook-mill and Ballydendran without the dreaded collision between her, Twice and myself coming to pass, but she seemed to have no ideas of going away. She spoke of her 'Ben-the-Hoose' as if she intended to end her days there.

For me the atmosphere of the house became more and more grotesque. Loose and Daze, like the innocents they were, were gambolling about making Christmas puddings and cakes and being secretive with coloured paper and tinsel string; all sorts of people, led by the Slaters and Sir Andrew, were besetting Monica, Twice and me (whom they seemed to regard as a single entity, and how shockingly right they seemed to be) with invitations to attend this meal or that, this party or the other. Twice was becoming daily more strained-looking, and daily, almost, Monica was adding another drink to her quota and a little more acid to her tongue. Then, just before Christmas, Monica's sister Sybil paid us a flying visit and stayed for two nights in Daze's room while Loose and Daze packed in together, and I was faced with that thing, the Loame world, in an even more pronouned form than at the time of Gerald's visit, for this time there were two Loame *women*, and two who were very close to one another, for in age Monica and Sybil were separated by only a year, Sybil being the elder of the two. They had all the nursery, the schoolroom and their Parisian convent life together as a background for themselves and as a drop curtain between them and the outside world — or that was how it seemed to me.

On the second afternoon of Sybil's visit, when Monica had gone in to Ballydendran to one of the many 'last meetings' at the works, Sybil came in to sit with me. I cannot tell exactly what happened, but first my happiness became dulled, then it disappeared altogether, and by the time Sybil had said goodbye and had gone Ben-the-Hoose for a meal before catching her train I was very miserable indeed and aware for the first time that my life and my future with Twice were not as secure as I had always thought.

I have always found it easy to remember trivial conversations, especially if in the course of them something has been

106

said to amuse me, but important conversations, by which I mean exchanges which have made some impact of unexpected shock on my deepest feelings, tend to escape my memory, so that I cannot remember now many of the actual words that Sybil spoke, but I can remember only too clearly the feeling of insecurity and desperate loss that she left behind her.

Sybil had once been described to me by Monica as a 'full-time convener of committees cum bazaar-opener' and all her utterances invariably seemed to me to have the detachment of view of the person who has met with you to discuss some problem that has no bearing either on your personal life or on hers. As I have told you at some length, I had been worried about Monica and her unhappiness, and I wanted more than anything to ask Sybil what was troubling her sister and what I could do to help her, but this was something that I could not do in a direct way in that closed world of the Loames, and especially with the 'bazaar-opener'. All I could do was try to keep the conversation on Monica and try to pick up hints from what emerged — I was coming to the idea that the trouble was a family one of some kind — so I told Sybil how very helpful Monica had been to us all at Ballydendran, how we would miss her when she went, how grateful we were and how I hoped that she realised that we were grateful.

'Grateful?' Sybil said, like a comment from the chair on an unimportant point that some committee-member had spoken on for over-long. 'I shouldn't bother about that if I were you.'

She lit a cigarette, smoothed her hair and flicked a speck of dust from the toe of her shoe, which actions might have been a rearranging of the papers in front of her and the phrase: 'Next, please.' We continued to chat aimlessly for a long time, but eventually we came back to Monica.

'I have been worried about her lately,' I plunged. 'She has seemed to be very restless and unhappy.'

'*You* shouldn't worry about *Monica*,' Sybil said in her light, clear voice and the emphasis on the 'you' and the 'Monica' was so slight as to be just discernible and no more. 'I agree that it is time she left this job she has been doing,' she continued, 'but, of course, I did not approve of it in the first place. She has been

107

very silly and difficult since 1945 when she came out of the service.' She frowned as if the bolt of flannelette for the Women's Institute sewing meeting were late in its delivery.

'The war may have upset her more than we know,' I suggested. 'One hears of nervous cases developing long after —'

'Nerves? Monica?' Sybil broke in with a polite, tinkling laugh of apology for the interruption of what I had been saying. Really, the laugh indicated, as chairwoman, I do not wish to interrupt the well-intentioned remarks of *any* member, but the time of the committee is limited. She rose to her feet and continued: 'Monica has been very spoilt and difficult since she grew up, Janet. I don't think you understand her in the least. The main thing that is wrong with her is that men spoil her — they always have. It is time she left here. I must see some of the family and make a plan about it.' She smiled at me graciously. 'In the meantime, you must concentrate on getting better and do not worry. It is extremely naughty of Monica to behave like this, but things have not gone too far. They can be put right. Fortunately, it is not too late. Don't worry, Janet. Just take care of yourself and get better completely. Goodbye.' And, very much the Country President who had got one more committee-meeting off her hands for another month or so, Sybil departed to the Ben-the-Hoose, leaving me feeling that I was so much visited, but very uncomforted, tenantry.

You cannot have read thus far in this chronicle without realising that I am a very simple-minded sort of creature — indeed, almost what Monica would call 'a natural' about many things, and especially about people that I like and love. If I like a person, I want to help that person in any way I can, and I do not want to hurt that person for anything in the world. I want the people I like to have everything that they want to make them happy, big things and little things, and I will always try to help them to get these things, so I wanted Monica to have everything that *she* wanted. Where my simple-mindedness comes in so strongly, though, is that I had never visualised a situation where she, or anyone else for that matter, would try to take Twice away from me. That is not the sort of thing that *I* would have thought of doing had I been in Monica's place, so it did not occur to me that *she* would think of doing it. But of course, as I told myself as I sat there after Sybil had left me, maybe thinking did not come into it very much. When *I* met Twice, would I not have loved him just as much and wanted him just as much even if he had been the husband of Monica? Did people think, in these situations? Did thought come into it? I did not know. I did not know anything, except that I loved Twice more than I had ever done and wanted more than ever that he should have what *he* wanted to make him happy.

You might as well, I told myself, put the thing into words and face it. There is no point in dithering about in your mind with vague phrases. Does Twice want Monica instead of you? Quite probably, came the painful answer in my mind. Why shouldn't he? There is not a single way in which Monica cannot make rings round you — she has brains, wit, looks, position, wealth, and she can *walk*, you know — she is a physically normal woman that a man can live with and enjoy as men and women were meant to live with one another, as you and Twice used to live with one another, remember? All that time ago? Away back before you fell on the bridge? Remember?

Yes, but I will walk again. One day soon I will walk, and then . . . Then? It will be too late. It is too late now. If Twice wants someone else, are you going to compete? You know that you won't. For you, he is lost right now, you know that. And the Loames do not betray one another. Sybil was not sounding a sort of gypsy's warning. Sybil was telling you of what is already a *fait accompli*. It can be put right, she said. Put right! Patched together, flawed for ever and ever. What was that phrase there? Gypsy's warning! Remember that day, that first day on the hill behind the Crook — that day a little over a year and a thousand centuries ago — when Monica told you you had been warned? Even then she could foresee this situation. She could always see further ahead than you could — it is natural with her and her kind to see away ahead, like giraffes having long necks and deep-sea fish having a special kind of eyes. They evolve that way. Oh, she could not foresee that you were going to fall down and break your stupid back — not that. But she could see then that you were not enough of a person to satisfy Twice, and she knew then, too, that she wanted him for herself. And if you were a poor sort of person then, what are you now? A cripple. You will walk again, you say. Oh yes. You will walk. Once again you will be a little pedestrian creature. Pedestrian. You will never be anything else. This accident, this illness, have been nothing more than an over-dramatic melting of the silly wax wings you made for yourself. From wax wings to plaster cast; you should write a nice dreary book about it — it would sell by the million to the morbid . . .

Remember, remember another thing — remember the night that Twice brought the marigolds in the Storied Urn — the night he made you believe you would walk again? Remember when Monica came in here and caught him by the shoulders? You knew that night — right then you knew that this was between them. Deep down and instinctively, like an animal that crawls along the ground on all fours — that is all you are — you knew it, and what did you do? You went into a screaming, slobbering debauch of rage — a sickening debauch — and now you are hurt in your feelings when a man leaves you for someone else.

He hasn't left me! He won't leave me . . .

In his mind he has left you. And can you blame him? Oh, it can be put right, as Sybil said, put right. Monica can be dragged away and you can hold on to him. Such a fine thing to do and be — a puling, pathetic cripple holding on to a man who is sick of you and wants to be free! Such a creative thing to do — to create a merry little hell on earth for three people, just to satisfy your miserable little ego . . .

Stop it, I told myself. You do not know that any of this is true. Sybil did not say anything. Sybil did not . . .

How does one come to know anything? Seldom does the deep knowledge, the understanding that twists in the mind and the heart like a bright knife, come from one person to another through the medium of the spoken word. This sort of knowledge is a piling up, a rising in temperature, an increase in speed until the moment is reached that is like the moment of birth of a typhoon, when suddenly all the elements are fused into a single blinding force that bursts over the astonished heart and brain. By going back to the beginning, I could trace the development of this thing from the moment when Monica stepped off the plane over a year ago.

There are times in life when all events seem to conspire against one, and this was one of those times for me. It was mid-winter and the Ballydendran winters are severe, so that the roads were either frost- or snow-bound, or sleet was driving before the wind which howled round the Crookmill chimneys, so that fewer and fewer people could come to see me. Twice was away a great deal, short trips of two nights down to the Midlands or London, and Monica came and went, her comings and goings leaving plenty of field for my speculation.

Suspicion is not a pretty weapon. It is no straight Damascene blade with a sharp point and two cutting edges, but a crude instrument, like the primitive knobkerry, with which the blinded mind blunders about, striking now inwards at itself, striking next at the heart, striking next at every small daily event, until nothing in range is clearly defined, but battered and bludgeoned shapeless and meaningless by this weapon of suspicion.

If Monica was away at the same time as Twice, she was *with* him in a sordid, furtive way. If she was at home while he was away, she was staying at home by arrangement with him in order to allay my suspicions. If they were both at Crookmill, I would suggest that Twice go through and fetch Monica to come to us for a drink or a meal. If he accepted the suggestion and went to fetch her, I knew — positively knew — that he could not live except within sight of her; if, as he often did, he responded with: 'Oh, why? Can't we just be ourselves alone for a little while?', I knew — positively knew — that he was afraid of betraying himself by having her in the room with us.

I was very unhappy, but I was fortunate in that I was not tortured by jealousy, for jealousy seems to be something that has been left out of my composition. I suppose that people love in different ways, just as they walk, speak and reason in an individual manner, and my way of loving does not admit of jealousy. I could imagine all sorts of physical contacts and emotional situations between Twice and Monica, and these imaginings made me very unhappy with a poignant sense of my own loss, but they did not make me jealous in the way of wishing to damage Monica or of wishing to vent spite against Twice. If Monica was the person that Twice wanted and she wanted him, they must have each other. There was nothing I could do because in my way of loving there was nothing to be done. All the love I had to give lay between me and Twice, and if he no longer wanted it the essence of it was a crippled thing which would for ever be a part of me, just as my crippled legs were part of me. I think that I have said that I am a simple sort of person, and in my mind I saw the position as simply and clearly as that; but life is not a matter of simple, straight-forward decisions taken in one's own mind and followed through. No. The business of living is more complicated than that.

If you love anyone as I love Twice, the love begets a detailed and deep knowledge of the beloved, and this knowledge, in turn, engenders a deeper love. It becomes an infinite progression of love, knowledge, more love, more knowledge. I knew, at this time, a great deal of and about Twice, and one of the many things I knew was that he would never leave me until I told him to go. I knew that Monica could bring all her desire for him to bear, bring all her ruthlessness to her aid, but that all her efforts would go for nothing against the hard core of the strange integrity that was at the centre of the character of Twice. He had loved the woman I had been, and if a combi-nation of events — Monica's coming and my accident — had caused a shift of emotion as an earthquake will cause a shift in the ocean bed, that did not mean that Twice would drift with the newly formed current. Twice was violent and passionate in everything he thought and did, and no doubt his feeling for Monica was violent and passionate like all his feelings, but I knew that, always, his greatest violence, passion and force were retained for the maintenance of his own moral standards. It would be a violation of these standards, I knew, to do

112

anything that would mortally hurt *me*, for he was aware that all that was deepest and most valuable in me was vested in my faith in him. I did not have, in Sybil's words, to have things 'put right' for me. Twice would never put them wrong.

What is so difficult to believe now, after many years, is that a set of circumstances had arisen which had convinced me that I did not want Twice to stay with me. And this brings me back to my way of loving. A love like mine has no desires except the happiness and welfare of the beloved. Compared with the unhappiness that I felt in Twice at this time, all my own ugly, torturing suspicions, all my self-pity, all my feeling of betrayal by Monica, all my sense of cruel loss were nothing. If only Twice were brought out of this deep, wordless unhappiness of his and back to happiness, nothing else would matter.

Life, as usual, did not stand still throughout the long cold days and nights when I spent so much time alone, trying to beat out some solution to my small but torturing problem. The Christmas parties came and went, I went on daily with my 'walking practice' with my crutches — horrid, cacophonous word for these horrid, unsightly instruments. Old Mattha's son, who had chosen to take a trip home from America, turned out to be a wealthy dyspeptic widower of about fifty and Loose and Daze were hot on his trail, competing hard to be a comfort to him, to the grim amusement of Mattha and earning his acid comment. Matthew, called after his father but known as Matt for differentiation, seemed to be utterly at the mercy of Loose and Daze, who controlled his life and his diet, commandeered him and his hired car for trips to Glasgow and Edinburgh, and knitted him mufflers and socks against the rigours of the Scottish winter. Matt came to be known as 'The Mat', for, indeed, very much like the proverbial doormat did the ladies pull and shake him between them and jointly tread him down.

Old Mattha continued to take a personal interest in Crookmill, and, in spite of the protests of Loose and Daze, I encouraged him, for his cynical, disillusioned attitude to most of life suited my mood at this time. On Saturdays he would arrive with a commandeered labourer, horse and cart and two commandeered grandsons who were forced to cut logs for the

113

Crookmill fires, whether they would or no, and Mattha would bring a kitchen chair, which was the most comfortable seat for his rheumatism, alongside my bed or wheelchair and give me the benefit of his views on anything and everything. I think it was the fact that I was a cripple that caused Mattha's unusual attitude towards me, as my being unable to walk rendered me sexless, and at the same time added years to my age to make me a contemporary of his own. At all events, he would talk to me as he did to no other woman, and even gave an impression of respecting my opinions, a compliment he paid to few men and to no other woman to my knowledge.

'An' hoo muckle longer is that reid-heidit bizzom gaun tae be stoppin' here?' he asked me suddenly one morning before Monica was quite out of earshot.

'Lady Monica?'

'Leddy Monica, if ye like,' he said sourly. 'Leddy or no', she's a bizzom like a' the rest an' a reid-heidit yin at that. Ah never could abide reid hair — hot-tempered they are, but there's mair nor that. Aye. They're hot in ither places forbye their tempers, the bitches.'

'Now, Mattha, that will do. I have known Lady Monica for a long time and she is a good friend of mine.'

'Freen's!' said Mattha with scorn. 'The bother wi' *you* is ye huv faur ower mony freen's as ye ca' them! Folk fur iver skitterin' aboot yer place as if it wis a bliddy hotel! *Ah*'d gie them their orders if it wis ony o' *ma* business! Freen's! Well, dinnae say Ah didnae tell ye!'

'Tell me what?'

'Ach, ye ken fine! It's a bliddy shame, that's whit it is! . . . Hoo's yer legs?'

'Fine. I'll surprise you all one of these days.'

I was glad when he went away that day. So far, the tangle between Monica, Twice and me had been a thing private to ourselves, for one could discount the secret world of the Loames and Sybil's knowledge, but old Mattha was the writing on the wall of the Ballydendran world. Although Daze called him 'that ill-natured old craitur' and Loose called him 'that nasty spitting old man', he was a realist with unblinded

114

sight and by far the most observant person who came to Crookmill. He had spent years in the observation of humanity, with special reference, it is true, to its foibles, follies and failings, and was qualified, therefore, to be the first of our surrounding world to see what was happening, but after him would come the deluge, with all the indignity of small-town gossip, comment and speculation.

Grimly I went on with my walking practice, for I now had matters reduced in my mind to the utmost simplicity. The only thing to do, I had decided, was to walk out; it seemed to be the only solution that would leave any of us with a shred of dignity — such a simple thing to do, provided one can *walk*. Everything turned on that, that once again I should be master of my own movement, no longer an object for help or pity, but someone with the power to make a decision for herself and act upon it, by walking away, unaided, into the future. This future, this what-might-come-after, did not matter to me and I did not think of it. I thought of nothing, almost, but the desperate need to walk, and despair brings with it its own strength and its own courage, and also, I found, its own secretive pride. I did not tell anyone how proficient I was becoming at my walking, because, you see, it was all I had at that time that was my own and so much had been taken away from me that I guarded my walking with secrecy in case, somehow, that should be taken away from me too.

One afternoon, towards the end of February, while everyone was out, I walked to and fro along the back passage of Crookmill six times, turning at the ends, without even once my courage failing me, so that I had to put out a hand for the support of Mattha's wall, and the next day I did it ten times, but now I had reached the stage when the number of times did not matter to me, for I was no longer clinging to the safety of Mattha's wall. The terrible fear of falling had gone. Suddenly I found in myself the knowledge that I could walk out of the house, down the rough road and away along the main tarmacadam highway at the foot of our hill. I was no longer afraid that I should fall. At last, at last, I could really *walk*.

I went back to my wheel-chair and sat down to enjoy my

jubilation, to triumph about my conquest of the fear of falling that had been the worst and most persistent aspect of my convalescence, to wallow in my regained courage, only to find that I had no courage at all. Now that I was physically able to walk out and away from Twice I did not have the mental courage to do it. Not yet. I must wait a little, keeping my walking a secret. I must wait until this new kind of courage that I needed came to me.

It was shortly after this that, one evening, Twice came home in the mood which always made my love a deep ache of tenderness. His tie was crooked, he had a smudge of black oil on his face, he was irritable with himself and with all the world, he was whistling 'Scotland the Brave' as he always did, without knowing it, when things were going against him. There was no conversation, still, but one had to say something. One always had to say something.

'I thought you were supposed to be a white-collar type nowadays?' I greeted him. 'How did you get your face into the oil?'

He threw his coat at the sofa and began to undo his tie as he came across the room towards my wheel-chair.

'Will you kiss me in spite of it or must I bath first?'

'Come and I'll tell you.' I kissed him on the oil patch. 'There. What's wrong?'

'Oh, everything. That new lay-out they've put in is all to hell and gone. It just won't *do*. I told that production bloke it wouldn't, but, oh no, they had to try it. Well, they've tried it now!'

'And?'

'They're going to pull it all out and put it in *my* way now. Waste of time, the whole bloody issue ... Can I have some tea?'

'Not a drink?'

'No. Tea ... Daze! Some tea, please!'

'You are in a real fan-tod, my pet,' I said. Twice always calls for tea at peculiar times when he is worried or discontented. 'Look, would it help to sit down and have a cuss about it?'

'I'm tired of cussing,' he said, but he sat down and began to roll his shirt-sleeves up over his powerful forearms. 'I'm fed up, that's all. Fed up to the back teeth!'

I felt cold inside. 'With anything in particular?'

'With everything.' He clenched his fists between his knees and sat looking down at them. 'This Managing Directing job is a poultice, to start with. I'm not an office-wallah! I mean, I don't mind writing a few letters and attending a few meetings and so on, but dammit, it makes me mad when they resent me walking through the assembly shop. Hell, I'm an engineer! I'm not a civil servant or an office boy or something! If I'd wanted to sit behind a desk and push a pen all day I'd never have learned to use a lathe or a micrometer. Dammit, if I'd wanted to choke myself on a diet of paper I'd have taken to the law or gone into a bank! . . . And, talking of paper, when the hell is Monica going to get out of those rooms through there?'

In these moods, his brain often flew off at tangents, but this time the fly-off was a little sudden and in an odd direction.

'Paper? Monica?' I said.

'I always intended to have myself a little drawing-office in that end room there. You *know* that!' he snapped crossly. He was partly right. It was something I *had* known about but had forgotten with all the other things I was trying to forget, this drawing-office of his. Daze came in with her tea-tray and he almost chased her out of the room.

'I wish to God Monica'd clear out,' he said moodily, poking spitefully at the sugar with a spoon.

I felt lost and bewildered. As I have said before, I am slow-witted and easily muddled and, in addition, I was now wandering into strange country, for Twice had not mentioned Monica to me for months.

'But, Twice, I thought you liked Monica!' I said stupidly.

'Oh, don't pretend to be Loose-an'-Daze and muddle-headed, Flash!' he snapped impatiently. 'It's nothing to do with liking or not liking Monica! I want a *drawing-office*, *here*, in the *house*, at Crook*mill*!'

'I see.'

'You don't see at all! When you say "I see" like that, it means "I wish to God everybody would shut up and go away so that

117

I can think this thing out" . . . Great God! You would think I didn't *know* you!'

'Stop bawling!' I shouted back at him. 'All *right*, I don't see! Why this sudden desperate urge to have a drawing-office through there? You have the latest model drawing-table in your office at the works and all sorts of fancy lighting — isn't that enough?'

'Monica isn't even company for *you* now! She hardly ever comes in here. And it isn't a sudden urge to have a drawing-office through there! I've *always* wanted it! The works! I haven't got *you* at the works! . . . Flash, you and I could have fun through there — I hate these evenings when I have to go back to the works to draw because it's the only time I get peace to do that sort of thing!'

'Twice Alexander, do I understand you to be making oblique love to me?' I asked in a silly, joking way, in order to cover the tremulous uncertainty that I felt shaking me.

'If you like it oblique — certainly. I'll make any kind of love to you at any time you choose. I'll do anything in my power for you. I thought you knew that. I love you, you see.' He paused. 'I thought you knew that,' he repeated.

I did not speak and he went on: 'But I have felt for a little while that you weren't in much of a mood for any kind of love-making.' He was not looking at me, but down into his teacup. Twice has very heavy-lidded eyes and the eyes themselves are very brilliant, so that when the lids come down to cover them his whole face takes on a curious, closed blankness. His mind is always at its most alert and penetrating when his face looks like that. It is very disconcerting.

'This — this dreadful thing that happened to you, Flash, is something that no one else can know about — not even me. Now that you are getting better, you may be finding that you are a different person from — well, from the person that loved *me*. That is what worries me so much. I don't know if you even want to talk about it.' He looked up at me questioningly, a quick flash of blue light.

'Talk, Twice,' I said.

He breathed out a sighing breath, rose and took a pipe from

the rack on the mantelpiece. 'This thing that happened has changed both of us.' He was concentrating hard on the pipe and the tobacco. I held my breath painfully. Here it was. I thought some miracle had happened, but no. The dreaded moment was on me after all. I sat still and looked straight ahead of me at the Animated Bust on the corner of the bookshelf. 'What happened was what I would have said was impossible,' he said. 'A year ago I would have said it was utterly impossible. But that accident has been like a wedge driven between us — I did not think that such a thing could happen. I did not think, a year ago, that any experience could come to either of us that the other could not share. I have tried my best, Flash. I have tried to feel as you felt, to think as you have thought. If I could have done all the suffering for you I would have done it, but I couldn't. All I could do was my own thinking and feeling and suffering and know all the time that you and I were drifting into two separate worlds. And the loneliness is the worst thing. It is getting worse, the blank, lifeless loneliness.'

'Loneliness?'

'Yes, my separate world is full of it and it is coming over me like — like a darkness, and soon I shall lose touch with you altogether, and then, I know, I myself will be lost.' He put the unlit pipe back in the rack, turned his back to me and began to walk away down the room. 'If this dreadful thing that happened to you, Flash, has made you so that you don't want me, we can arrange things somehow. I will know that it isn't your fault and that you are not deliberately being cruel to me. I know that you would not hurt me if you could help it. But if this thing has killed in you what was between us, as the baby was killed, tell me. That would be kinder than just going on like this from day to day. But, Flash, if you *can* come back out of that separate place you have gone away to, will you try to come? If it is difficult, let me try to help, but I wish, Flash, that you could come back!'

The length of the large room was between us and I was blind with tears of shame and sorrow, but I rose from the wheel-chair.

'Twice,' I said, 'I am coming back.'

He turned and stared, his hands held out, but his feet rooted to the floor by his fear to move, as I walked the length of the room towards him.

'You see what I mean by separate worlds?' he said later, when he could speak coherently. 'I would never have believed that you could practise your walking in secret like that and never tell me of your progress. It was a cruel thing to do, Flash! What made you do it?'

'I don't know,' I told him. 'It was a thing I had in my mind. I wanted it to be a secret until I could walk well enough to — to walk right up to you.'

I have told in some detail of these mental reactions to my state of physical paralysis, but this does not mean that I feel that these reactions were in any way unique. I think that the balance between the mental and the physical in any human being is of extreme delicacy and that the mental and physical are linked more closely than the physiologists on the one hand and the psychologists on the other would lead us to believe in their approach to the ills that affect mankind. To be in the physical situation of having apparently healthy legs that will not move is in its essence macabre and I do not find it extraordinary that a mind encased in a body in such a situation should tend towards the macabre in the thoughts and ideas it generates. At all events, during the time that I was tied to my surgical bed, I generated for myself a fine set of what my friend Tom would call 'MacAbers'.

Tom pronounced the word 'macabre' as if it were the name of an old Highland crony of his and, indeed, it has something of this meaning in his mind. His acquaintance with the word came from the title of a book we have at home which is *Tales Grim and Macabre* and which is a collection of ghost stories and other queernesses, mostly by Le Fanu. Tom, after reading the book several times, persists in his belief that 'macabre' is another word for 'ghost' and gives the whole thing a tang of his own countryside by referring to ghosts, invariably, as 'MacAbers' — and quite a clan of them there is, too, up there in Ross-shire.

And so after my long sojourn among the MacAbers I emerged into a world that seemed to be entirely refurbished. It was the same world, with the same people in it, that I had known before my accident, but it was like an old house and garden, long known, that had been redecorated and refurnished, relandscaped and replanted. It all lay before me to be rediscovered and I had all the time in the world to go about in it, savouring in leisure and with pleasure all its fresh newness and old memories.

Part IV

Part IV

When one is completely happy it is very easy, I find, to lapse into the attitude of: 'Pull up the ladder! I'm on board!'

In the midst of my own new-found happiness and security I was still aware that Monica was far from happy, but, with utter selfishness, I did not want to think of unhappiness and I pushed the thought of Monica aside. This was very easy to do, for she was away a good deal although she was still the tenant of Ben-the-Hoose, and it was made easier still by the fact that, being able to walk again, I found myself extremely busy. Every day, I discovered some new place that I must walk to and walk back from — an old elm tree three fields away, a certain gate that broke the hedge that bordered the main road and — great adventure — the little waterfall in the burn, quarter of a mile up the hill behind the house. Dram and I were so busy walking — and we could run a little now, too, in a flat field where nobody could see us — that we had no time to think of anything else. And at weekends, when Twice was at home in daylight, we all three of us would go walking, which was pure bliss. Time flowed past me, with its flotsam of the small events of day by day, but I was so full of happiness that I noticed events only vaguely, like strangers passing by on the other side of a golden trellis.

By the end of March Loose and Daze had The Mat worn practically to a shred with all their attentions to him, and the rest of us were beginning to wonder if he would get away at the end of the month back to California without finding himself imprisoned for bigamy, when one evening he arrived at Crookmill, looking as wondering as ever, accompanied by his father, old Mattha, who was as sardonic as usual.

'He go' a tellygram,' said Mattha, who invariably behaved as if his successful son were not only half-witted but stricken with dumbness into the bargain. 'He's no' tae gae back tae Amerikky the noo. His boss is comin' ower here an' he's tae wait here fur him an' gae back wi' him la'er on.'

'Isn't that nice?' said Loose delightedly.

'Isn't that grand?' said Daze delightedly.

'Iphm,' said Mattha and spat out through the kitchen window. 'Ah thocht yees wid be pleased. That's the wey we cam' rinnin' richt doon tae tell yees.' And he leered at them with hideous sarcasm.

'Really!' said Loose indignantly.

'Well!' said Daze indignantly.

'Reely! We-ell!' mocked Mattha and spat again through the window.

'Stop that!' said Loose and Daze in one voice.

'Whit?'

'Spitting like that!' said Loose.

'Through the window!' said Daze.

'Ah wish a' the folk Ah ken didnae dae ony waur nor spit!' said Mattha and marched off into the garden.

Throughout this scene Matthew had stood blinking through his spectacles with that look he always wore of wonder at this world in which he found himself — as well he might — and showed neither embarrassment at his father's behaviour nor indignation at his treatment by Loose and Daze, nor did he seem to share my amusement at the exchange between the three.

'You know, Matthew,' I said, 'I don't think I even know what your job *is*?'

'Fruit farming,' said Daze.

'Fruit canning,' said Loose.

I wished that just for once someone would allow Matthew to

speak for himself and I looked at him and tried to convey as much in a glance.

'I am what the English call a market gardener,' he said. 'The Americans call it truck gardening, but here in Scotland, where we say what we mean — when we get the chance to speak — I am what they would call a fruit and vegetable grower.'

I took what, in south Scotland, they call 'a second look' at Matthew, met his twinkling eyes behind his rimless glasses and discovered that he was not at all 'The Mat' of our imagination, but a genuine, if more polished, chip off the old granite block that was Mattha, and I knew that once again Loose and Daze were wasting their hunting time.

'Of course,' he continued, 'since I ply my trade in a big country I do it on a biggish scale. I manage six fruit and vegetable farms for the Garvin Canning Company of California.'

'Peaches an' a' the like o' that,' said Mattha from outside the window like someone in an Edwardian play. 'Peaches!' He turned aside to spit. 'Gi'e me a goo' stick o' rhubert an' ye can keep a' yer peaches!' He disappeared.

Matthew laughed. 'I've always wanted to thank you, Mrs. Alexander, for your kindness to my father,' he said.

This took me completely by surprise. 'Nonsense! It is your father who has been kind to *us*! But for him, this house wouldn't have been habitable in the first place, not to mention all he does about the firewood and the garden.'

'We-ell,' said Matthew, 'when both parties are satisfied it is a good piece of business, but it's not everybody that can do business with my Old Man.'

'Well, I happen to like him,' I told Matthew. 'And you must bring your boss to see us when he comes.'

Now this is the kind of thing that I do without effort or even conscious volition. Twice says that it is my Highland instinct of hospitality which makes me automatically say a thing like that when I am at a loss for a topic of conversation, and maybe he is right. He is also right when he says that you never know where it is leading you, like the time that I met an acquaintance at the Waverley Station in Edinburgh and told him to bring the friends he was meeting along to our hotel for a drink. The friends turned out to be two very large African gentlemen in blankets and bracelets, and old Alex, our Writer to the Signet cousin, looked quite faint when we introduced them.

Anyway, in the snarling teeth of past experience I invited Matthew to bring his boss to see us and dismissed the whole thing from my mind. I should have known that Matthew was the success he was largely because when he said: 'I certainly will,' what he meant was: 'I certainly will.'

I have probably mentioned already that my birthday is in March, but this is a different year, and Loose and Daze, being born birthday-celebrators (but not their own — you would think they had never been born) and anniversary-rememberers, and who had not had a hospitality orgy since New Year, threw themselves into a frenzy of cake-making and party-preparing. It began by being 'a few people for drinks', and then it was altered to 'starting earlier and having tea as well because of people like Mrs. Slater and Mrs. Webb who don't really drink'; and then it was decided to extend it over supper because 'poor Matthew won't get back from Glasgow until about seven and won't have any party at all'. Fortunately the day fell on a Saturday, except that that was almost a misfortune too, for Twice said: 'Why not invite the whole boiling lot for the weekend and have done with it?' and I thought for a moment that Loose and Daze were going to take him seriously. Monica was away, which in one way was a relief to me, yet in another way it made a little grey smudge on my bright happiness and I said as much privately to Twice when we were alone one evening.

'Oh, well, it can't be helped,' he replied banally.

He never spoke of Monica now except in a distant way and with a strong air of constraint. I did not like it, not only because I disliked that attitude to Monica when once she and Twice had been such good friends, but because it was the only constraint that lay between Twice and me. More and more I was coming to think that my sick imaginings and the mischievous machinations of old Mattha's sour mind had spoiled and tainted their friendship, and the thought was worrying me, but I had not the courage to say outright to Twice: 'I thought you were in love with Monica once'. Not even as a joke could I say it, for I knew that to tell him such a thing would hurt him deeply.

'I wish she were here for my birthday, though,' I said

'Don't start to *harp*!' he told me, grinning. 'Kate told me that when you were small you could harp on about things you wanted or wanted to know until you drove the household half crazy. Monica isn't here and that's that. No good your starting that I wish-t business.'

'Yes — I always pronounced wish with a "t" at the end ... I *wisht* I had a pencil that would write red!'

'That's it — that's just what Kate told me.'

'Anyway, it works. So I *wisht* Monica was here.' Twice was silent. 'You don't?' I asked.

'*I* wisht I had a drawing-office. I also wisht the whole situation was cleared up.'

'What situation?'

'Monica in general. She is running about hither and yon like a hen with its head cut off.'

'I think she is unhappy about something, Twice,' I ventured.

'*I* can't help *that*,' said Twice, 'and I still wisht I had a drawing-office. Can I give you another small dram?'

'Ouf!' said Dram sleepily in his deep voice from his place on the floor.

'Not you, you oaf!' said Twice and drowned the subject of Monica in the gurgle of whisky into the glasses.

I gave a lot of thought to that '*I* can't help *that*' with its emphasis on the first word and the last. Knowing Twice as I did, it was a tacit acknowledgement of his awareness that all was not well with Monica, and at the same time it was a disclaimer of all responsibility to try to help her. Six months ago Twice would not have taken that attitude to Monica, and there was no other person of our merest acquaintance to whom I could imagine him taking such an attitude. Monica must have done something that had angered him very much in order to cause it and I could not imagine how or when, for they had never quarrelled, and when they were together at Crookmill they still maintained, most of the time, the sparring, good-natured fellowship they had had from the time of their first meeting. Yet, was the attitude the same? No. Since the night my first muscle had moved, Monica's replies had often had a poisoned edge of bitterness that had not been there in the earlier days.

Childishly I continued silently to 'wisht' that Monica would arrive for my birthday, but the day came, the party got under way with the arrival of Mrs. Webb at three in the afternoon, but Monica did not arrive. It is difficult to describe the disappointment I felt. What Twice calls my Celtic Twilit Conscience was working on this thing, which meant that I was feeling that all the 'bad things' I had thought about Monica, which were not true, were now avenging themselves upon me, so that Monica was not coming to — and did not even write a postcard about — my birthday, and it was all because I had 'betrayed my friends' and it was 'all my own fault' and it 'served me right' and I was conscience-stricken and miserable.

Of course, the thing about parties is that the thing that they are being given about has no ultimate bearing on the success or failure of the party. A party can get given to celebrate an engagement of marriage and the two 'engagees' can be as miserable as sin in the course of it, but that fact has no ultimate bearing on the success or otherwise of the party. A party seems to depend for success on two people present having been in the same bad spot during the most recent war, or on two people present having been at another party in Chicago the night the host's mistress dotted him one with a champagne bottle, while for failure it depends on the drink running out or two lady guests arriving wearing identically the same hat except for the colour of the feather.

Neither of these two untoward things happened at my party, and it was a great success in spite of the fact that I was missing Monica so badly. Several of the new staff of Slatersub came to it, and also a director of the parent company, who, with his wife, happened to be spending the weekend with the Slaters. The couple were a Mr. and Mrs. Lester, and Twice brought them to me as soon as they arrived. When the usual pleasantries of introduction were over, Mrs. Lester drifted away with the Slaters, but Mr. Lester, who was a large man, manoeuvred himself between me and the rest of the room and said: 'I have been very anxious to meet you, Mrs. Alexander. I have heard a great deal about you.'

Many people, I suppose, have the poise and savoir-faire to deal with this sort of remark, but as I can never think of anything to say except: 'Thank you very much. Here I am,' I smiled in a gormless sort of way and said nothing at all.

'A charming place you have here,' he said next, looking round the room.

We chatted for a little while about the house and the garden, and houses and gardens in general, and then: 'Are you fond of travel, Mrs. Alexander? Like my wife? Or are you the stay-at-home sort, like Mrs. Slater?'

I felt that the question was not idle and I replied as truthfully as I could: 'I don't think I am definitely either sort, Mr. Lester. I am not a very definite person at all. I simply enjoy most things that come my way, I think. Before the war I travelled a little on the Continent and enjoyed it. During the war I was confined in one place for several years while I was in Air Intelligence and I didn't find it unbearable. Since the war I have been mostly here at Ballydendran. I like this too.'

'I heard of your long illness. A very trying business. You are really well now?'

'Oh yes, thank you. Perfectly. I am a matter of great pride to the doctors and people who looked after me — it is rather a pleasant experience.'

'The paralysis itself must have been far from pleasant.'

'Oh, well, one soon forgets that.' I was bored with the subject. 'I understand that you are on the export side of the firm, Mr. Lester? Does that mean that you and Mrs. Lester travel a great deal?'

'It means that, roughly, we are at home for only three months or less in the year. Not that we *have* a home — only a service flat in London . . . But I wanted to know what you would think if we gave your husband a few overseas assignments?'

I looked at him. 'I wouldn't have any opinion, Mr. Lester. It would depend entirely on what Twice thought.'

He laughed. 'This is stalemate — *he* says it would depend on *you* ... Alexander, come here a moment, my boy!' Twice came over to us and Mr. Lester continued: 'Your wife says it all depends on you.'

Twice turned to me. 'Mr. Lester knows what I think about the job the firm is offering me, Flash, and I'll tell you about that later. But when he made the offer this afternoon I told him that I didn't get married in order to travel off to the ends of the earth and have to live on a diet of letters. But if you would travel with me, that would be different.'

'Well,' I said, 'I got married on the "Whither thou goest, I will go" principle, but I don't know if I would like not having a home, like Mrs. Lester.' I looked round the big room with its wrought-iron fire-basket and all the things we had made and all the things that people had given us. In that moment I was full of possessive love for the Animated Bust, even. I looked back at Twice, but it was Mr. Lester who spoke.

'It would not be quite like that for you, Mrs. Alexander. As I visualise it at the moment, you wouldn't be out of the country for more than six months at a time. Most of the trips would be considerably shorter, in fact.'

'And then come back here?' I asked Twice.

'Yes, Flash.'

'I'd like that!' I said; and that is how, more or less, Twice and I got into a new way of life and Twice became chief consultant for the factory plant section of the firm.

Later in the evening, when he told me all about his new job, his eyes glittering with enthusiasm, I said: 'What a dope you were to hesitate! The salary and expenses are fantastic!'

'It will be a fantastically expensive way of life too!' he reminded me.

'Well, I'm thrilled to bits, anyhow, and so are you! And don't try to be blasé about it!'

'I can't be that. To be truthful, Flash, I was getting fed up to the back teeth with Slatersub. I am not constructed to be a little cog in a big machine. I'm like Mattha — I like to "work tae ma ain haun" '. I like a job that is all mine, that I can leave my trademark on, so that after I am dead people can say: "Alexander, the fool, did that — bloody awful, isn't it?" or "Alexander did that — he wasn't a bad craftsman in his day". This job gives me that sort of chance. Wherever I plan a layout, that plan is mine and I have to stand or fall by it. It makes me sort of the modern version of the itinerant craftsman, you see?'

'I see.' I smiled at him. 'And I become the modern version of the camp-follower, with all expenses paid.'

'Don't be deluded, my pet. You are going to have to work your passage. I haven't given you your proper birthday present yet — what about a portable typewriter?'

'Of course! Now you really *are* talking! I'm not really the camp-following type.'

'As if one didn't know,' said Twice.

He was pleased with his new job because it made, as he had said, an 'itinerant craftsman' of him, but Mr. Slater, who was the only other person who knew as yet of the appointment, looked as if at any moment he would burst with sheer pride, that out of all the men in the vast organisation Twice had been chosen for this plum of a job. I was pretty proud myself, at that, but did not dare to air my pride to Twice who did not think of his new job in terms of promotion or personal advancement at all. Twice has much of the isolation of mind of the single-handed craftsman and does not think in terms of personal advancement. He sees only the job to be done, the machine to be constructed, the production lay-out to be planned, and is quite unhampered by any questions of personal profit or loss, or the jockeying for positions of power or prestige which are always a feature in some degree of any large enterprise. We shall never be wealthy, for if Twice can earn enough to provide bed and board, with a little left over to pay our way into an occasional concert and to buy pipe tobacco and whisky, he is perfectly happy as long as the job is going well. If the job is not going well he is a devil incarnate, and a palatial residence and all the music, whisky and tobacco in the world would not make anything else of him.

133

At the age of thirty-nine, as he was at this time, he had enormous physical strength and vitality, and when everything was going well he effervesced, spilling energy around him like a bubbling fountain. He was in such a mood one Sunday morning about a month after my birthday, when I was at my desk writing my weekly letter to my father, and, having no better way of using his spare energy for the moment, he was rolling round on the floor playing with Dram. A table that carried a vase of flowers fell over with a crash and the vase of water fell plumb into my lap.

'Twice!' I sprang up, shaking icy water from my skirt and legs. 'Honestly — for heaven's sake, you and that damned dog! Get out of here!'

'Sorry, Missis,' he said from where he sat on the floor with his arm around Dram's neck. I was angry until I looked at them staring up at me with wide eyes in contrite faces. 'How do you get so damned *young*?' I asked, exasperated.

'I don't know.'

'Well, you are making an old woman out of *me*!' I said and went away to change my clammy, uncomfortable clothes. When I came back he had wiped the floor and set the table and vase to rights again.

'I am very sorry,' he said. 'But the vase isn't broken ... I say, Flash —'

'Yes?'

'You *are* older than I am, you know.'

'Only six weeks!' I countered.

'No, I mean *really* older — and far, far wiser.'

'Thank ye kindly. Well, be a good boy until I finish my letter.'

'Flash?'

I put down my pen and turned round. 'Yes, darling?'

'I think it was being ill that made you so much older.'

'I'm sorry about it.'

'I'm not! I couldn't love you more than I did before, but I *admire* you more now.'

'That's very civil of you, darling.'

'And I never tell you often enough how much I love and

134

admire you, so I thought I would tell you this morning.'

'Thank ye kindly again. I love and admire you too.'

'That's nice,' he said in a satisfied voice. 'Would you mind if I kissed you, just to seal the agreement?'

'Not at all.'

'Whit a cairry-on an' it the Sabbath Day!' said the voice of old Mattha. 'But folk's only young an' daft the yince ... Ah cam' in becuz Ah thocht yees wid like tae ken that that yin ben there is roarin' an' greetin'.'

'Who? Loose?' Twice asked.

'Whae else?'

'What's wrong with her?'

'Ah niver speired. Ah dinnae haud wi' her at the best o' times as ye weel ken an' specially no' when she's roarin' an' greetin'.'

'Come on,' I said to Twice and we went along the back passage. Loose was mopping her eyes and sniffing when we went into Monica's living-room.

'What's up Loose?' Twice asked.

'It was the telephone!' sobbed Loose, staring at the inoffensive black instrument on the table.

'The telephone?'

'It was Lord Beechwood, all the way from London. Monica's missing.'

'*Missing?*' I almost shouted. I wanted to shake Loose. 'What the devil d'you mean?'

She began to cry again. 'Well —'

Daze now came into the room with a lugubrious face, and at sight of her Loose began really to bellow, so Daze began to cry too.

'Oh, God —' I began to bawl at them.

'Go easy!' said Twice. 'What about a cup of tea?'

'Ah jist thocht that wid be the next caper,' said Mattha, creaking through the doorway with a tray, a teapot, an odd assortment of cups and two bottles of beer. 'Here ye are. But Ah'm no' fur yer tea — tea at a' times o' the day tans the stamach, that's whit it diz. Here, yous yins — for the love o' God tak' some tea an' redd up yer faces! Whit's that reid-

135

heidit wee bizzom at noo? Is she in the jile?'

'That's not the way to go on, Mattha!' said Daze.

'Gaol! Really!' said Loose.

'Weel, whit are yees greetin' about? *Whaur* is she?'

'We don't know!' shouted Loose. 'Nobody knows! Nobody has heard a word from her for seven weeks! They've rung up *every*body, and the bankers say she hasn't cashed a cheque for *eight* weeks and none of the shops where she has accounts has seen her and none of her friends or anybody, and she's *missing*, and so is her car, and the family is going to call in SCOTLAND YARD!'

And at the end of this tirade Loose and Daze gave a loud bellow in one voice and dissolved into a fresh flood of tears.

'Great God Almighty!' said Twice and went away back along the passage to our own part of the house.

Dumbly, and feeling very, very frightened, I followed him. When I reached our living-room he was standing staring out of the window, and in an automatic way I went to my desk and sat down. The unfinished letter lay there with a large blot in mid-sentence that had been made when the vase and table fell over. 'Twice and Dram have just knocked over a table so this is all for this week. Love from Janet,' I wrote, and put the sheets into an envelope. I had just finished addressing it when Twice turned round.

'Flash —'

I looked straight into his eyes. 'Yes?'

'Flash — Monica wouldn't have done anything — stupid?'

'It depends on what you mean by stupid — Monica can do some very odd things.'

'Flash — there's something — I didn't want to tell you — ever — but —'

I stared at him. 'Twice, what? What *is* it?'

'Flash, don't be angry. It wasn't my fault. At least, I don't think so. I couldn't help it —'

'You couldn't help what? What are you talking about? What ... Great Heaven! Don't stand there looking like Loose and Daze rolled into one! What do you mean, Twice?'

'I didn't want to talk about it — ever ... I thought one

136

time you knew and then it seemed you didn't —'

'Knew what?'

'About Monica.'

'*What* about Monica?'

'She wanted us to go away together.'

'Wanted —? Away together?'

'Yes.'

'When?'

'From — oh, a long time back.'

'No,' I said. 'No, I didn't know. Twice, you had better tell me about this, hadn't you?'

'There's nothing to tell. That's all.'

'Darling, it can't be *all*. Listen, I'm not angry as you call it, and I'm not hurt or *any*thing, but if you could tell me a little more of what happened and what was said between you and so on, I might be able to think of what Monica may have done . . . She fell in love with you, I take it?'

'That's what she said.'

He had gone round behind me so that I could not see his face, but his voice betrayed a dreadful pained embarrassment and shame.

'When was this?'

'Oh, away back — when she first came to live in the Ben-the-Hoose.'

'And you?'

'I — I told her not to be a fool.'

'I see. And then?'

'Then you got sick and she came at me again. She —' He stammered a little and then fell silent.

'Go on, Twice. I know Monica. She said you were tied for life to a cripple who would never walk again — is that it?'

'That and more and over and over —'

'And you?'

'I — I — it is a shocking thing to have to say — I'd feel better, somehow, if —' He broke off and suddenly came round to stand in front of me. 'I'd feel better and less ashamed — It was an unreal thing she had, a sort of delusion. I could feel it . . . I'd feel less ashamed —'

137

'Less ashamed about what?' I asked as quietly as I could.

'I'd feel less ashamed if it had been a real thing and I had jumped into bed with her!' he burst out brutally. 'But I couldn't! She was hysterical and revolting! What I did was —'

'Yes?'

'I turned her over my knee and smacked her bottom!' he said, all in one breath and on a falling note.

'Twice!' In spite of everything and all my worry I began to laugh and could not stop.

'It isn't funny, really,' he said shakily, staring at me.

'Sorry. I couldn't help it . . . Where did this smacking take place?'

'In a hotel room in Birmingham — *my* room. And she had nothing on but a pink satin thing. But I was so goddam mad at her for following me down there like that —'

'All right. I know how you must have felt, my pet. When did this happen?'

'That last time I went south — Monica hasn't shown up here since.'

'What happened after you — smacked her?'

'She started to cry, and I was sorry for losing my temper and then —'

'She came back to the attack again?'

'Yes. So I called her everything I could think of, picked up my bag and walked out of the place.'

'Everything you could think of? Can you remember any of the things you thought of?'

'Oh, trollop, harlot, nymphomaniac — I pretty well threw the book at her. And got very childish too, when I think of it. I told her she was too undignified to be human and that I'd as soon get into bed with a polecat and that I belonged to the world of *people*, not brute beasts and so on. I think that's about all. But do you wonder I didn't want to talk about it? Do you wonder I feel ashamed?'

'No, I don't. It was a shameful position to get yourself into.'

'Get *myself* into? Listen, *I* didn't make the running! That's what's so humiliating! It's — it's AWFUL to be hounded round the country by someone who doesn't interest you in the least! Interest! I began to think there must be something wrong with me when I couldn't raise even a flicker of interest. Interest! I've never been so revolted in all my life!'

'I wish I had known about this sooner, Twice,' I said.

'Why? Anyway, I thought you *did* suspect something, but I did not want to bring any of it into words between you and me. It isn't the sort of thing that belongs with you and me. And, anyway, what could you have done? It would only have led to some sort of filthy scene. I know that you and I can have ourselves quite a hair-tearing when we feel like it, but ours is just usually good healthy bad temper. This thing of Monica's was unhealthy and revolting — it is difficult to talk about it now without feeling sick.'

'That is just the point — that word unhealthy. There is something wrong with her, Twice. Where in the *world* can she be? It didn't occur to you to worry about her all this time — since Birmingham?'

He stared at me, frowning. 'Well, no. The Birmingham thing was nothing special to me. Or to Monica, I thought. It was the first time I had laid hands on her, but otherwise it was just a bigger and better scene than the smaller ones we had had in dozens before. It never entered my head that she would disappear like this. I was delighted when she didn't turn up here again — thought I'd got her choked off at last.'

'You used the word unhealthy, Twice. Did you mean it literally; I mean, did you get the impression that Monica was — well, sort of crazy?'

'Not literally. No. I mean — oh, Christ, how embarrassing all this is! Even to talk about to *you* which is like talking to myself . . . No, I meant more that, for me, *any* hole-and-corner affair like that, especially in our circumstances, with you ill and everything, was unhealthy and revolting . . . No. She was sane enough, if that's what you mean. Good heavens, only a person with a good brain in good working order could have handled those last days of the old Slater firm as she did . . . But wait, there *was* something odd in the business, too. I always had the feeling that the hounding of me that she went in for was unreal — spurious. Sort of *contrived* — you know,

139

unnatural. Words are difficult. I can't explain what I mean. But I used to say to myself that it couldn't be real, this business of a bloke like me being chased by a female scion of the nobility, you know? Then I would tell myself that she must have some sort of slumming complex and that maybe that was why she had picked on you for a friend as well as me for a lover. ... When I say slumming, like that, what I mean is, escape — out of her own world and into another ... But the queerest thing about it all was her attitude to *you*. I used, naturally, to drag your name in and her reaction always was: You leave Janet out of this! It is nothing to do with Janet! This is between you and me! ... That was always the attitude except when she was using your illness as a lever, you know.'

'It couldn't have been very amusing for you, all this, Twice. It's no good saying that I'm sorry that I ever brought her here — that doesn't help. But I *do* wish we knew where she is now!'

'If her family, with all their resources, can't find her, we can't,' Twice said. 'Flash, you won't tell anybody about all this carry-on?'

'I can't see that telling about it would do any good,' I told him. 'At this stage it would only be humiliating for everyone.'

'She has always been fairly highly sexed, hasn't she?'

'No. Not really,' I said. 'I wouldn't have said so. Men always fell for her like ninepins — understandable, when you think of her, isn't it?'

'Lord, yes. I give you that. I merely happened to be otherwise engaged, as it were.'

'She used to take it all in her stride. During the war, especially in our unit where there weren't many women and everyone was fairly confined, she and I were always having the odd whirl with someone. Nothing very serious. And quite often we would agree that we had more fun in one another's company than we had with the boy friends. No. She wasn't sexy in those days and she didn't lose her head. That's why I feel that something's gone wrong with her. That business with you is not the Monica I knew. I *wish* I knew where she is!' I got up. 'Still, it's no use sitting here wishing. I suppose Loose and Daze are still through there bawling. I'll have to make them

140

understand to keep their big mouths shut in Ballydendran, at least for the moment.'

'I agree,' Twice said. 'No use in having a local wonder if it can be avoided.'

To comfort people like Loose and Daze is not difficult. Their minds are strangely childlike, and in a fatalistic way they expect to fall down and graze their knees occasionally; they expect things to go a little wrong for them, but for them, as for most children, there is always some 'bigger' person around who has to do the comforting and all the real worrying that has to be done. To put a rein on their tongues is a more difficult matter, so when the crying had stopped I became extremely serious and stern with them and implied that if one whisper of the mystery of Monica leaked out in Ballydendran they would both leave Crookmill forthwith and: 'You know how Ballydendran would gossip about *that*!' I ended darkly. When they had sworn that they would be trampled by a herd of elephants before they said a word, I returned to my own end of the house, unjustly cross with them both for the very weak ineffectiveness that made them so nice and harmless. Monica, I thought, was at least effective.

'Listen,' Twice greeted me, 'I've had an idea. Don't accuse me of having sex on the brain, but isn't it possible that Monica, having drawn a blank with me, has gone off somewhere with one of the many boy friends?'

'It's possible, I suppose.' I took thought for a moment. 'In fact, it's highly probable, I suppose, if one can believe what one reads about women and sex generally. But I have an odd feeling about this. I don't somehow *see* Monica in — in —'

'Loitering in the fields of dalliance somewhere?'

I laughed. I had to.

'What's so comical?' Twice asked.

'Nothing really. It was just odd that you should bring out that particular expression at this moment.'

'Why?'

'Oh, the usual thing,' and I went on to tell him about Monica and me and the fields of dalliance. To tell him of this, to reconstruct a little of Monica's and my past, was comforting to me in this situation of nagging worry about her.

From the earliest day that I can remember, my home and my family were dominated by my grandmother, a tall, fine-looking, eagle-eyed old woman — in fact, a typical Highland crofter's wife, but not at all like these bonneted and shawled old crones that you see sitting at firesides in Victorian prints having the Bible read to them by Queen Victoria. Indeed, I would like to have seen Queen Victoria — or anyone else — calling unexpectedly on my grandmother in order to read the Bible to her on a day when she was getting the butter ready for market. That would have made a picture worth printing. From morning till night, the house, yard and steading rang with her commands.

'Are you men going to sit there all day smoking your pipes? That won't get the hay in!'

'Janet, take the little pitcher and get me some spring water for the butter. And don't spend all the morning staring about you! Go straight to the spring now and don't dally!'

'Kate, get that table cleared and bake a few scones — there's hardly a morsel of food in the house!'

'Janet, take this jar of jam east to old Granny Fraser — she's very fond of rhubarb jam, the poor old craitur. And be back by tea-time and don't dally!'

'Janet, go out and get some tatties for the hens' pot and quick now and don't dally!'

'Janet — don't dally!'

And in moments of utter exasperation she would add: 'That Janet! She is just my old Uncle Rory all over again, the idle wastrel!'

These last words in my mind were one word which was spelled: 'Idolwastrel' and in my mind the idolwastrel was a fat, benign, brown creature with a paunch who sat all the time, cross-legged and dallying, on a nice stretch of moorland like the three miles between our house and old Granny Fraser's. Sir Torquil Daviot, the local baronet, whose study I had once visited with my grandfather to discuss a matter of some march

142

fencing, had a small bronze Buddha which, when I asked what it was, I was told was an 'idol' and I think this is why my familiar, the idolwastrel, had this form in my mind. I was very fond of my idolwastrel, who accompanied me everywhere I went for a long time, although I knew it was a sin to have this 'thought person' and I knew that it was even more of a sin that I should feel so much in sympathy with him, for, of course, my grandmother knew everything and was right about everything and everybody had to do what she said, and my grandmother would tell you that idols were 'sins of ignorance', but that dallying and waste of time and waste of any kind were far bigger sins because you 'ought to know better'.

Then, to make matters still more sinful, I read the phrase 'the fields of dalliance' somewhere and realised at once that these fields, and not the moor between our house and Granny Fraser's, were the true home of the idolwastrel and myself. The fields of dalliance were green water meadows — something I had never seen but which sounded cool and beautiful — 'with daisies pied' and strewn with asphodel, eglantine, daffy-downdillies and all the plants of poetry which, by mind-sight, were far more beautiful than any of the real flowers that I knew by eyesight and by local name, and the idolwastrel and I dallied together endlessly in these fields, the idolwastrel, in the extraordinary way of childhood, contriving to dally without ever uncoiling himself from his cross-legged, sitting position, although to reach the fields of dalliance at all you had to travel away, away to a far, far country and, in hard fact, often found yourself wandering away up over the Greycairn moor instead of coming 'straight' home from old Granny Fraser's by tea-time.

When I had told Monica of these fields of dalliance she had said: 'How very strange! I have never thought of them as being in the open air at all — and certainly they weren't water meadows. I have always known they were fields 'd'alliance' — places where people get together, you know, like ballrooms and double beds!' I think that this goes to show in some degree the difference that background can make to people. My grandmother probably never had cause to use the word 'alliance' either in English or in French, but 'dally' was a word that she used as frequently as any in her vocabulary. Monica, from her earliest days, probably heard the word 'alliance' being bandied about all the time but had never heard the word 'dally', being, as my grandmother would have told you, had she known Monica, of a family that had nothing to do but dally all day and for ever if it wanted to.

But now the only effect that my leit-motif about the fields of dalliance had on Twice was to make him say: 'There you are! Double beds! The old sex thing again! I tell you, that damned woman is rolling in the hay somewhere, with *some*body!'

I immediately felt angry with Twice, and in some queer way that I could not explain this certainty of his that crept into every discussion of the subject that now dominated our lives invariably hurt and exasperated me to the point of ill-temper. The days rolled past and we all lived in a network of telephone calls which got nobody anywhere, except to fray the nerves of Twice and myself with our ugly knowledge of the prelude to the disappearance. Twice was extremely bad-tempered about the whole thing too, but for reasons different from mine.

'Drat her! You can say what you like, Flash, but this is no way to behave. Would *you* do this to *your* people?'

My weekly letter to my home, written every Sunday, was almost part of my religion, as was my father's letter to me, also written on Sunday, part of his.

'That's different,' I said. 'And Monica's people are not as worried about her as mine would be about me. I once said that the Loames had a world of their own, but actually *each* Loame has a world. Her people are more annoyed than worried — annoyed because she hasn't turned up for this meeting about the Derbyshire estate and they can't get on with the business until they get her signature. Their relationships to one another are different from ours — I realised that when Sybil was here.'

'Sybil's stab at the *Times* Agony Column was no good, either?'

'Apparently not.'

'Flash, I hope to God she is all right. She was drinking like a fish for a bit.'

'You can't drink for free and she has never cashed a cheque —'

'Unless she has another bank account they don't know about —'

'Twice, I wish you'd stop worrying and worrying at this like a dog with a bone! It doesn't do any good!'

'It wasn't *you* that smacked her behind! I feel like a monster!'

'Oh, shut up! What I ought to do is smack *both* your behinds!'

I was now feeling cross at Monica as well as worried about her, for now, by her very absence, she was dominating the atmosphere of Crookmill, and, what was utterly exasperating, she was putting me in an uncomfortable position with all its inhabitants. I find that I can be talkative and garrulous to an amazing degree about anything unimportant, but in critical situations I find no release of outlet in mere words, and the people around me were beginning to accuse me of harshness, lack of sympathy, lack of proper feeling by word, look and gesture. Old Mattha was a perfect pest.

'Nae word o' that wee bizzom yet?'

'No.'

'Ah bet ye she's droont at the bo''om o' some river wi' that damt caur. She aye drove it as if the divil wis on her tail. It's no' a year ago that a man wi' a caur went ower the side o' the Divil's Beeftub an' naebody kent for a fortnicht, wi' the snaw an' a'.'

'There is no snow just now, Mattha.'

'A caur could stot aff the road a' the same! She aye drove it as if the divil wis —'

'Oh, shut up, Mattha! Everybody is worried enough without you beefing around the place!'

'Gettin' crabbit'll no' help ye! Nor the poor wee lassie aither!'

'Poor wee lassie! I thought you didn't like her, anyway?'

'That wis diff'runt ... Och weel, if ye dinnae care, ye dinnae care ... Matt's boss fae Amerikky an' his sister are comin' doon here the-day.'

'Oh? They've arrived, then?'

'Aye, on Setterday. They're gaun tae stop here fur a week. Matt's got rooms at the Shepherd's Crook fur them.' He gave a malevolent chuckle. 'Ah said tae pit them up in oor garret, but Matt said oor plumbin' wisnae gidd enough. An' us wi' a bath an' an inside closet an' a'! Plumbin'! . . . Ye ken that man Morrison up the Toon?'

'The plumber?'

'Plumber? He couldnae wipe a j'int tae save his life! Niver feenished learnin' his tredd.' He snorted. 'He's pit a new board ootside his hoose. Ye ken whit it says on it?'

'No. What?'

'Sanitary Ingineer! Did ye ever hear tell o' the like o' that? It seems there's nae plumbers nooadays. They're a' — whit's yon word your man disnae like?'

'Technologist?'

'Aye. They're a' technologists. In ma day there wisnae ony technologists.' He spat into the cabbage patch. 'An' Ah'll tell ye anither thing there wisnae in they days.'

'What?'

'This thing that that bolshie bastard doon at the railway ca's proletariats. We wis a' in the bar o' the Royal the ither nicht an' he says we wis a' proletariats. No' me, Ah says. Oh, but ye are, says he. Whit wey? says Ah. Because ye *are*, says he. Awa' tae hell, says Ah, Ah'm no' a proletariat an' niver wis, Ah says, an' wan mair funny word oot o' yer heid, Ah says, an' Ah'll warm yer lugs fur ye, ma lad.'

'And what happened then?' I asked. I could listen for hours to Mattha's views and experiences, especially now, to get away from the eternal subject of Monica. Mattha spat into the cabbages again. 'Ach, his wife cam' in an' gi'ed him a cursin' an' took him awa' hame. Pare sowl! If Ah wis mairrit tae a wuman like yon, Ah'd likely be a proletariat masel'.'

When, later, I told Twice that Mattha had the idea that a proletariat was a henpecked husband, Twice pointed out that Mattha might be right at that if one defined 'proletariat' as many people did as a 'down-trodden mass'.

Matthew did not let any grass grow under his feet, but brought his 'boss' and the sister to see us that very evening,

146

and once again I discovered that I had fallen into the trap that catches me so frequently. I always preconceive ideas of people, and almost without fail I am, as Monica would say, 'quite wrong'. Because Matthew was a man of about fifty, I had made up my mind that his 'boss' would be a man of at least sixty, and I had mentally supplied him with spectacles and a slight paunch as worn by Matthew himself. I was therefore rendered speechless while I rearranged my ideas when Matthew presented a very tall, rangy, loose-limbed, fair man of about thirty, who had an engaging smile and a very small, turned-up nose, while the elderly maiden sister that I had been expecting turned out to be a miniature creature of about five feet tall, about twenty years old, with a crop of fair curls, a wide curly smile and a nose even smaller and more turned-up than her brother's.

'I'm Jim Garvin, Mrs. Alexander,' the young man said, 'and this is my sister Martha. We're certainly pleased to meet Matt's friends.'

I looked at Martha's hand, engulfed in the broad hand of Twice, and thought that I had never seen anything so unlike a 'Martha' in my life. She was so small in stature that she had to look upwards at everyone, which gave her face a childlike innocence which was merely intensified by her sparklingly mischievous smile and I could see that clumsy protectiveness that large men can generate already beginning to ooze out of Twice. I was conscious of a similar feeling in myself towards Martha.

'And is this your first visit to Scotland?' I asked her.

'It is,' her brother replied for her. 'She never wanted to come to Europe before, but now she's gotten herself a Scotch boy friend and that alters everything.'

'Oh? And where in Scotland was he born?' I asked.

'He was born in Boston, Massachusetts,' said Martha, 'but that only makes Scotchmen Scotcher. His name is Ian Macdonald.'

'That's the Article!' said old Mattha, pushing glasses of whisky into our hands. 'Another danged Heilan'man!' and he went back to Twice at the sideboard, pouring the drinks.

'Say, that old character, Matt's father, just kills me!' Jim Garvin said. 'I can hardly understand a word he says!'

'Just as well,' I told him. 'His language is just about the bottom half the time . . . And is the boy friend over here now too?'

'Not yet he isn't, but he hopes to get over in the fall and go back with is,' said Martha. 'I hope to get me a kilt before he gets here.'

'The kilt wouldn't suit you,' I said firmly. 'You must have a tartan skirt and a good sweater, though.'

'Aw, gee, I'd have liked a kilt!'

'Your Ian would prefer a skirt, I feel quite sure,' I said.

'Why?'

'Well, it's difficult to explain —'

'You mean — it's a "just because"?'

I smiled down at her with delight. 'That's exactly what it is — it's a "just because"!'

She wrinkled her nose, smiling back at me. 'It was Ian that told me about "just becauses". They have far more of them in Boston than we have out west, but he told me that there were *hundreds* over here. He says that "just becauses" — quote — are the hallmark of a true civilisation.'

'Your Ian sounds like a very wise young man.'

'He's quite cute, too,' said Martha, sipping her drink thoughtfully.

I found her entrancing and did not want the party to break up, for she seemed to have brought with her out of the distant west of America some of the golden light of her own country. Playing this radiance over the people in the room, she caused me to see in them things I had never seen before, and she even gave new outlines to the familiar furnishings.

'Flash,' said Twice, coming over to us with Jim, 'Jim and Martha are determined to drive up to John o' Groats.'

'You bet!' said Martha. 'I want to see *all* of it!'

'And I've been telling Jim not to miss Reachfar.'

'Reachfar?' Martha enquired. 'Say, that's a cute name! What is it?'

'The name of my home,' I said. 'Certainly, you must go

there — it's only a few miles off the main north road.'

'Reachfar,' she repeated. 'That's just about the cutest name for a place that I ever heard. Who thought of it?'

'Oh, lord!' I began to laugh. 'Nobody knows. We spell it as we pronounce it, as if it were English, but I think it is probably a corruption of some Gaelic name.'

'Would you mind if I was to borrow it?'

'Borrow it?'

'For the cottage Ian and I are going to have up at Cape Cod? We want a name that's good and remote —'

'It's remote, all right,' Twice said.

'I am sure my father would be delighted to think that there was a Reachfar at Cape Cod,' I told her.

In the end Jim and Martha Garvin stayed for three weeks at the local hotel and that was long enough for My Friend Martha to come into being, but by the end of the second week of their stay there was still no hint or hair of My Friend Monica, and we were all getting more cross with one another as we became more worried and day followed day. Her family also was getting beyond the discreet enquiry stage now and beginning to consider a general hue and cry, with all the attendant publicity that would ensue. The most that we knew was that she must be somewhere in Scotland, England or Wales and that her car was probably with her, for her passport was at the London house and the car could not be traced in any garage.

I prayed to see a telegraph boy cycling up the road to Crookmill, but day after day the only emissary of the post office was the red van with the letters. One evening Lord Beechwood came on the telephone and told us that he was going to institute a police enquiry the following day. This was it. I had not been really anxious before, it seemed now, but real anxiety set in at the thought of police action, just as a sick person often feels more sick when first taken to a hospital. We slept little that night, were low in spirits the next morning while Daze drooped around getting breakfast, and suddenly I saw the telegraph boy turn the corner at the bottom of the road.

'Twice! A telegram!'

We both rushed to the gate. "Morning!' the boy shouted. 'The van's got a puncture, so I brought your letters!'

Hope deferred does indeed make the heart sick. I took the dreary bundle of letters from him, walked into the house and burst into tears.

'Oh, come, Flash! Dram and I can't bear you to cry like that!' said Twice while the dog lay at my feet and whined. 'Here's the letter from Reachfar — shall I open it?' I nodded. ' "My dear Janet and Twice",' he began to read, ' "We hope that you are all well at Crookmill and that the dog is behaving himself. George and I have been very busy with the turnip in the West Park this last week" ... Gosh, Flash, I wish I could write a hand like your father! ... "but we have had grand weather for the hoe-ing which was just as well with the weather bringing the crop on so much earlier than we expected. Monica has been —" ' Twice's eyes seemed to pop at me. 'Great God, Flash!'

'*What?*' I yelled. 'Go *on*!'

"Monica has been a great help to us. You would hardly believe how quick she was at learning to handle a hoe but she seems to be clever at everything and can bake as good a scone as anybody. She is still enjoying her holiday and we will miss her when she gets tired of Reachfar. She took George and me down to Dingwall Market last week in the car. It was a fine outing but the cattle on sale were poor quality compared with last year. Of course it was a bad winter and the spring grass —"

'God damn and blast her!' I exploded. 'I never even *thought* of Reachfar!'

'Neither did anybody,' said Twice.

'And, of course, I didn't mention in my letters that she'd disappeared. Honestly, for sheer low cunning she takes a lot of beating. She gambled on the fact that Dad would think we knew she was up there — and got away with it. She knows his letters are always mostly about the crops and the cattle. The cunning little beast! Just you wait —'

'Just *you* wait until I put a call through to London though,' said Twice. 'And calm yourself. What are you going to say to Lord Beechwood?'

That was easy, and all over within the first three minutes of the telephone call, but after I had given Lord Beechwood the Reachfar address and had put down the receiver I was still jittering with a rage that, even then, seemed excessive and unreasonable. Grabbing a piece of paper and a pencil, I drafted a telegram: 'Contact your father London address immediately failing this will inform Sandison family in entirety repeat entirety your behaviour stop this will doubtless induce smacking more serious than Birmingham affair stop do not imagine you have either courage or impudence to visit Crookmill but telegraph not effective to tell you what a fool you are Janet.'

'Send that,' I said to Twice.

'As is?'

'As is.'

'All right — then may I leave home for a fortnight until the fight is over?'

'There won't be any fight.'

'Well, you should know,' said Twice.

By lunchtime the reply was back from Reachfar. 'Have telephoned papa stop leaving here for London now stop cannot apologise or explain will visit Crookmill soon Monica.'

'You see?' I said to Twice. 'No fight.'

'And *you* don't feel like having a fight? As I see it, Flash, your *friend* Monica has treated you abominably. What *do* you feel about her?'

'I honestly don't know, Twice. At the moment I am merely relieved that she is all right. I haven't got it thought out yet.'

But there was not much time for thought at Crookmill these days. The spring, that lovely season at Ballydendran, had come dancing across the hills, trailing her pale-green skirts, and had touched with her pink-and-white hands the hawthorn in the hedges and had scattered her golden largesse of daffodils, and Loose and Daze, inside the house, were in a frenzy of spring-cleaning while Mattha, outside in the garden, was driving his conscripted labour like a Scottish Simon

Legree. And periodically, of course, the two forces would cease their labours of cleaning and gardening to indulge in an exchange of hostilities.

'Get that bliddy cloot aff that young gress!' Mattha would bellow.

'You and your old grass!' Loose would answer back.

'Cloot! That's the sitting-room carpet!' Daze would add.

'You an' yer bliddy kerpits! An' yer cleanin' an' yer skitterin' aboot! . . . Here, whaur ye gaun wi' that hammer o' mines?'

'I want to nail down the —'

'Nail doon yer behind! Ye couldnae hit a palin' stab! Gi'e *me* that hammer afore Ah get sweerin' at yees! Whit *noo* are yees needin' nailin' doon? If iver Ah saw twae weemen creatit by the Almichty as a cross fur folk tae pit up wi', it's yous twae!'

Strange things happen, and one of these was that Mattha, Loose and Daze had settled down into a state of armed neutrality that dated from the time of Monica's disappearance. Less than a year ago we used to have a weekly crisis when either Loose or Daze would tell us that unless that 'dirty, spitting old man' was forbidden the place *they* could not stay. There were no such crises now. They had frequent battles in the kitchens and in the garden, but they had, all three, apparently decided that the world contained all three of them and that the fact could not be altered.

And another change that I noted in my mind as I watched the three of them disappear into the Ben-the-Hoose with the hammer was that Loose and Daze were different. They would always in some degree be huntresses — though neither very chaste nor very fair — for they had been born that way, but their liking for one another now dominated their marauding propensities against the male of the species. Men were all very well, they seemed to indicate, but a nice evening spent with Loose or Daze, either at home or at the cinema, had a great deal to commend it, and really — although you wouldn't admit this in public — much more restful and comfortable than having to entertain a gentleman.

They knew, of course, of Twice's new appointment, and

152

when they were first told of it the uppermost thought in their minds was: 'But what about Crookmill?'

'Well, what about it?' Twice asked.

'Will you be selling it?' Daze asked fearfully.

'Good lord, no! Flash and I have to have a home somewhere!'

'The kitchen will get very damp if it's shut up for a long time — it's kind of close to the burn on that side,' she told him.

'Oh, we won't shut it up. We'll be able to let it quite a bit to people from Slatersub.'

'Oh!'

'But, Daze, we thought that you and Loose would maybe stay and look after it for us, anyway,' I said.

Their nice, foolish faces became bright with pleasure. 'We could pay you rent for our rooms!' said Loose.

It made me want to cry. 'Don't be foolish!' I said. 'You *get* the rooms for looking after the place while we're away.'

'Oh!' they said, and rushed off to vent their delight in a fresh orgy of baking and cleaning.

It was Loose or Daze or both, of course, who discovered that Martha's twenty-first birthday fell during the third week of her stay in Ballydendran and I was at once asked if we could have a party.

'What sort of party?' Twice asked, looking up from his book.

'Well, we thought,' said Daze, 'seeing they're Americans and so daft about Scotland we would have a sort of supper with scotch broth and haggis and a raisin dumpling and things like that —'

'Ah dinnae like haggis!' said Mattha, appearing like an evil genius. 'Sheep's guts, that's whit it is! Gi'e me a gidd mealy puddin' an' —'

'You be quiet!' said Daze.

'Wait till you're invited to the party before you say what you want to eat!' said Loose.

'*If* then!' said Daze.

'Sheep's guts!' said Loose in antistrophe.

'Be quiet, the lot of you!' I shouted before the thing could get out of hand. 'All right. Give an evening party but cut out the

153

haggis — nobody will eat the darn thing, anyway, and it wouldn't be the real thing at that. I'm fed up with all this food rationing. Daze, you'd better write to my aunt at Reachfar and see if she can send down some ducks or something.'

'Will we get a gidd big raisin dumplin' biled in a cloot?' Mattha asked wistfully. 'Ah huvnae had a bit o' raisin dumplin' since the New Year.'

'It's the suet —' said Daze thoughtfully.

'Suet?' Mattha asked. '*Ah*'ll sin get ye some suet!'

'How?' asked Twice, who was always interested in Mattha's machinations.

'Weel, that new man Burnside doon at the slauchter-hoose wis speirin' at me in the Royal the ither nicht aboot the slauchter-hoose drain — it seems the sanitary man's efter him aboot it an' they cannae get it tae clear richt. That drain has aye been a bother — it was that auld Mick Fairlie that laid it an' Mick wis half-Irish. Ye niver ken jist whit kin' o' a twist an Irishman will pit in a drain — or in onything else — they jist cannae seem tae help it, like.'

'And do *you* know where the bend in the drain lies?' Twice asked.

'Och, aye. Ah wis at the biggin' o' the slauchter-hoose when Mick pit it in.'

'But you haven't told Burnside?'

'Fur the price o' wan beer f'ae Burnside? Ah'm no' that daft. Forbye, Ah havnae muckle time fur him. He's a hell o' a man tae blether.'

'But you might tell him now?'

'Ah micht.'

'Mattha, you are an old twister!'

'*Me?*' squeaked Mattha, scandalised. 'Kennin' aboot drains is verra specialised knowledge, that's whit it is. An' specialised knowledge is worth a pun o' suet when Ah'm needin' it or Burnside's drain can be stappit for a' eternity for a' Ah care. It's no' *me* the sanitary is efter!'

So, dependent on the delivery of the suet, Mattha was promised his 'dumplin' in a cloot', and Loose and Daze had begun to plan a raiding expedition by bus round all the local villages in search of currants and raisins, when Martha danced into the room and said: 'I've got a package for you, Janet! Matt and Jim are bringing it.'

Matt and Jim staggered into the room with a huge wooden crate.

'What on earth is that?' I asked.

'Currants and things to put in cakes,' said Martha. 'You said one night they were hard to get here.'

'Holy Moses!' said Mattha. 'Whaur's ma hammer?'

He, Loose and Daze fell upon the crate and soon the floor was littered with packages of dried fruit of all kinds and little drum-like containers of vegetable shortening.

'I ought to start a shop!' I said. 'Martha, I can never thank you. But where did you get them?'

'New York,' said Martha, as if it were a shop round the corner. 'I cabled Ian and they came over in the *Queen Mary* with a friend of his.'

'Prunes!' said Twice. 'Golly!'

'Noo, that's a thing Ah niver get nooadays,' said Mattha, 'prunes an' rice puddin'. Ah used tae be real fond o' prunes an' rice, an' it's a gran' thing fur the workin' o' the inside intae the bargain.'

'You can't get *rice*, you old fool!' said Loose and Daze in one voice.

'Shut up!' Twice hissed at them. 'Want the *Queen Elizabeth* to come in next week with a cargo of rice?'

Loose and Daze went into their customary frenzy of preparation, I did a certain amount of telephoning to bid the guests, and the evening of Martha's birthday party came along. Martha had then, and still has, the ability of the child to grasp at simple pleasures with both hands. She was, in spite of a background of great wealth, completely unspoilt and also completely unsophisticated and brought to everything the freshness that a child brings to a new experience. When she arrived at Crookmill on the evening of her party she was like a child attending her very first celebration. Twice told her so as he welcomed her.

'But it is!' she cried. 'It is the first time for my *Scottish*

155

birthday party!'

Twice and I had decided to give her a circular silver brooch with a cairngorm set in it, and when, with quick fingers, she had it out of the box and pinned to her dress she cried: 'Look, Jim, look! Gee! Look at my Crookmill cairngorm pin!'

'If I know anything about the parties around this joint, you'll be saying Crookpin cairnmill gorm in an hour or so,' said a deep, insolent, American-accented voice from the doorway. 'Howdy, folks! May I meet your new friends?'

Elegant to the last burnished hair, Monica sauntered into the room.

'Good God!' Twice muttered and slid away in the direction of the kitchen.

'Hello, Monica,' I said. I felt as if roots had grown out through the soles of my feet into the carpet. 'Come right in.'

She came towards me. 'Have a dram,' I said.

'Merci bien.' She gave me her sidelong glance.

She came close up to me so that her back was to the room and the people, while my back was against the wall.

'I know you are too *bien-élevée*,' she said softly, 'to slap my face in front of your guests. That's why I appeared tonight.'

'I'm not going to slap your face, anyway,' I said.

'Why not?'

'It wouldn't be one bit nice,' I said, quoting a refined woman whom we had both loathed during the war.

She raised the veil of eyelashes and looked straight at me for a second. 'I see,' she said.

'That's good.' I handed her a drink. 'Try to behave yourself.'

'I'll be ever so nice,' she said, 'and help to make your party go.' She glanced round the room. 'Who is that two and a half yards of potential cowboy over there? I think you had better lead me to him.'

'Come along,' I said and moved in the direction of Jim Garvin and Martha, but she took my wrist in her hand, arresting me for a moment.

'I *can* be nice,' she said, looking at me wide-eyed for another instant.

'I know,' I said. 'You can be very, very nice.'

But, not for the life of me, could I be 'nice' to Monica.

After I had made the introductions between her and the Garvins I moved away round the room, but very shortly Martha was at my elbow.

'Say, Janet, is it a "just because" not to talk about it?'

'About what?'

'Lady Monica's title!' Her eyes were sparkling with excitement. 'I collect them — ones I've met, I mean — and I've got five Lady Surnames, but this is my first Lady Christian-name and it's just wonderful!'

I went across with Martha to where Monica was talking to Jim Garvin, Sir Andrew and Mr. Slater.

'I understand,' Jim said as we came forward, 'that Lady Monica here has just gotten over a disappearing act. I'd have thought nobody could disappear in a country this size with your police system!'

'But I'm smarter than most!' said Monica.

'Damn' silly affair from start to finish!' Sir Andrew barked.

'Of course it was!' said Monica. 'And all a misunder-standing, anyway. You know I hate writing letters. And I was certain that Janet's father would mention when he wrote that I was up there —'

'Damned liar!' I thought, and as if she had heard the thought she shot a glance at me.

'— and so he did, in the end,' she finished with a grin.

'Well, don't do it again!' said Sir Andrew. 'You know, Slater, I've just been looking at these drawings again and —'

'Monica,' I said, 'do you know what a "just because" is?'

'A "just because"? No. Is it a thing like a *Suivez-moi-jeune-homme* — you know, a little fluttery ribbon at the back of a hat?'

'No,' I said. 'Nothing like that. Martha knows all about "just becauses".'

'A "just because" is a thing that you do or don't do for no very obvious sorta reason — like drinking soup in a certain way, you know?' Martha asked earnestly.

'Oh!' said Monica, equally earnestly. 'That must be the

157

American for it. In English, that's a "why-why-not".'

'Why?' I asked, drawn even against my will into the old word nonsense between Monica and myself.

'Why not?' said Monica. 'Because of the March Hare — why ask riddles that haven't any answers? — why not? — but a "just because" is a very nice name for them too.'

'Say,' said Jim Garvin to me, 'I've lost the place. This is the darnedest conversation I have ever been mixed up in. Where were we at?'

'At "just because",' said Monica. 'Why?'

'Why not?' said Jim.

'You keep out of this,' said Martha. 'You see —'

As Martha hesitated, I said: 'Martha wondered if there was a "just because" why she shouldn't talk about your title, Monica, and I said I didn't think so.'

'Lord, no!' said Monica. 'Ask away, as Janet's father would say. It's very civil of you to take an interest in our primitive customs — I find the British peerage quite fascinating myself.'

'Let me get everybody another dram,' I said and collected their glasses.

Twice was busy at the sideboard with Mattha in his Sunday suit as head-waiter. 'There you are, Mattha,' he said, putting a final glass on Mattha's tray. 'Don't get them muddled or Loose and Daze will be reeling and we'll get no supper.'

'Them twae? It's a mortal sin to gi'e them even a teaspoonfy o' the Article. Ah've tellt ye till Ah'm tired that ye should get port wine f'ae the grocer fur them!'

He went off about his duties, which he did very well and with great pride, never forgetting to assure all whisky-drinkers that their glasses contained 'the Article'.

'It's a long time since I saw you,' I told Twice as I put my four glasses on the sideboard. 'A small one for Martha, please, and three ordinaries for Monica, Jim and me.'

'I've been taking cover,' said Twice, busy with his decanter. 'How is she?'

'Chastened,' I said.

'She'll never be that.'

'Everything is comparative,' I told him, 'and relative —

Einstein will tell you that. Get yourself a drink and come on over.'

'All right.'

He picked up his glass and we went over to the little group in the corner.

'— and if you got married,' Martha was asking eagerly, 'what would your husband be?'

Monica tilted her head so that the red-gold curtain of hair fell away from her face as she looked upwards. 'We would be Mr. James Garvin and Lady Monica Garvin,' she said.

'Not Lady *James* Garvin?'

'No. For that, *he* would have to be Lord James Garvin and the son of a duke.'

'Too bad, Jim!' said Twice. 'Have a dram, Monica!' and he handed her her glass.

'Ah've been listenin' tae ye, ye wee bizzom!' said Mattha, appearing behind Jim Garvin like Mephistopheles in an ill-produced play. 'Whin Ah wis at the schule, we used tae learn whit they ca' poetry an' Ah mind a bit aboot kind he'rts bein' mair nor coronets—'

'And it was also about some rather parvenu people of Norman blood!' said Monica scathingly. 'Besides, *you* have about the unkindest heart I know, Mattha Vere de Vere. How are you, anyway?'

'No' muckle the better for the askin',' said Mattha. 'Ah hear ye've been up in the Heilan's?'

'I liked the company up there,' Monica told him.

'Ah'm gled ye enjoyed yersel'. Iphm. Weel, Ah'm awa' tae get a dram fur masel' noo an' then gae ben tae the kitchen an' see whit them twae's at noo.' He turned to Twice. 'An Ah'll kin'le ma pipe an' hae a bit smoke when Ah'm ben there an' if ye're needin' me ye ken whaur tae get me.'

'The perfect butler,' said Monica as he creaked away. 'This damned place is madder than ever.'

'Not really, Monica,' said Twice.

There was a brittle uneasiness among us and I could see that the Garvins were aware of it. I could feel Twice's mind darting about, like my own, like a fish in a trap, seeking a way out and becoming more and more panic-stricken by the instant, when Monica's voice, very cool, very Loame, with the garnered experience of generations of difficult situations behind it, said: 'There are some things that never fail to surprise one.' She looked thoughtfully from one of the Garvins to the other, then at Twice and me, and then back to the Garvins. 'When Janet first told me that she was going to marry Twice I didn't think it would work at all. Now they are the happiest couple I know. I always have to remark on it. It is most disconcerting how wrong one can be.'

Just like that, without uttering one word that was not the truth, yet without saying one word that disclosed anything untoward, she swept aside the tension, confessed to her own feeling of guilt and contrived to convey a form of apology. The sheer impudence of it left Twice and me speechless.

Not, now, that the party would have been marred if Twice and I had been permanently stricken dumb. Monica had taken it over, and played all her cards of her looks, her wit and the glamour of her title for the Garvins. I was conscious all the time that, socially, I should be grateful to her for making Martha's birthday an evening that she would remember, but to be conscious of what one should be is a very different thing from what one is. If we were all what we know we should be, most women would be a combination of Cleopatra, Madame Schiaparelli, Juliet and Mrs. Beeton or something like that instead of the combination of shrew, last year's hat, raw juvenile and tin-opener that they mostly are, so perhaps it is not surprising that I, who should have been the gracious hostess of Crookmill, was tending to stand around in corners and seethe the kid of my spite at Monica in the milk of my human unkindness which was away past boiling point and sadly curdled by the time the party was over.

As a result of the party, the Garvins once more postponed their departure from Ballydendran, and when they were not driving to the Border Abbeys or to the Trossachs or to Stirling or to Edinburgh they were at Crookmill. Monica either drove about the country with them or stayed in the Ben-the-Hoose, packing, but as Twice and I had arranged to take over from her the furniture she had acquired, the packing seemed to be the merest excuse, though for what we were not sure.

She seemed to spend quite a lot of time alone, she was no longer giving parties, but I did not interfere — indeed, I tried not even to think of her because of an unpleasant feeling that I did not at the moment want any truck with her. Strangely, her most welcome visitor and the person who spent most time with her was old Mattha, and after each of his visits to her he would come back to his chair by the stove in the kitchen, which he regarded as his own, and sit smoking his pipe, one gnarled old hand holding its bowl and the left elbow resting on the chair arm, the forearm upright, the palm turned outwards, as if the hand were about to push aside a screen that would expose some searched-for truth to his gaze. I have always liked old people, standing as they do in their wisdom between the long past of their remembered experience and the utterly unknown of their short futures, and time and again, in old people, I have noticed this waiting, upheld hand.

'Aye,' he said to me one day, coming out of one of his waiting silences. 'the lad was tellin' me that ye wis thinkin' on a bit trip tae the Heilin's yersel's.'

He frequently referred to Twice as 'the lad'.

'Yes,' I said. 'Twice has a backlog of leave due to him and we thought we'd go up with the Garvins and Matthew. My family haven't really seen me walking yet.'

'Aye, that'll be fine fur them. Ah've niver been tae the Heilan's. Ah've seen Loch Lomon' an' Ah wis tae Perth yince tae a ca''le show, but that's no' the Heilan's.'

'Would you like to come, Mattha?' I asked him. 'My father and my aunt and uncle always ask about you and they've never seen you since that awful time when I was so sick.'

'Ah wid like it fine,' he told me. 'Folk is no' their richt sel's when a body is as seeck as ye wis yon time. Ah took tae yer faither, though Ah cud see the pare man wis that anxious he wisnae like his richt sel' at a' . . . Aye, Ah wid like it fine. But there widnae be room in the caur, naw, nor in the Reachfar hoose aither, Ah'm thinkin'.'

'Oh, we're taking two cars — after all, the Garvins are going on to John o' Groats — and they and Matthew are booked at the hotel, anyway. There'll be plenty of room at Reachfar. If you think your rheumatics will stand the long seat in the car, come, Mattha!'

'Mebbe Ah will. An' thank ye . . . A fine cairry-on, makin' a trip tae the Heilan's at ma age!'

'How old are you, Mattha?'

'Och, no' that auld. Ah'll be seeventy-seeven come Michaelmas. Ma faither lived tae be ninety-three an' a' his ain teeth. Ma teeth are no' near sae gidd as his wis — it's a' they dentists — but he wis faur waur wi' the rheumatics nor me. Ma faither wis a beer-drinkin' man — Ah believe on the Article fur the rheumatics masel' . . . Aye, that fellah Garvin has a bit notion fur the wee yin ben there,' he said suddenly.

'Who? Monica?' I pretended to be surprised to please Mattha, but I was not surprised, really. As I had told Twice, men fell for Monica like ninepins.

'Whae else? Did ye think Ah meant that auld harridan Loose as ye ca' her? Loose by name an' Loose by naitur. Mind ye, she's no' near as damt aggravatin' as she yince wis . . . Naw, he has a fair notion fur the wee yin.'

'What makes you think that?'

'Whit?'

'About Jim and Monica, of course!'

'Ah've seen a wheen o' cocks on a wheen o' middens. Ah ken the signs.'

'Oh!'

'D'ye think she'll tak' him?' he asked.

'I've no idea, Mattha.'

'Och, weel, if *you* dinnae ken, naebuddy diz.'

'Why should *I* know?' I asked him as I put my cake in the oven.

'Whit's in it?'

'What?'

'That cake.'

'Cherries.'

'When are ye gaun tae mak' a richt gingerbreed? Them twae — Daze an' the ither yin — cannae mak' a richt yin.'

'All right. I'll make one now,' I said.

'That's the ticket. Mak' a richt gidd black yin an' kin' o' saft … It's you that kens her better nor onybuddy else,' he reverted to the subject of Monica. 'She's got plenty o' money, hisn't she? She's no' broken-doon, like some o' the gentry?'

'No. The Loames are not what you'd call broken-down,' I agreed.

'So she widnae tak' him fur his money. Aye. He wad suit her fine. He's no' as damt saft as ye micht think.'

'I don't think Jim Garvin is soft at all!' I protested.

'He's saft aboot *her*, though. But every man mak's a neddy o' himsel' aboot some wumman. Ah've been a neddy masel' in ma time.'

'Then that makes it conclusive,' I said.

'Nane o' yer impidence! *Your* lad's no' a neddy, though.'

'No?' I said, watching treacle run out of one of Martha's beautiful cans from New York.'

'Naw. It wid be a clever wumman that wid bamboozle *him* — yin as fly as *you* as a ma''er o' fack.' He creaked up out of his chair. 'Weel, sittin' here on ma backside'll no' get the kin'lin' sticks cut.' He knocked his pipe out into the coal bucket. 'Ye should ask the wee yin ben there tae come up tae the Heilin's wi' us.'

'Why? She's only just back from Reachfar!' I turned away from my baking to make the protest.

'She wid like fine tae get comin', Ah'm thinkin',' he said and went away out to the woodshed, leaving me standing in the middle of the kitchen floor.

It may be my early training by my grandmother that makes me have so much respect for age and its opinions, but I do not think so entirely. I think it is logical that an average intelligence that has watched the world for seventy-seven years should have opinions more likely to be valuable than an average intelligence that has only some forty years of observation on which to base its opinions. I was also of the belief that Mattha's intelligence, to start with, was of a higher level than my own, and I tended to give weight to his opinions.

163

I was not vitally interested in his idea that Jim Garvin 'had a notion' for Monica. In the time I had known her so many notions had been entertained for her by so many men that I would have been more interested had I been told that Jim Garvin could not bear the sight of her. After all, even Twice, who was eccentric enough, apparently, to prefer me, had been the first to agree that Monica was an eyeful, a heartful and a mindful for any man who had an open eye, heart and mind. No, the facet of Mattha's discourse that interested me was his suggestion that Monica should join the expedition to Reachfar. *Not* John o' Groats — Reachfar. And it interested me because the very idea of taking her with us on our holiday was repugnant to me.

You know how it is when there is something you know you ought to think about that you would rather not think about so you think about any other thing under the sun in order to escape from thinking about the thing that really needs thinking about? You travel round it in a muddle of loose thought and repetition just like that sentence back there. At least I do. I have not got the courage of my friend Edna who has added a phrase to our family vocabulary. Edna is British by birth but regards New York as her spiritual home — it is to her what Moscow was to the three sisters — and in the aftermath of the 1939-1945 war her husband was working in Buenos Aires and Edna was down there with him and, as Damon Runyon would say, it began to come on Christmas.

'I want to go to New York for Christmas,' said Edna.

'Well, you can't,' said her husband. 'I can't get the dollars for a trip like that.'

'I want to go to New York.'

'Now, Edna, don't be silly. Dollars are not allowed for pleasure jaunting. You *cannot* go!'

'I want to go to New York for Christmas,' Edna said.

'Listen, there's no point in going on like that! You need dollars to go to New York and I can't get the dollars. If I were as rich as Croesus I couldn't get a *permit* to buy dollars for a pleasure trip!'

'I PREFER NOT TO THINK ABOUT THAT,' said

Edna. 'I want to go to New York for Christmas!'

Well, like Edna, I preferred not to think about Monica going to Reachfar with us, but, unlike Edna, I did not have the courage to say so, even to myself. Not me. I believe that if anyone were to ask me I would say that I am one of these forthright people who face things squarely, look facts in the face, study a problem from all angles, but that would be what Martha would call a 'lotta hooey'. I am not like that at all, for, instead of facing up to this problem about Monica, I began to hold a large, foaming-at-the-mouth indignation meeting inside myself. 'The impudence! She creates a year of merry hell in my life, chases my husband round Birmingham in a pink satin nightgown, and now she wants us all to have a happy holiday together at *my* home with *my* family! The impertinence of it! And suborning old Mattha too! The absolute —'

The whipped-up, internal indignation meeting did not last long, proving very unsatisfactory, and almost without realising it I slipped from thinking of Monica and Reachfar to thought of Reachfar only. I think I have already said that my home and my childhood are never very far from my thoughts, especially when the things that I have to think about at the present time do not please me.

I had not been home since my illness, but my family — of course my grandparents were dead now — in the persons of my father, my uncle and my aunt had all been down to Crookmill at various times since I had been bedridden. Tom had not come, for he was very old and had never been south of Inverness even in his youth, holding the very reasonable view that there probably was a city called Edinburgh, just as there probably was a country called Peru, because he had met people who said they had been to those places and he also knew that there was a big, reddish star, because he had seen it himself, which the minister said was a special sort of star called a planet and its name was Mars, but Tom had no urge to visit either Edinburgh, Peru or Mars. Reachfar would do fine for him, he said, and look at that now, he said, that branch on that tree shaped just like a big capital 'S'. He had never noticed that before, he said, although he must have passed that tree a thousand times; and do you know, he said, that the swallows are building in the old chaff-cutter of all places? At over eighty Tom would, no doubt, still be seeing new things at Reachfar to marvel at, I thought. It would be good to see him again. And Reachfar. But one did not want Monica at Reachfar ...

The year had now passed the peak of mid-June. It was warm in my nice kitchen and the air was rich with the smell of baking gingerbread and the scent from the garden vegetables that lay by the sink and the odour from the little piece of mutton that Mattha and I would have for our lunch. I was enjoying myself in my own kitchen, with plenty of flour and eggs and all the good things that had come out of the New York crate. Twice would not be back until the evening, and Loose and Daze had gone with Matthew and the Garvins on a shopping expedition to Glasgow. I could have an orgy of baking and make as much mess as I liked and enjoy to the full my recovered ability to use my hands and my body for the small, satisfactory tasks that had to be done around my own home. I would make a huge Black Bun, I decided, to take to Reachfar for Tom.

I plunged into the store cupboard again and laid hands on a fresh packet of raisins and another of currants — Daze would be mad, but let her be! Martha had given the crate to *me*, after all! I had the mixing bowl full of a rich and glutinous mass of fruit, spices, pepper, sugar, treacle and flour all moistened with a little whisky when Monica came into the kitchen, the acme of elegance in a new silk-tweed suit, a cocktail shaker in one hand and two glasses in the other.

'What in Christendom is that?' she asked, sniffing over the bowl.

I was panting a little with the effort of moving the wooden spoon round in the mixture. 'Nothing in Christendom. As Martha would say, strickly pagan, this — Black Bun.'

'Crikey! Have a snootful of gin and french for elevenses. Nothing like it for making spoons and things go round. I came to tell you I'm going to Edinburgh.'

'Oh?' I put a cloth over my bowl of mixture and got my tin of cigarettes from the dresser.

166

'I've an appointment with Alex.'

'Haven't seen Alex in ages,' I said. 'Give him our love.'

I took the gingerbread out of the oven and put it to cool as Mattha came in with a basket of logs for the sitting-room fire.

'That's the Article!' he said.

'No. It's gin,' said Monica. 'Want one?'

'Naw. Rot yer guts, that's a' it is. Ah'd raither hae a bo''le o' beer.'

'In the passage cupboard,' I said. 'Help yourself.'

He took a large tumbler from the dresser and disappeared with his basket of firewood.

'That old article,' said Monica, 'thinks, in his own parlance, that the sun shines out of your behind!'

'Nonsense!' I said. 'And I don't object to that sort of parlance from Mattha — it's in character. In you, it isn't.'

'Sorry,' she said. 'Sometimes one's character gets a little frayed and tattered at the edges.'

My mind veered away from this intimacy. 'That suit isn't frayed or tattered at the edges,' I told her. 'You look very smart.'

'Like it?' She looked down at the sleek line of the skirt. 'It's one of Paul Caraday's — he's a squealing pansy but a coming boy in the rag trade. Inge has given him all her clothes for this South American tour. That should help him.'

'Help him? It will make him.'

Inge was Monica's fabulously smart and wealthy sister-in-law who figured in all the shiny magazines and was invariably mentioned in the Sunday press of the type that periodically lists the World's Best-dressed Women.

'How *is* Inge, by the way?' I asked.

'More of a bitch than ever. What I can't understand is how it doesn't show in her face. But it doesn't. She looks like a well-groomed Nordic angel with dew in her eyes, and her tongue drips more venom than ever. How Philip stands it, I don't know. Insulation of some sort, I suppose. Of course, she's first-class socially — it's in the family she's such a cow . . . Do you ever get sick to death of your family, Jan?'

'I don't think so,' I said. 'Of course, I don't have a big lot

167

of them or such a mixture of them as you do.'

She tipped the shaker over my glass. 'Sorry it isn't a full second wing,' she said, pouring what was left into her own glass. 'It was just the dregs of a gin bottle. Filthy word, dregs. Makes you think of all that glub a dredger shovels up . . . I've got frightfully sick of the family lately.' I made no comment. 'I can't lay my finger on why, quite. But that hoo-ha I had to go down to about the Derbyshire place was just about the end. It's not a place that anybody cares a damn about — it came into the family about 1800 through a marriage. It's a nice enough house, Georgian, not very big — but none of us has ever lived there. It has always been let, but it's bigger than most people want now, so it's been empty for a couple of years. Some farming people have the land on rent, but they don't want the house and the garden and so on, and a girls' school wanted them, so Papa thought he would sell. Golly, did the balloon go up?'

'Why?'

'God knows! Nobody else does. There were about thirty Loames sitting round a table all bawling about a house that they had never seen — half of them hadn't, anyway — and a house that didn't belong to them at that. Aunt Pat was accusing Papa of laying waste her Edward's inheritance, and Uncle Egbert was accusing him of Communism, and Cousin Lorimer was saying: "Give it for a youth hostel" — he is always twaddling on about the nation's youth but he has been careful to stay a bachelor. But what they were all after, really, was that the Loame family must be rent by a major difference of opinion at all costs. Everybody must be suspicious of everybody else's motives. My family must always be in a state of civil war. They'd make you sick. When I think of other families' ways of living — Here, I've got to go . . . Want anything from Edinburgh?'

'No, thank you.'

'All right. I'm off.' She ran along the passage but ran back to push her head round the door. 'I say, tell Twice I've borrowed that spare jack of his. I don't know where mine is. I think I must have left it at Reachfar.'

I was taking the cloth from the top of my mixing bowl as I heard her car drive away down the stony road from Crookmill to the main highway, and as I began to plough my wooden spoon through the mixture again I wondered what the reason for her visit had been. I had not been alone with her since she came back, except for the few moments at Martha's party, and as far as knowing what was in her mind went I had not been alone with her now. Monica was not as easy to fathom as Mattha, I thought. And, of course, I myself had not helped her to be forthcoming. But she had used Reachfar as an exit line . . .

'Whaur's she awa' tae noo?' Mattha asked, putting his beery tumbler in the sink.

'Edinburgh.'

'She's a hell o' a leear, that lassie,' he continued. 'She can tell lees by sayin' a thing an' she can tell them by sayin' naething an' she can tell them sideways an' backsideforemost. Tellin' me it wis gin yees wis drinkin' — as if Ah didnae ken the smell o' the Article at ma age!'

'It *was* gin and vermouth!' I said, springing to Monica's defence. 'The article, as you call it, is in the black bun I'm mixing.'

'Och, weel, nae hard feelin's. She's a hell o' a leear a' the same even if she tellt the truth by accident aboot the gin. She's hidin' somethin', that's whit she is.'

So well she might be hiding something, I thought. She had plenty to hide if one thought over her past behaviour.

'It's a black bun, ye said?' Mattha peered into the mixture. 'Aye, it hiz the richt smell. Ah'm very fond o' a bit o' black bun.'

'It's for Tom at Reachfar.'

'Och, aye, Ah've heard aboot him, the auld sowl. Och, weel, he'll be sharin' it wi' us, likely . . . Did ye tell the wee yin to come on up there wi' the rest o' us?'

'No, I didn't,' I said snappishly as I measured the flour for the pastry case for my bun. 'And stop bullying me, Mattha. I don't know where you got this notion that Monica wants to go back to Reachfar, but no doubt if she wants to come she will tell me so.'

'There's nae need tae get yer dander up!' he said. 'An' Ah'll tell ye somethin' fur nothin' — she'll *no* tell ye, an' ye can pit that in yer pipe an' smoke it!'

'What's all the mystery? Why shouldn't she tell me?'

'Ah dinnae ken, but she'll no'.' He lit a spill of paper at the stove and began to suck at his burned and bitten old pipe. 'This bliddy thing's stappit again!' he said. 'It's the teebacca — fu' o' taur, that's whit it is!'

The pipe sucked and gurgled and stank. I left my pastry and went to Twice's pipe-rack in the living-room and took out a pipe that had been given him at Christmas which he did not like because the bowl was too small and the stem too slender for his strong teeth.

'Here!' I said to Mattha. 'Fill that one and see if it's any better.'

'Hey, that's wan o' the lad's pipes!'

'He doesn't use it. He'd bite through that stem in a week. He said you were to have it.'

'My, but that's a richt bonnie sweet wee pipe! Ah'll be richt prood o' it. The lad's a fine fellah, ye ken, lassie.'

'I know that,' I said, concentrating on my pastry. Nobody knew better than I did what a fine fellow Twice was.

'He's no' a man that wad like tae come atween freen's an' —'

There was a loud, unmistakeable rattle at the back door, a rattle as of the large head of a large dog requiring immediate admittance.

'That's Dram, Mattha,' I said, holding up my floury hands. 'Let him in for me, please.'

'My, my!' said Mattha as Dram trotted in with a big rabbit in his mouth. 'My, but ye're gettin' tae be a richt fine poacher o' a dug! Here, gi'e me that rabbit ere Ah kill it fur ye.'

'Take it outside, for goodness' sake, and kill it!' I said. 'Dram, why the devil don't you kill your things before you bring them in?'

Dram looked at me as if to remind me of what I had said the day he brought in the butcher's cat — dead.

'It's a fine young yin,' said Mattha, coming back with the dead rabbit. 'Ye widnae conseeder makkin' a rabbit pie wi' it?'

170

'I might, if you would consider skinning and gutting it for me.'

'Och, Ah'll sin dae that. Ye ken whit Ah think?'

'What?' I asked, lining my cake tin with pastry.

'That wee yin ben there wid be a bliddy sight better if she'd been brocht up richt.'

'Brought up right?' I repeated foolishly.

'Aye — tae ken aboot cookin' an' bakin' an' bein' usefu'. What gidd is it tae a wumman tae live a' her lane in the ben end o' the hoose even if she *can* speak French an' Eyetalian? The bother wi' that wee yin is that she doesna want a man o' her ain kind an' the ither kin' dinnae want *her* . . . Och, weel, come on, Dram, ye article, ye. You an' me maun sort this rabbit fur the Missis.' He creaked out into the garden and left me to my baking.

My mind veered away into escape from the thought of Monica again and I began to think of Mattha's phrase 'sort this rabbit'. In the Scotland of Mattha's generation the verb 'to sort' has a meaning that I have not come across elsewhere. It means to 'put to rights' and a parent, annoyed at a child, will say: 'If ye do that again I'll *sort* ye!' meaning 'If you do that again I will punish you in such a way that it will put you to rights for ever about that particular thing'. And, in Scotland, we may ask a carpenter to 'sort' a piece of woodwork for us or a shoemaker to 'sort' a shoe, by which we mean: 'put it to rights, repair it, make it usable or wearable.' So Mattha was making the rabbit fit for kitchen use by 'sorting' it.

A nice, homely word, I thought, with a flavour of the native earth about it, except for that one extraordinary Shakespearian phrase 'a sort of traitors'. That collective noun, a 'sort' of traitors. Why a sort? Assortment? Sort. Covey and school had a collective sound, a *probable* sound, for what they described, for one could think of the comfortable fat partridges in a cosy covey, and the whales, especially the pompous kind that blow a fountain out of their noses, as a school of philosophers blowing wind and water into the air. But a sort of traitors? It was strange that the same word could feel homely and comfortable in one context and ugly and cacophonous in

171

another. A sort of traitors. Traitor. The word suddenly turned into a picture of Monica that rose like a cloud over the horizon of my mind. I pushed the picture and the word into limbo and escaped again, but not for long.

It is true that Monica had been very much in and on my mind for weeks, but today it was as if I had had a fresh injection of her when she had unexpectedly appeared in my kitchen in the fashionable new suit. There had been something exotic about her as she had stood there, the acme of moneyed elegance, against the utilitarian enamel draining-board of the sink. Physically she had momentarily taken on again the glamour that had always coloured her image in my mind.

This mind of mine is a little like the west attic of Reachfar as it was in my grandmother's time. My grandmother never threw anything away, but put anything she was not using at the moment in the west attic and I spent a lot of time up there on wet winter days. In those days many strange things were acquired by a household such as ours, for if a farm changed hands, there would be a sale and my grandmother would send my father or my uncle off with instructions like this: 'Try and get the chain harrows if you can manage the price at all, and if that big hamper that Mrs. Morrison used to have for her eggs comes up and is going reasonable try and get it for me. It's on the big side for us, but the two egg baskets are fair done.' Usually the hamper would come back to Reachfar, but not alone, for a thing of that nature would be filled with odd saucers, a colander, a few nails, a horse blanket, a chamber-pot, a screwdriver and a mirror from the servant's bedroom and sold as a lot. At Reachfar the hamper would be cleaned and go into use while the rest of the lot would be sorted through and what was not wanted for immediate use would go up in the west attic. The west attic was a very interesting place. It being known that I was familiar with it and its contents, I was frequently 'sent up for a patch', which meant that I was shown my uncle's trousers, perhaps, complete with hole, and had to find a piece of the tweed from which they had originally been made, for Mr. Grant the tailor made all the family's heavy clothes and had to deliver the clippings along with the garment. To be sent for a patch was a dull job, for it meant looking through all the big-rag bags that hung on a row of pegs and most of the materials in them were very dull — grey and brown tweeds, old pillow-cases and scraps of flannelette shirting. One winter day, though, I was sent to find a patch for my grandfather's heaviest jacket which was probably half a century old, and I sorted through about six bags without finding the right thing, so I took the seventh bag right off its peg, held it up by the bottom corners and, with an impatient shake, tipped its entire contents into the middle of the floor. When I had thrown aside the bag, on the top of the dun-coloured heap was the most beautiful scrap of material I had ever seen. It was some sort of brocade, I suppose, but to me it seemed to contain all the jewel colours of the Indies as well as gold and silver, and it lay there in the dusty gloaming of the attic glowing with an exotic light. In this light the walls of the attic receded to the far boundaries of the world and a gorgeous procession of caparisoned elephants, peacocks with spread tails and men and women with yellow skins and feathered headdresses and robes of silk hung with jewels, floated past before my astonished eyes, while the bells of a thousand temples sounded in my bemused ears.

Monica, in my mind, had always had something of the quality that that scrap of brocade had had that first day I saw it among the heap of drab clippings in the west attic. She could always open for me a vista of far places, of strange customs, of another world. In cliché parlance, I suppose that she had spelled romance to me, caught me in romance as in a silken web, and, in spite of all that had happened, she had done it afresh today, in my own kitchen, by my own sink.

I ought, I supposed, to tell Monica that Twice and I wanted her rooms so that Twice could have his drawing-office, hasten her departure from Crookmill and put an end to the whole absurd situation, but I knew that I would not do that. I did not know why I would not do it. I knew merely, but with certainty, that I would not do it. Then, as Twice had pointed out, the normal reaction to behaviour such as Monica's would be anger. 'Your *friend* Monica has treated you abominably,' he had said. Yes. To be angry and quarrel with her would be the standard, conventional reaction, but I have always tended to look askance at conventional reactions because, for me, they are so often false. My natural reaction was not to be angry with Monica or to quarrel with her. If those had been my reactions, they would have been translated into actions long ago. My temper is not the sort that waits to decide if it is going to go up in a blaze. It is of a highly combustible quality, my temper, and goes off with a bang at the first spark of the sort that ignites it. So, in this case, what Monica had done was not to make a spark of the temper-igniting sort. No. There was nothing of the clean, sudden fire about what she had done. No. What she had done had induced in me more of the sly, furtive festering of a poison in the mind.

I was spending a difficult, unhappy day. After Mattha and I had had our lunch I began to bake again. It was part of my escape apparatus, as I have since recognised, for I like to work with food, and the materials and utensils of cookery all have associations of smell and taste and texture and colour that come from my earliest childhood which was a very happy time in my life.

As I opened a tin of cinnamon and the fragrance rose from it, I thought of church at home when I was very small and the minister reading the hymn in its entirety in his soft, Hebridean voice, before the congregation began to sing:

> '*What though the spicy breezes*
> *Blow soft o'er Sea-lion's isle ...*'

for that is how I heard the words, a sea-lion being an animal in one of my picture books, when I had not heard of the island of Ceylon. I was, for a long time, convinced that aromatic spices grew among the polar ice-floes where the sea-lions lived and that this was why they were so expensive and had to be used so sparingly.

Then, when the minister had finished reading, Big John the Blacksmith, in his sober, grey, Sunday clothes would rise from his special chair behind the communion table, give his tuning fork a firm yet respectful 'Ping-oing!' on the oak of the pulpit stairs and in his enormous melodious voice sing out:

> '*From Creenland's icy mountains,*
> *From Intia's coral strand . . .*'

and gradually the rest of us would gain courage from him and soon all would be singing.

And I went on to remember now that it was big John the Smith who first made me realise that a person is not just one person, that Big John, in his leather apron, with his hammer in his hand and his pipe in his mouth in his smithy, was not all there was of Big John the Smith. When I was very small and first went to church I did not connect the grey figure behind the communion table with Big John at all. In my mind, although I did not mention it to anyone, I thought that the figure in the church was a tame angel who belonged there, put there by God to help us with the singing, and that his tuning fork was the sort of thing that so many biblical people had, like Moses having a staff and Aaron a rod. And then came the great evening when I was allowed to stay up really late for the first time and my family took me to a concert in the village. The concert was to make money for a thing called the Red Cross which helped the soldiers who were fighting in a war that had started in 1914, and Tom and I used to make money for the Red Cross too, so we had to help *other* people to make money for it. Tom said: 'It's chust a plain matter of neighbourliness an' fair-dealing. Next time we have a pair of rabbits or a pound or two of rasps to be selling for *our* Red Cross, we canna be asking Mrs. Macdougall to buy from us if we'll not be buying a ticket for her concert for *her* Red Cross.'

I was very excited, not being quite sure what a concert was, but inclined to the belief that it would be something like church because I had been told that 'everybody would be singing', but it could not be exactly like church either, because my grandmother, my mother and my aunt were 'helping with the tea' and you did not eat at church except bread and wine at Communion and children were not allowed to go to church on

Communion Sundays. I do not remember a thing about the concert except that, suddenly, the minister said: 'And now our good friend Big John the Precentor will sing the "Cooper O' Fife" for us —' and this person who was this thing called a precentor and was also the tame angel from the church but, strangest of all, was my friend Big John the Blacksmith came on to the platform in his Saturday suit and second-best boots and began to sing the funniest song I had ever heard in all my born days, with a jingle at the end of each verse that made you tap your toes on the bare wooden floor of the schoolroom.

This two-or-three-peoplishness of Big John the Smith was one of the most remarkable discoveries I had made in my lifetime until then, I think. For many Sundays afterwards, when he was being the tame angel in church, I used to wonder if the wind might change and he would stay like that and, if so, where in the world would Tom and I take Dick and Betsy, our plough horses, to have their shoes attended to? However, the wind did not change at the crucial moment. Big John remained, angel and blacksmith too, and, indeed, was still remaining in his house beside the smithy which was now a garage as well at the crossroads, some two and a half miles east of Reachfar.

Reachfar. Monica. What *was* all this about Monica and Reachfar? The place meant a great deal to me, for so much of memory for me was tied up in its every stone and tree and crystal spring rising among the heather of the moor, but it had none of this meaning for Monica. It was true that most of the people who visited Reachfar were entranced by it, but visits were usually made in the summer, for short periods, and the visitors did not know the rigours and isolation of its long, harsh winters, when the panoramic views were blotted out by a bleak grey curtain of bitter sleet and the wind lashed in fury across the dead brown morass of the moor. It was true that Reachfar had a steadfastness, a security of thick old walls settled down among their traditional pastures, but what age and sense of traditional security there was at Reachfar, compared with the manor of Beechwood, were as events of this morning compared with the happenings of all the yesterdays

176

of a thousand years. Reachfar had nothing for Monica, I told myself, and Monica had nothing for Reachfar. Drat Mattha and his old man's notions and funny ideas! The rest of us would go north as we had planned and Monica could do what she liked. There was no *room* for her, anyway. Besides, she was only just *back* from Reachfar. Why should she want to go up there again?

Impatiently, I jerked a tray of cinnamon buns out of the oven, knocking the corner of the tray against the oven door, so that some three or four of the buns went sliding across the polished linoleum of the floor.

'Oh, damn and blast it!' I exploded.

'Is it safe to come in?' Twice enquired from the doorway, while Dram sidled between his legs in the direction of the nearest bun.

'Hi! Let that alone!' said Twice. 'What's on the floor is mine!' Dram sat down, his eyes still on the bun. 'What went wrong, Missis?'

'Oh, nothing. Just a touch of clumsiness.'

'No harm done.' Twice picked up the spilled buns and slipped one to Dram who yelped and dropped it again. 'All right. Let it cool. I like them hot.' He began to eat what he had salvaged. 'Any tea going?'

'In a minute or two, pet. You are early.'

'I know. Where's everybody?'

'All out, except Mattha, Dram and me.'

'Hurray! Let's have picnic tea in the garden. I'll do the carrying.'

'All right.'

'What a lot of grand smells, though! What on earth have you been doing?'

'My, but her an' me's fairly had a richt day o' it, the day!' said Mattha through the window. 'We've got gingerbreed an' chirry cake an' rabbit pie an' rhubert tairt an' black bun — hey, whit's they ye're eatin'?'

'Cinnamon buns — want one?'

'Ah widnae see yin gaun straucht by me!' Mattha reached in through the window.

We carried our tea out into the back garden where Mattha had caused to be built a bench that served as a table, and Twice carried out wooden chairs from the kitchen.

'My, but it's gran' weather!' said Mattha. 'This is jist the very dab — Ah've got news fur ye, lad!'

'What?' Twice asked.

'Ah'm comin' up tae the Heilan's wi' yees.'

'That's fine, Mattha!'

'Ye'll mebbe hae tae stop whiles on the road tae let me get oot an' stretch ma legs so that ma knees dinnae get ower stiff.'

'Oh, we'll easily do that. We'll leave early in the morning and take our time on the road. Pity it wasn't tomorrow we were going — we could have taken the rabbit pie for our lunch.'

'Maybe Dram will catch another rabbit,' I said. 'Will you, Dram?'

'Uff!' said Dram obligingly.

'That brute can bliddy nearly speak,' said Mattha. 'It wis yon time she was sae seeck — she wis fur iver bletherin' tae him . . . Aye, Ah'm lookin' forrit tae seein' the Heilan's.'

When we had finished tea and Mattha had thanked Twice for his new pipe and had got it drawing to his satisfaction, he gave a crust to Dram and rose: 'Ah'm awa' doon tae that auld Jeanie Robson tae see if Ah can cadge a wheen eggs aff her. The Missis here has been gaun a bonnie length wi' the eggs the-day — there'll be nane fur yer breakfast the morn Ah'm thinkin' . . . Aye, Ah'm fairly lookin' forrit tae seein' the Heilan's. It's a peety the wee yin's no' comin' wi' us, and her that anxious tae get comin'.'

He creaked away round the corner of the house and I glared malevolently after him.

'Monica, he means?' Twice said after a moment.

'Yes,' I said shortly.

'If she wants to go to Reachfar, why doesn't she go?'

'How the devil do *I* know?' I was suddenly very cross indeed. 'Where is she, anyway?'

'Edinburgh.'

'Doing what?'

I stared at Twice. 'How do *I* know? Look, I'm tired of this!

178

What's got into you and Mattha? You'd think Monica was some sort of idiot and I am her keeper. She told me she was going to Edinburgh and would be out for lunch. I didn't ask her *why* she was going to Edinburgh or what she was going to do there. Why should I? It's none of my business. I'm sick and tired of all this —'

'Have another cup of tea and keep your shirt on. Can't a bloke ask an idle question? *I* don't care if she's gone to Edinburgh to climb the Scott monument . . . No word of her getting out of the Ben-the-Hoose?'

'No.'

Twice poured tea and fiddled with the sugar spoon.

'Flash, what *is* this about her wanting to go to Reachfar and yet not going?'

Twice has the knack of making me feel contrite just by looking at me. 'I'm sorry I was ill-natured,' I said. 'Maybe I've been in the hot kitchen today for too long and have developed a touch of cook's temper . . . It's Mattha — he has this idea that she wants to come with us to Reachfar and that she won't come unless I specially invite her. He has niggled on about it all day!'

This was not strictly true, in fact, but it *felt* to me as if Mattha had been nig-nig-nig-nagging all day and there are times when how things feel comes nearer to the truth than actual facts.

'Then why not invite her and see?' said Twice.

'I don't *want* to invite her!' I said sharply, and as soon as I had spoken the words I was surprised at myself. All the nebulous nasty thoughts of the day seemed suddenly to become a solid, concrete wall between me and Monica.

'Why not?' There is a relentlessness about Twice.

'I just don't. I don't know why.'

'There must be a reason.'

'Reason! Why should there be a reason for every silly little thing?'

'If a person is reasonable, there must somewhere be a reason for doing or not doing every silly little thing.'

'Oh, rubbish! I just don't want Monica around Reachfar, then!'

'Why not?'

'Twice, do you have to go on and on and *on*?' I tried to keep my voice calm. 'It seems to me that people are losing sight of certain aspects of this Monica situation — especially you and Mattha. *He* knew about her carry-on with you and was extremely mean-minded about it while it was going on, but now he has swung about and talks about her as if she were a misunderstood angel. It doesn't seem to occur to either of you that I am being damned reasonable with her. Most women in my place would have told her a thing or two by now —'

'Don't talk like an idiot!' Twice broke in. 'You are *not* most women, whatever that may mean. In point of fact it would be better if you *did* tell Monica a thing or two — whatever *that* may mean. Why don't you?'

I glared at him. 'I don't know. That's just the trouble — I don't know what I want to tell her. I have never been in such a muddle in my life about anything. It would be conventional, I suppose, for me to haul off and tell her to clear out of here, out of my life, that I never want to speak to her again and a lot of stuff like that. But it wouldn't be — true.'

'True?'

'No. It wouldn't give me any satisfaction. If it would, I'd have done it long ago. There is something in the whole situation that seems to me to go deeper than that, something that a conventional blazing row between two women about a man won't satisfy.'

'You are sure you are not just shrinking from the idea of a row about a man, as you put it? You are not the type that fights about that sort of thing, you know.'

'I know. But it isn't that. No. It's not just that I don't want a row. After all, Monica and I could separate without the actual disgusting vulgar mechanics of a row. No. It's not so simple as that. It goes deeper,' I repeated.

'I think you should invite her to Reachfar,' said Twice.

'Edna! I want to go to New York for Christmas!' I snapped. 'I'll do nothing of the sort! I don't *want* her at Reachfar, I tell you! Why *should* I have her there?'

'All right, Flash. Leave it. But I don't like to see you unhappy like this. But leave it . . . Come for a walk up the hill before supper. Dram! Where's that hill-climbing, burn-paddling-in, rabbit-catching dog?'

Dram came galloping round the house and we went for a walk up the hill.

Nobody said any more about Monica and Reachfar, and Monica said nothing about it either, but do you know how the air can become heavy with a thing like that? I felt that Loose, Daze, the Garvins, Sir Andrew, the Slaters and even Mattha's conscripted-labour grandsons were all wondering why Monica was not coming to Reachfar with us, although my senses told me that not one of these people was even thinking about it, for they did not even know that she wanted to go. But there are times when what your senses tell you does not matter — you do not live entirely by your senses. I, when I come to think of it, use my senses only for things like eating and drinking, washing my face and interviewing the butcher — I do the large remainder of my living by some means that does not seem to have much connection with my senses.

And my senses, of course, were very active about telling me that there was no reason in the world why Monica should not come to Reachfar with us. My family liked her and so did the other people who were going, and there was plenty of room for her in the house when we reached it, but my feelings told me that I did not want her with me at Reachfar, even if every-body else wanted her to be there, and my feelings were darned if I was going to ask her to come. Indeed, I was prepared to treat Monica as if all that had happened while I was ill had never happened at all, except for this one thing. I was not going to invite her to Reachfar — not, ever, again. So, in this state of deadlock, time passed until it was the evening before we were due to make the journey.

The weather was still bright and hot, and Loose and Daze were in the kitchen making jam while the rest of us were out in the garden beside the burn. The Slaters and Sir Andrew had called in and Twice and Mattha had gone into the house to bring out some drinks, and Dram was standing in the burn in about four inches of water, with his mouth hanging open and looking, on the whole, extremely silly.

'Come out of there, you fool!' I said to him.

He went on panting and did not move.

'He's washin' his feet afore he goes fur his holidays,' said Mattha, arriving with a tray of glasses. 'He's near as wyce as masel'.'

'Have *you* washed your feet yet?' Monica enquired.

'No' yit, but Ah'll dae it the nicht. Whit are ye for, Mrs. Slater? We've got limmonade an' beer an' a little o' the Article.'

Mrs. Slater accepted some lemonade and said: 'I wish I was going up with you. Maybe it'll be cooler up there. My, but's been a hot summer!'

'It will be lovely at Reachfar,' Monica said. 'Probably just as hot as here, but it's not so humid and far more pleasant.'

'Are you going north too?' Mr. Slater asked her as Twice went round the whisky glasses with a jug of water. He was standing beside Monica, the jug poised over the glass she was holding towards him.

'No,' she said. 'At least, I don't think so.'

There was a second of silence after she spoke, and then Twice put some water into her glass and came over to pour water for me. I had a lonely sort of feeling suddenly, the kind of feeling that when I was a child I used to describe to myself as 'an Ishmael', a feeling of lonely separateness from the world, of isolation within a heavy black cloud. The longer the friendly talk around me went on, the more pronounced became the feeling, so that by bedtime I had about me an Ishmael like a ton of black cotton-wool and I sat at my table, brushing my hair and glowering at myself in the looking-glass, while Twice said goodnight to Dram in his bed in the passage. In the glass I saw Twice come into our room and close the door, but I could not speak. (A major Ishmael makes you dumb — it is one of the ways that it cuts you off from communion with your kind.) Twice sat down on the bed, took off his shoes and socks and sat wriggling his toes for a moment before he came over to stand behind me.

'Flash, will you do something for me?'

'Of course. What?'

'You shouldn't promise until you know what it is.'

'Don't be silly. What is it?'

'I want you to invite Monica to come with us to Reachfar.'

I felt cold now, as well as black and ugly. I laid down my hairbrush very carefully.

'Why?'

'I don't think I can tell you why. I don't think I know why. I am just asking you if you will please invite her.'

'I don't see why I should.'

'I am just asking you to invite her.'

'But, Twice, I don't *want* to! You know that!'

'I know. But I am still asking you to invite her.'

'You won't tell me why?'

'I don't know why.'

I looked into his mirrored face and rose. 'All right, I will.'

'Now?'

'Now. She won't be in bed yet.'

I walked out of the room, along the passage and into Monica's Ben-the-Hoose. I did not want to do this, but Twice wished me to do it, so I would do it. Monica was standing in the middle of her bedroom in a white cami-knicker with large pink polka-dots all over it.

'Hello,' she said.

'Hello. Monica, I just had an idea. Why don't you come to Reachfar with us and then Loose and Daze can have their jam-making orgy all on their own?'

'Why, Janet —'

Suddenly she seemed very small, alone and naked — all the Loame armour had disappeared and only the absurd pink polka dots seemed to be between her and the world.

'What about it?' I asked.

'I'll love to! Thank you, Janet, very, very much.'

'We start at seven,' I said. 'Goodnight, now.'

When I got back to our bedroom the Ishmael was blacker and thicker than ever, because of the way that Monica had looked at me and had said: 'Thank you very, very much.' And now Twice was looking at me too.

'She says she would like to come,' I told him.

'Thank you very much for asking her, Flash,' he said.

'Oh, I wish you would all stop *looking* and *thanking*!' I burst out. 'What's the matter with you all, with all this intense rubbish about Reachfar? I don't care a damn if the whole Loame family comes up there and brings its Habsburg noses and all and holds one of its stinking committee meetings in the middle of the moor! I'm going to bed and you can all go boil yourselves!' I hurled my clothes at a chair, hurled myself into bed and pulled my thick, black Ishmael all in tight about me.

In the morning Twice, Mattha, Dram and I went first in our very old Bentley, the Garvins and Matthew came next in convoy in their large, smart, hired, chauffeur-driven limousine, and Monica brought up the rear in her Jaguar. My Ishmael was still upon me, but less intense in the morning breeze than it had been the night before and it was fairly easy to forget about it in the company of Mattha, who, in his best suit and stiff white winged collar, was sitting with Dram in the back seat and providing a running commentary on everything we passed. We stopped for our picnic lunch some way north of Perth, before tackling the long run over the moors through Aviemore to Inverness, and shortly after we started again Mattha leaned forward and tapped Twice on the shoulder.

'Are ye sure ye're on the richt road, lad?'

'Aye, Mattha. Why?'

'It's awfu' kin' o' eerie an' no' ceeveelised,' said Mattha, looking about him uncomfortably. 'Whit kin' o' folk could live amang a' that heather an' hills an' a' them stanes?'

'Folk like Janet,' said Twice.

'Aye? Mebbe it's nae wunner they're kin' o' diffrunt fae ord'nar' folk!'

'You'll like it better when we get further up, Mattha,' Twice assured him.

'Weel, Ah wid hae muckle need tae!' said Mattha.

We stopped again a little way south of Inverness to drink some tea and to let Mattha and Dram stretch their legs again, and the other two cars came up and pulled in alongside of us.

'By the way,' Twice said, 'that in there' — and he pointed —

'on the other side of the road, is Drumossie Moor where the Battle of Culloden was fought.'

'Say,' said Jim Garvin, 'there ain't much of this country where you haven't had a fight at some time or another, is there?'

'It's they danged Heilan' folk,' Mattha commented. 'They'd fecht wi' their ain shaddahs at the drap o' a hat an' aye aboot somethin' that ord'nar' folk widnae gee their ginger aboot.'

'You Borderers aren't exactly men of peace either,' Monica said. 'We've got a picture at Beechwood of a bloke that looks exactly like Twice that was caught stealing cattle.'

'I didn't know they made pictures of cattle-stealers,' said Twice. 'Not traditional treatment for a reiver, was it?'

'This wasn't a traditional reiver — or maybe he was. He was being held as a hostage, but he jumped into bed with my great-great-cousin about sixty times removed and ended up owning the Yorkshire property. Quite a character. Then he went over to Holland and got himself killed in a tavern brawl.'

'Did he and your great-great-cousin have any children?' Martha asked in a practical way.

'Oh yes. Ten or eleven.'

'And what happened to *them*?'

'Nothing much. They just went on. The present one, the head of the family, is that cove who is always asking questions in the House about foot-and-mouth disease and the excise laws. They are still interested in the same things — cattle and strong drink ... Well, Mattha, what do you think of the Highlands?'

'No' very much,' said Mattha, lighting his pipe. 'Scenery an' history. Iphm. Folk cannae get muckle o' a livin' oot o' scenery an' history. Although, mind ye, it's gey interestin' tae think o' that pare sowl Prince Chairlie makkin' his last staun' jist ower the dyke there.'

'I think Prince Charlie is just the most romantic thing!' said Martha. 'And if I have a girl I'm going to call her Flora. I can't call the boy Charles because he'll have to be Ian the Fourth.'

'Have *two* boys and then it'll be all right,' Twice suggested.

'My, aren't you the brightest thing?' laughed Martha.

185

It should all have been very pleasant, relaxed and entertaining, but I did not feel in the least pleasant, relaxed or entertained, and when we were at last on the stony, uphill road that led up to Reachfar, the road that I had always hitherto travelled with such a joyous sense of journey's end, I felt actively gloomy and unhappy.

Part V

Part V

As usual, my father, my uncle, my aunt and Tom had seen the cars coming over the last four miles or so from the little back window of the scullery, the only window in the house which looks to the north, for, to get to Reachfar from the south, you have to go past it, as it were, and then turn back and make your climbing approach from the north side. As we arrived at the east gable of the granary the welcoming committee was there to meet us, with two collie bitches fanning their plumed tails round the feet of the people.

'Hello, everybody!' I called. 'Hello, Fly! Hello, Moss! Dad, where's Fan?'

'I sent her down to Johnnie's at Lochside. She's in heat and I didn't want her spoilt with that yellow-coloured brute of yours.'

'Bad luck, Dram!' said Twice, and Mattha cackled lewdly.

I jumped out of the car and ran towards my father and the others, but pulled up short at the sight of their faces. There was a moment of silence until my father said, 'Aye, Janet. You're on the move again, right enough!' His voice was full of a quiet, thankful wonder that made me want to cry.

'I sometimes thought never to see her like that again,' said my aunt and turned away to wipe her eyes.

The other cars came up the hill and came to a stop beside ours. I hated them all. Wrapped in my black Ishmael, I had forgotten that I was hobbling about on crutches the last time any of family had seen me. I felt ashamed of myself, bitterly ashamed, and my world became darker than ever.

In the bustle of introductions and welcome and carrying of luggage and Dram taking a dislike to the turkey-cock whose like he had never seen before, I hoped that my black mood would pass unnoticed, and I think it did — except for Twice, of course. At bed-time, when the Garvins and Matthew had gone away with instructions to come up the next morning and everyone else had gone to bed under the crowded roof of Reachfar, I knew that Twice was watching me covertly, but he did not say anything. And the next morning he did not say anything either, but went away, as soon as we had all had an early cup of tea, to look round the place with Mattha, Tom, my father and my uncle. This left my aunt, Monica and me all cosy together in the kitchen where my aunt was preparing breakfast. Monica began to help her, which I resented in a queer, ugly way, so I went out into the yard, and from there away on to the moor, where the dewy mist still hung among the fir trees, for it was only about seven in the morning as yet.

About a quarter of a mile from the house, above the spring-fed well which supplies our water, there is a place on the moor where the fir trees grow taller than in other places, and they are more closely ranked too, so close that the heather does not grow on the damp ground beneath them, which is covered, inches deep, soft and resilient, with a thick brown carpet of dried fir needles. This place has always been known to me as the Thinking Place, for, in its dim quietude, unvisited by birds and bees, there are no flowers or even grasses growing and nothing to ensnare a mind that can wander too easily from mundane things into the realms of enchantment. It was to the Thinking Place that I went this morning and sat down inside it, deep inside, on the fir-needle carpet.

I sat in there trying to be rational and reasonable and sensible and all these things which people try to be about their feelings and emotions and thereby waste their time. Words like 'rational and reasonable and sensible' do not apply to feelings and emotions, and feelings and emotions cannot be made to comply with their laws. Rational, reasonable and sensible are words for applying to things like the design of mass production lines and alimony agreements in the divorce courts and such things where emotions and feelings and most of what is valuable in humanity have been thrown out of the window.

This morning, in the Thinking Place, I no longer tried to escape from the thought of Monica. Instead, I tried to face it and the pain that it brought, for of course as soon as I faced the problem I discovered that Monica simply was not the person that I thought she had been. I do not think that anyone enjoys the realisation that he has been wrong in an estimate; or the discovery that he has been cheated over a period of years; or the knowledge that where he has given love and friendship it has been repaid with selfishness and disloyalty. The more I thought of what had happened, the greater became my feelings of resentment and hurt against Monica, and yet lurking behind these feelings was the thought that something was wrong. Somewhere in my chain of reasoning there was a false step, so that the conclusion was spurious. Monica was *not* like that. The Monica I had known since 1939 was neither selfish nor disloyal.

My mind, divided into two, argued with itself. On the one hand there was the factual record of what Monica had tried to do, and on the other hand there was — what? That was the difficulty. On this other hand, there was no factual record, there was nothing except some deep-rooted conviction of falseness in that factual record which existed. It was as if all that had happened were recorded on a balance sheet which showed a convincing statement of assets and liabilities — a balance sheet that any accountant would accept as a true and accurate record — and yet, for no reason of a logical kind, I had, looking at it, a deep conviction of falsity. The more I studied it, the deeper the conviction became; and the deeper it became, the more illogical I felt; and the more illogical I felt, the angrier with myself — and, of course, with Monica — I became. Round and round in circles I went, to come back again and again to the same point — this thing that had happened was simply not in character with the Monica I had known. Either I had been utterly wrong in my estimate of her or some unknown factor was at work.

It is easy to be wrong about people. In fact, people are the hardest things in the world to be right about. At least that is what I think, although I know that plenty of people will say that they knew So-and-So was Such-and-Such the very moment they laid eyes on him. I do not have that sort of eyes. Probably, in her own words, I had been quite wrong about Monica.

I had gone back to the beginning and was going over all that had happened for perhaps the tenth time when: 'Flash!' Twice's voice called. 'Are you in there?'

I hesitated for a moment before calling back.

'I brought out some breakfast. Want any?'

'Yes, please. Come on in.'

He came though between the trees with his basket, dodging the low-spreading branches. 'Gosh, it's hot already. When we came back and you were out, I asked for the basket, but I made a wrong guess and went to the picnic pond first.' Twice knew most of my private places on Reachfar. 'You must go to the pond,' he said, bringing scones and butter and boiled eggs and tea out of his basket and laying them down on the brown carpet. 'It is like Wordsworth's lake, only it's a crowd, a host of double-buttercups that won't scan ... Been having yourself a nice think?'

'No. Not very nice.'

'Two eggs for you and two for me. Do you know why a black hen is cleverer than a white one?'

'No. Why?'

'A black hen can lay a white egg and a white hen can't lay a black one. An old man who was a mole-catcher taught me that when I was four.'

'I once skinned some moles,' I told him, 'and tried to cure the skins to make me a fur tippet, but they got very stinking and Tom had to bury them.'

'So it wasn't a nice think?' Twice said, making a tidy job of peeling an egg. 'Listen, I have been thinking too.'

'Oh?'

'Yes. Has it crossed your mind that you and I are a little unpopular around here?'

'Here? What on earth do you mean?'

'Just that.' Twice frowned at his egg. 'You haven't had any time with the family yet, but, take it from me, you and I are in the dog-house.'

'But what for?'

'I have no idea. And also, forbye and besides, as Tom would say, a very queer thing is going on.'

'What?'

'The power company is running electric light into Reachfar and Monica is putting up the money.'

'You're demented!' I said. 'You've got things all wrong. The family would never do a thing like that! They have never borrowed a shilling in their lives, even for a necessity, and they would never do it for what they term a luxury . . . Please pass me that second egg.'

'I didn't say anything about borrowing. Listen. Monica is giving them a present of the electric light, to quote your father verbatim, and when I raised my eyebrows a little when he said it, it was then that it was finally borne in on me that you and I were in the dog-house.'

'Why?'

'Look, Flash, it's no good glowering at *me* like that . . . Your father said to me: "And I want you to mind, lad, that this is between Monica and us and is no business of yours or Janet's either".'

'Let's pack up this basket,' I said. 'I'm going back to the house. That brat Monica is going a lot more than a little too far.'

Trembling, I began to hurl the remains of our breakfast into the basket.

'Listen, Flash, go easy!' said Twice.

'Easy! Holy blistering cow! Who does Reachfar belong to, anyway? Or you? Or me? Or the Sandisons? Or are we all just a remote villeinage of the manor of the Loames? Come on!'

The blood was singing in my head as I marched — literally marched — across the moor back to the house. An hour ago, if anyone had asked me, I would have said that I was a fairly civilised being and that all that stuff about your feet being on your native heath was what Martha would call 'a lotta hooey'. But for me it is not. Out of some dark abyss of time there rose up through that heather and moss from that boggy, infertile ground, into me, a blood-and-soil rage as inflamed and senseless, as lustful and remote from reason as anything that ever caused a clansman to wave his claymore round his head and shout: 'Christ! And no quarter!'

It all came, of course, to a crashing anticlimax. My rushes of blood to the head — my big moments when I feel immense — invariably do. I am the sort, by fate, that if, like Juliet, I tried to take a phial of poison, the apothecary would have sold me an emetic by mistake. That is why, if I stop to think at all, I try to avoid big moments. I have a haunted feeling that they are not in my stars. So, expecting to find a houseful of people sitting round the breakfast table and spoiling for a scene that would shake the roof-tree, all I found when I got to the house was my aunt, alone in the kitchen, baking scones in huge quantity. I felt like a deflated balloon and had just as little air in me.

'Where's everybody?' I asked, on a dying note due to the emptiness of my lungs.

'The whole boiling lot of them is off to Inverness,' she said, 'Tom and all, cocked up in the front of the car beside the chauffeur with his Sunday suit on like an old laird. Where have *you* been? Up among the heather gawping about you like a crow, I suppose. You know, Twice, when she was a bairn there was times when we would be thinking she wasn't all in it — the way she would spend hours up there in the moor, all on her lone, just looking about her.'

'Never mind that now,' I said. 'They tell me you are getting the electric light?'

My aunt became quite still, her floury hands suspended over the baking-board. 'Yes, Janet,' she said after a moment and squared her shoulders.

I had a curious sensation that I was looking at an older edition of myself in fighting fettle. I had often been told that I resembled my grandmother, my aunt, my father, my uncle, but I always accepted these remarks as the things that people say to make conversation and never attached much significance to them. We are a tall family and well enough built and put together, but these things are commonplace among Highland people. Our men are not specially handsome, nor are our women startlingly beautiful, but maybe Twice is fairly accurate when he says that there is nothing reach-me-down about us and that we have the distinction of line that belongs to a garment made by a good tailor. My aunt is one of the most beautiful women of our women of this recent generation, and at this moment looked very decisively outlined indeed, not only in face and body, but also in mind and spirit.

'Quite a revolution at Reachfar!' I said, deliberately provocative, lighting a cigarette and tossing the spent match at the fireplace so that it fell on the whitened hearth, a thing that my aunt loathed.

'Aye,' she said, picking up the match and putting it in the fire, 'and Reachfar will take it kindly if you'll be civil to the lassie that's giving it to us.'

'Oh yes, of course!' I said in an affected way. 'I think it's jolly decent of her! I'll remember to thank her and be ever so grateful. And *you* will have to remember, too, to behave like the grateful tenantry!'

That did it. She laid down the rolling-pin with exaggerated care, wiped her hands on her apron, squared her shoulders again and faced me over the table.

'She didn't want me to tell you,' she said ominously quietly, and turned to Twice, 'nor you either. She said it was something that should be left alone.' She turned back to me. 'But I didn't make any promises and I am not going to leave it alone. Now, just you listen to *me*. God alone knows what the lot of you down at Ballydendran and that daft family of hers did to that lassie, but may God himself forgive you for it, for *I'm* not finding it easy. If you had been here the night she fell out of that car of hers out there, *I* would have sorted you, my lady!'

'*Fell* out of her car?' I asked, and Twice and I both subsided on to chairs at the side of the table.

'Surely — at ten o'clock at night. George had to go right off to Achcraggan for Doctor Mackay.' She suddenly narrowed her eyes and looked at us in a different way. 'You didn't know how sick she was? She hasn't told you anything?'

'No! Sick?' said Twice.

'She hasn't told us *anything*!' I almost shouted. 'She just came back to Crookmill and said she'd had a fine holiday. What was wrong with her?'

'What they call a nervous breakdown — she was nearly off her head. I thought she would have told you by now — but no.' Her voice hardened again. 'No. She didn't want you to know — she tried to get me to promise that I wouldn't say anything to you, but —'

'Never mind that now,' I said. 'We can have a row about it afterwards if you like, but tell us what happened first.'

She glared at me, drew a long breath and visibly quelled her anger. 'I don't understand these kind of illnesses, but we were very lucky. Doctor Mackay has young Alasdair home and in the practice now, and Alasdair got a man from the Air Force base who is a kind of nerve specialist or something to help him with her and we — your father and George and Tom and I — we just did what they told us . . . What did you *do* to her down there among you?'

'We didn't do *anything*!' I said.

'Her family, then?'

'What do you mean, *do* to her?' Twice asked.

'Well,' my aunt rounded on him belligerently, 'if you didn't do anything to her, why was she so frightened that you two and her family might find out where she was?'

'I don't know,' I said.

She narrowed her eyes at us again suspiciously. 'Well, neither do I,' she said drily, and then took thought again for a moment. 'Mind you, Alasdair and the Air Force man said that it was maybe just a notion she had about being so frightened of you all. They said that when people get into that state they imagine things, but I never believed that, somehow. There must have been *some* reason why she was so frightened. You'll swear to me for certain sure that none of you were bad to her down there?'

'Well, she and I used to have the odd argument at the works —' Twice began.

'Och, it wasn't a little thing like that — this was some big, hurtful sort of badness — and it wasn't about *you*, anyway, lad. No, it was about this one here.' She jerked a hand towards me. 'It was aye "Don't tell Janet!" and "Don't let Janet know!" and "Janet must hate me!" and sometimes it was "Don't tell Mama!", but it was mostly about Janet.' My aunt swung round on me. 'I know fine, my lady, that you can be a wicked thrawn limmer when it comes up your back — now, for the last time, WHAT DID YOU DO TO THAT LASSIE?'

'Aunt Kate, I swear to you that I didn't do anything at all.'

'She didn't, you know, Kate,' Twice added.

'Well, I have to believe you both. But I was certain sure you had done something terrible to that wee craitur ... Well, maybe Alasdair and the Air Force doctor were right after all. Maybe it was all just notions that she had.'

'How long did this notion business go on?' I asked.

'Och, for about ten days. Then one day she looked up at me when I took in her breakfast — we had a devil of a job getting her to eat for the first whilie — and she said: "I suppose I have been making the hell of a fool of myself?" You know that way she has of speaking? So I said, Aye, that was so, but we were all fools sometimes — Alasdair said not to cross her at all — and I told her to come now and eat her breakfast for me like a clever bairn. That's how she was, just like a bairn, a lost bairn. So she gave me that look of hers — you know how she does, out of the tail of her eye — and after that she got better every day. But it took a whilie for her to let your father tell you in a letter that she was here. She said: "Janet will be angry, and she'll be quite right." But we kept saying that that was nonsense and that we wouldn't *let* you be angry, and in the long run she gave in about it. But I got a fright when that telegram came in from you, but when she read it she seemed quite pleased and happy and then she went off south to see her father ... It's funny that she never told you she was sick.'

My aunt was still inclined to regard me with suspicion.

'Monica is funny in lots of ways,' I said defensively.

'Aye. That's true too,' she agreed thoughtfully and began to work at her baking again. 'Of course, these fine-bred sort of folk — they're not like the rest of us. Still, your father and George and me — we were all gey angry at you two, letting her get into a state like that.'

'But, honestly, we didn't *know*!' Twice protested.

'It's all very queer, but I have to believe you both,' she said at last. 'And then, of course, she took this notion about the electricity and nothing would do but she would get her own way — she can be as thrawn as yourself, Janet, when she makes up that red-headed little mind of hers. She felt that we had been good to her when she was sick — as if anybody could have turned her away from the door that night she came in here — and I know what it is like when folk won't let you thank them. So I just told your father and George and Tom that the right thing to do was to take what she was offering to us in the spirit it was being offered.'

'I think you were perfectly right, Kate,' I said. 'I am sorry I was wicked about it to start with.'

'I don't blame you for being wicked about it when you didn't know the reason.'

'Monica won't notice the cost of it,' I continued, knowing that at last she had accepted my innocence of being 'bad' to Monica. 'And it will be a wonderful thing for you all here, especially in the winter. Are you getting an electric cooker?'

'Your father and George are giving me one. It will be very handy on the cold winter mornings to get a cup of tea in a hurry. And Tom has lifted five pounds out of the Post Office to buy me an iron.'

'Crikey! I bet the Post Office got a shock! Tom has never taken out a penny in his life!'

'That's not true,' my aunt said. 'He lifted five pounds when you went to the university to help with your books. You didn't need it, but he'd always said he'd do it and he did it.'

'Did he? I never knew that.'

'He didn't want you to know — but it's an old story now . . .

And when I get a run to Inverness myself I am going to buy something I've aye wanted.'

'What's that, Kate?' Twice asked.

'A lamp to sit beside my bed with a fancy shade on it. A pink shade. That's a fine thing — to be as old as me and be getting something you've wanted for thirty years. Every time I've put out that stinking candle at night I've thought on a nice electric lamp with a fancy shade. I've hated the stink of candles and paraffin since I was a bairn, and when the lights come in I think I'll take all these rotten old lamps outside and take the hammer to them!' she ended with spirit.

'No,' said Twice, 'don't do that — we can wire them, you know.'

'To burn electric instead of paraffin?'

'Yes.'

'Well, we'll see.' When my aunt has a spite at anything she takes a deal of convincing that it can be improved in any way. 'I'm still going to have the wee new one with the fancy shade for beside my bed, though.'

Twice and I left her to her baking and retired to the granary stairs, where we sat in the sun and stared out across the broad landscape.

'Well,' I said, 'things are starting to sort themselves out.'

'But I wonder why she didn't tell us she had been ill?'

'I don't know.'

'You know what I think, Flash? I think maybe the whole carry-on with me was part of the illness. That would explain the queer unnatural feeling I had about it. And another thing, I think that maybe the illness was partly your fault and mine — especially mine.'

'Why?'

'Look at it this way. You went and fell over the bridge and, to put it briefly, the whole boiling lot of us at Crookmill lost our heads. The first few weeks were pure hell. The doctors couldn't tell us what had happened — they knew a bit of your spine and a bit of your pelvis were broken — they couldn't find any broken bones round your neck or your skull, but the awful thing was that they didn't know, and had no means of telling, whether certain nerves were actually severed or whether the immobility came from bruising, shock or what-have-you. It was a nightmare. For days we did not know whether you would be able to see or speak —'

'You mean, I might have been a drooling idiot?'

'I was told that there was a definite risk that you might be completely helpless. Then one day you said: "Hell!" quite quietly, just like that, and then you moved your right hand and opened your eyes and one knew that you could *see*. You can imagine what happened.'

'I can't imagine any of it,' I said.

'You know by this time the kind of fool I am — I had to let off steam somehow. I ramped round the house, hugging every-body and everything — the nurses, Dram, Loose and Daze, the Animated Bust and, of course, Monica ... Yes, I did ... Although I knew that Monica had indecent notions in her mind that I had been laughing off for weeks and we had been doing nicely, I forgot all about all that. I wasn't thinking of Monica at all — I was thinking about nothing but you — and myself, of course — so Monica got the whole hoop. When I look back on it, I was impossible. Every time you made a little improvement, I would go demented and finish up, as often as not, bawling salt tears on Monica's shoulder. One forgets these things, because one *wants* to forget them. Loose and Daze never came in for it — it was always Monica. And I know why now.'

'Why?'

'Because, actually, she has a capacity for sympathy similar to yours. She was genuinely as pleased and thankful as I was about every improvement you made. You *must* believe that. That was why she was able, practically, to keep me sane, Flash. If she hadn't been there I don't know what might have happened.' He paused and then went on: 'She is very *like* you in so many ways. She has the same sympathy and generosity of feeling and patience and steadfastness — it is difficult to explain that, in spite of everything, her basic loyalty to *you* and her love for you never faltered. Every time you made a little step forward, she was as pleased —'

'I know that is true,' I said, remembering. 'She was alone with me the night that the first muscle moved in my leg. I think she was even happier than I was. You had prepared me for it by making me believe that it would happen, but Monica was taken by surprise and — yes, she was genuinely pleased ... Yes, I can see the strain she was under, and I can see how it could all lead to a breakdown, but what I *still* cannot understand or accept, Twice, is her pursuit of *you*. You said it started almost as soon as she came to Ballydendran — before I was ill?'

'Yes. It did.'

'And now?'

'Since she came back — that night of Martha's party — she has been perfectly normal, the little I have seen of her. It is as if the whole thing had never happened except that — tacitly — she admits that it did. I don't pretend to understand that part of it.'

'You are sure she has no — feeling of that kind now?'

'Certain.' Twice was embarrassed, and so was I, as if we were conscious of discussing an indecency. 'One *can* be certain. It was such a blatant, obscene sort of thing that if it were there still I would feel it — I am sure of that. Let's not talk about it any more. Let's just go canny and see what happens ... This morning, by the way, when the lighting project was sprung on me, I offered to do the wiring of the place.' He grinned at me. 'Being conscious of being somewhat unpopular, I thought it might help to recover us in the family graces. Will you give me a hand? All the cable and switches and stuff are in a crate in the barn.'

I rose from my seat on the steps. 'We might as well start. Come on.' We walked along the yard to the barn. 'I have raked about and thought and cogitated about Monica in this rubbish heap I call my mind until I don't know where I am. A practical job will be just the thing. Let's concentrate on this wiring.'

In the initial stages the wiring involved a lot of climbing about and measuring, and, naturally when Twice and I were involved in it, argument. Twice, as must be obvious by now, has a lot of patience with me about most things, but when we do any constructional or engineering job together, and I am singularly ungifted in these ways, he has not any patience at all. He is not even reasonable. When I measure something and say: 'Seven feet eight inches and a wee bit,' he gets angry out of all proportion and bellows: 'And what the hell is a wee *bit*?'

When the two cars came back from Inverness we were still clambering about among the rafters of the barn, accompanied by the two cats who lived up there when Dram was at Reachfar, and as we were now at the stage of quarrelsomeness when we were hardly speaking to one another I was glad to give my end of the steel tape to Jim Garvin. Like every other thoughtless action one perpetrates, this led to the Garvins staying at the local hotel until the wiring job was completed and they did not go to John o' Groats until nearly a month later.

However, on this afternoon when I came out of the dusty dimness of the barn into the sunlight Monica's Jaguar and the Garvin's smart black saloon looked like those cars that commercial travellers use, with odd-shaped packages sticking out all over them, and the young chauffeur from Glasgow was untying some rope that held a white-enamelled electric cooker half-inside and half-outside his big luggage boot.

'I have the contrivance for to be ironing the clothes!' Tom told my aunt. 'Canny, now! It's heavier than you might be thinking.'

'And this is from Jim,' said Martha, struggling with a long, untidy package, taller than herself, and a large cardboard box.

'Mercy me! What is it?' my aunt asked.

'Come inside and open it and see!' said Monica.

The standard lamp with its big parchment shade was unpacked and set up and everyone was dumb with admiration.

'And here's the cooking thing,' said my uncle, helping the chauffeur and my father to carry it in. 'There, lad. Just in this corner. That's fine.'

'And this is from me,' said Martha, and began to unpack and set up on the table what must be the pinkiest, frilliest, fanciest-shaded, bedside lamp in the world. 'It's for you, Auntie, for your bedroom.'

My aunt sank on to the nearest chair and stared at it like a child at its first Christmas tree. It is the only time that I have ever consciously wished that I were as wealthy as My Friend Martha. If I were, I would go around looking for middle-aged women like my aunt, sturdy, sensible women, who had made do with candles all their lives, hating the smell of them night and morning, and I would give them all electric lamps with frilly, fancy, pink shades — or blue, if blue was their favourite colour.

'Well, Mattha,' I said, 'what do you think of Inverness now?'

'It's a real bonnie wee toon when ye see it richt,' said Mattha, 'wi' the river an' a' they suspension brigs an' the folk a' speakin' English-like, like the folk here. The shops is a bit backward, compared wi' Glesca, but that's tae be expeckit. Here, whaur's yon parcel o' mines, Matt?'

'Here it is,' said Monica, handing him a large, square package.

'There ye are, Mistress — this is fae Matt an' me,' he said, handing the package to my aunt. 'The yin Ah hae to hame is bigger nor they yins, but they're better nor nothin'.'

With wonder, my aunt unpacked four cylindrical bakelite objects.

'What's that things?' my father enquired.

'Bed-warmers,' said Monica, 'and a hell of a job we had getting them, too.' She was ripping the paper off another square package as she spoke. 'And this is strickly non-electrical. Let's have some water, Aunt Kate, and let's all have a noggin. I need it.'

'Here, ye wee bizzom,' said Mattha. 'Hoo mony bottles did ye manage tae cadge roon' Inverness?'

'You mind your own business.'

'An' an auld man wi' the rheumatics like me cannae get even a hauf-mutchkin o' the Article when Ah'm needin' it!' As he spoke, Twice and Jim came into the kitchen and Mattha transferred his acid remarks to them with: 'Aye, so yees smelt it, did yees?'

'Holy cow!' said Twice. 'Are you going into the electrical business?'

'Look at my lampie for beside my bed!' said my aunt.'

'Monica,' I said quietly in a corner by the dresser, 'it is very kind of you to have made all this possible for my people and —'

'Kind?' she said, with a hard, bright look. 'Oh no, I am never kind.'

She moved away from me with her whisky bottle and began to pour into the glasses which Twice was setting in a long line on the dresser, leaving me firmly snubbed in my corner. I felt wounded to my very heart, with a shoot of intense pain as physical as the pain of toothache, which momentarily can distort all the senses, so that sights and sounds become unfamiliar and unreal. For a moment the familiar Reachfar kitchen and the people that filled it swung crazily, tilted into a mass of distorted lines and angles, before settling back to normality so that I could again recognise the faces that I knew. Twice pushed a glass into my hand, and with a long breath of relief I looked round at them all — my father, old Mattha and tall Jim Garvin — they were all there, unaltered, these people that I knew. And there was one stranger, the beautiful woman in the pale yellow linen dress who was smiling up at my uncle over the rim of her glass. Her name was Monica — Monica Loame — known locally as My Friend Monica. That name and the fact that she was beautiful constituted almost all of her that I knew. Apart from these minor facts, and a few more of equal unimportance, I knew nothing of her at all. And she did not want me to know. I felt as sad and bereft as if I were in the presence of death . . .

Now, everyone had a glass in hand and we were all standing round my aunt, who sat nursing her frilly lamp on her knee, and there seemed to be electrical appliances and lengths of flex and discarded packing lying everywhere, and my father said: 'Well, I'm not much of a one for speaking — hey, Twice, why are ye not giving the driver-lad a dram?'

'I'm still on duty, sir,' the chauffeur said.

My father put his own glass down on the mantelpiece. 'What's your name, lad?'

'Grant, sir. John Grant.'

'Well, with a name like that, a wee droppie whisky can't make you incapable and your supper will sober you up before Mr. Garvin needs you again.'

'Sure!' said Jim.

'Give the lad a dram, Twice,' said my father, and when the chauffeur had accepted the drink he picked up his own glass again.

'As I was saying, I'm not one for speaking very much, but I want to tell you that we are pleased to see all you visitors at Reachfar. And I want you all to drink to the day when we get the poles up — they are halfway here already — and the lights come in to Reachfar, for I'll tell you a very queer thing. I am thinking that you will all travel a long way before you see another house that has been lit by nothing except the kindness of its friends. That's all.' He raised his glass and drank and then turned away to light his pipe.

'Gee!' said Martha. 'That was so cute I wanna cry!'

'Well, don't!' said Monica harshly, 'or you'll all start bawling.'

She turned away. 'Mattha, lend me your matches, you mean old devil!'

The chauffeur snapped a highly efficient lighter for her cigarette and everybody began to talk at once, while my aunt worked off her emotion by bustling about, picking up boxes, brown paper and string.

It was a between-season time at Reachfar, for the hay was in and the harvest was not yet on, so that my father and my uncle and Tom had leisure time, especially as they were now reducing their cultivation and had rented off several fields to their younger, wealthier neighbour on the west march. They sat about with Mattha, smoking their pipes, while Matthew, Jim and Twice went on with the wiring and Monica, Martha and I helped my aunt with the meals and the washing-up. The line of little pylons was now marching across the moor at a great rate and Twice had applied to Ballydendran for some more of his backlog of leave, which had been granted. It was continuously fine weather and Reachfar was at its smiling best and everybody was gloriously happy and — all that was how it seemed on the frothy surface.

'What an extraordinary gaggle of people we are here, when you think of it!' Monica said suddenly one evening when she, Martha and I were sitting on a gate smoking. 'If you read about us in a book you wouldn't believe it.'

'That's what's wrong with books,' said Martha.

'How d'you mean, wrong?'

'They're supposed to be believable. Real things aren't, quite often.'

'Maybe you're right at that,' Monica agreed.

'If any book had told me that the best bit of my trip to Europe was being right here on this gate, I'd have said it was a lotta hooey,' said Martha. 'Just fancy goin' all that ways to Europe to sit on a gate, I'd have said. Of course, I don't go much on books, anyways.'

'Why not?' I asked.

'Oh, I *read* them,' she said, 'but I never believe them. I took against them when I was about seven.'

'Why?'

'Cinderella and the glass slippers — expecting anyone to believe that a girl could dance in glass slippers. No, for me books are strickly for the birds. Ian says I'm illiterate. Maybe I am. But the way I look at it is, history isn't books. History is the real thing, and although some of it is kinda hard to believe — your old Queen Elizabeth that had the Armada, now *she* takes a bit of believing when you look at her face and then read about her beaux — but you know where you're at with it. You just *gotta* believe it, because it *happened*. But when I was at college we had a literary society and it was kinda snob to be a member so I go and get myself mixed up in it and we get to reading a book by some French guy — it was translated into English, of course — all about how he felt when he woke up in the morning and how he felt about some guy he knew and how it came over him when he saw some old dame in the street —'

'Marcel Proust?' Monica asked.

'That's the guy! How did you know? Anyways, I just said to myself: This ain't believable and it ain't any fun, and why did he write it, anyways? So I retired from the literary society and started going to the cookery classes . . . Anybody got another cigarette?' Monica gave her one. 'Thanks. Not that I have anything against this Proust guy personally. But *I* don't feel like that in the morning or about the guys I know or in the street, and I'm not specially interested in a guy who *does* feel that way so why read books about it? Now, if I could get a book that tells about how I feel sitting right here on this gate, I would read it. That would be worth reading and it would be believable, too.'

'The only snag is,' Monica said, 'that *you* would have to write it.'

'Who are you kidding?' Martha jumped off the gate. 'There's Auntie going to put the baby chicks to bed. I'm just crazy about that old hen and these chicks.'

She ran away down the yard, and through narrowed eyes Monica watched her go.

'There goes a highly individual attitude to literature,' I said.

'Highly,' said Monica.

She then slid from the gate and walked away from me into the house.

The days were full of little incidents like this. In the main people worked or sat around in groups of three or four, the women attending to the household duties, the younger men occupied with the wiring, the older men coalescing naturally into a group of their own, but in the evenings, when these groups shifted or merged, I noticed that Monica would sit with or go for a walk with any one member of the Reachfar community except myself. During the working part of the day, too, I noticed, the natural trend of the housework was to leave me in the kitchen with my aunt while Monica and Martha made beds and attended to other parts of the house, and Monica made sure that she and I were never alone together.

My family, an observer would say (and the observer would be quite right), are simply sons and daughters of the soil, but a thing that I have noticed about simple sons and daughters of the soil is that they are amazingly and awkwardly perceptive and can arrange to make you aware of what they perceive without recourse to the use of words. My aunt and, in a slightly less virulent degree, my father were bending upon me looks that mingled contemplation and suspicion and were obviously reverting to the opinion that at Ballydendran I had been 'bad to' Monica. The air daily seemed to me to become more dense with their disapproval and displeasure, until I decided that the only thing to do was what, mentally, I refer to as 'bringing up the heavies', which is my private description for taking the advice of my Uncle George.

My Uncle George holds, and has always held, a curious position in the family. Between him and my father there is only about a year of age, but most people who know the Sandisons will tell you of Duncan Sandison — or 'Reachfar' as he is frequently called — and having described this man and his croft in some detail, they will probably tell you that he has a daughter 'down in the south' or that his widowed sister keeps the house of Reachfar or some other little thing and then they will add, very much as an unimportant afterthought: 'Oh, aye, and there's a younger brother, George, that gives him a bit hand about the place.' To all appearances George has always been the satellite of my father, the devoted follower of my father, a nice, kindly fellow enough and very comical when he feels like it, but 'not the man that Reachfar is, och, no!' This is, however, precisely where people who think they know the Sandisons are quite wrong. George is the devoted brother of my father, but he is no satellite of anyone, no mere shadow of another man's thought and will. He is a highly original thinker and a keen observer who chooses to screen the originality and the keenness behind a mask of clownish foolery. People who 'know' the Sandisons would be amazed to know, as the Sandisons know, that George, in many ways, has a hundred times the intelligence and sharpness of wit of the big brother of whom he has always been the devoted 'second string' and admirer.

My uncle differs from my father and my aunt — and, indeed, from most people — in that he thinks but gives no judgments, observes but passes few opinions, and believes so firmly and absolutely in the human right of freewill and self-determination that it is easier, on the whole, to draw blood from a stone than to obtain advice from him, so I was very gratified one morning at breakfast when he said: 'You wouldna care for a right good long walk the-day, Janet?'

In his eyes there was the look of ancient mischief that had often been there when I was a child when he was speaking to me in front of the rest of the family and contriving to convey a message that was private to us two.

'I might,' I said, showing no undue enthusiasm. 'Where to?'

'Up over the moor to Greycairn.'

'That's fourteen miles before you get back! Are you daft?' my aunt asked. 'Janet can't walk like that nowadays.'

'Ach, if a poor old done craitur like me can do it,' said my vigorous straight-backed uncle, 'I thought maybe she would manage if we took our time.'

'I'd like it fine, George,' I said. 'I haven't been up to Greycairn for years. What are we going for?'

'To buy a few lambs,' said my father and turned to George. 'And tell Johnnie that if they're not down here within a week he can keep them. If there's a lazier man alive than young Johnnie Greycairn, I've yet to come across him.'

'If Janet comes up, we'll bring the lambs home with us,' George said.

We walked the rough six-odd miles to Greycairn through the bright sunshine where the larks rose singing round us, in an atmosphere that was intimate, on the surface, as that between two chance travellers in a railway carriage but which, in its depths, had the strange intimacy of blood and family mind. Monica's name had not been mentioned, but I had come to know before we were the first hundred yards on our way that George and I were out here alone on the moor because of Monica and that, now, all I had to do was to await his chosen moment. It came when we were about two miles back on the way to Reachfar, with the flock of lambs, attended by Moss and Fly, spread in a white mass in front of us. He gave a long whistle on a falling note and the two collies went wide of the flock and lay down among the heather and tussocky grass and the white mass lost urgency as the lambs began to nibble at the pasture. George sat down on a convenient boulder and took out his pipe.

'Aye, a bonnie enough few lambs,' he said and looked away to the hump of Ben Wyvis in the western distance. 'Janet, I'm sorry for that lassie Monica.'

I said nothing, and for a moment the silence was broken only by the nibbling of the lambs at the grass.

'Your father and Kate,' he continued, clearing the ground, 'will have it that you and Twice did something to her that time before she was sick, but that's chust an idea they've got and it's nothing like that that's wrong with her. The thing that is wrong is something in herself . . . I heard a song on the wireless once — ye hear a wonderful amount of foolishness on the wireless one way and another although it's a fine entertainment in the wintertime. I thought at the time that this song was chust about the foolishest thing I had ever heard, but now I'm not so sure.' He paused to light his pipe and after he had burned three matches down to his fingers he went on: 'Aye. This song was called "Poor Little Rich Girl". Aye. I can kind of understand it. I wouldna get the same pleasure out of taking that puckle lambs home if it didna matter one way or the other if we had them at Reachfar or not. But the wintering for them is there and we have to use it. But with Monica it is not chust the money alone. The money would be nothing to worry about if she was foolish, like so many folk that have too much money. If she was like that daft ould craitur over at Dunlochy that spends a fortune on her home for stray cats. But Monica has more brains than to be content with a puckle cats. Or if she had been born with a face like a turnip lanthorn, it would have been an interest for her to be going to beauty parlours as they will be calling them and be dressing herself fancy and all the like o' that. But Monica is held all ways — with the money and the brains and the looks an' a-all. Aye. I am sorry for her. It is a pity that she isna married with a clan of bairns round her feet.'

'Poor little rich girl again, George,' I said, making my first comment. 'She has been surrounded by a rabble of admirers ever since I have known her. Look at Jim Garvin now. It is like that with every man who lays eyes on her.'

With narrowed eyes George stared at the hump of the distant ben.

'All except Twice, I suppose,' he said quietly.

My breath left me so suddenly that it was as if my thorax had collapsed. 'Whatever do you mean?' I managed to ask.

'Ach, nothing much. It was chust a notion I got that last time I was down at Crookmill. Of course, I never thought to mention it to anybody until now.' This was his method of indicating that his 'notion' had not occurred to my father or my aunt. 'But that is chust a caper that took her, that nonsense that she had about Twice, and you shouldna be holding it against her.'

'I'm not!' I snapped shortly. 'It's *she* who's holding it against *me*!'

'I'm not surprised,' he said calmly. 'She is awful fond of you, Janet, and she is terrible ashamed of herself. As long as you are not holding it against her, then, you'll have to speak to her and put things right.'

I felt angry suddenly. 'Speak to her!' I said. 'I can't get within miles of her!'

'Aye. So I've noticed. We'll have to see about that. She's terrible fond of you, Janet, and the best of us goes wrong and does foolish things whiles. You'll not be wicked to her?'

My anger became tinged with almost tearful self-pity. I felt that I was being 'put upon', badgered and generally misused by everyone in this situation with all these accusations of being 'bad to Monica', 'being wicked to Monica' and 'not understanding Monica'. In mental muddles of this sort I do not think in the heroic verse of the Shakespearian soliloquy. Not me. My mind explodes like an erupting volcano and throws up smoke, flames and boulders and lava in the form of a series of disjointed petty curses and slang phrases: 'God dammit! Wicked? Who's wicked to whom? What have *I* done? Did I chase Twice round Birmingham in a pink satin —'

'Listen, George,' I said, pushing a large bung I have for the purpose into the crater of the volcano inside me. 'I think everybody has an exaggerated idea of my importance to Monica. What I think or feel doesn't matter a tinker's cuss to

211

Monica. It never has. Why should it? In her life I am very small fry. I liked *her*, of course. For me, she had all the glamour and strangeness of another world. She had all the brains and beauty I didn't have myself. But I have nothing to give *her*. It was just one of these war situations, our friendship. She was out of her own world and amused herself exploring my world for a bit. I agree that there's something wrong with her just now, but I don't think it turns on *me*, as you all seem to think.'

'You are wrong, you know, Janet.'

'Oh, for heaven's sake, let's take these lambs home!'

'You'll think about this, though?'

'Oh, I'll think about it!' I snapped and told myself that I was sick with thinking about it already.

George rose, whistled to the dogs, and the flock gathered in and began to move ahead and we followed them in silence over the moor until we came within sight of the gate above the house where Monica and Martha were sitting on the stile and chatting to two men with guns over their arms. George whistled to the dogs again and the flock stopped moving and began to drink at the pond. 'You can be a thrawn brat,' he said quietly. 'I know that what she did on you is hard to get over, but she did not mean it. And you and your talk about your world and hers. That's a big part of what's wrong with the craitur — she *has* no world of her own. Janet, when you get the chance, when things are quieter here, you have to try and help her. Mind that, now.'

I stared at him sulkily and defiantly. 'Who are the two blokes at the gate?' I asked.

'You'll think on what I've said, Janet?'

I looked into his grizzled, ruddy face. 'Yes. I will,' I agreed. He looked down towards the gate. 'That's young Sir Torquil and young Alasdair, the doctor. They were up in the west fishing, but they must be back. They come round for a shot now and again when they have the time.'

'Young Sir Torquil' was a man of about my own age, but I had never seen a great deal of him since my childhood, for I had been away from home and he had spent his life in the Army until he came home to take over the estate from his ageing father. I remembered, now, that the estate was not much of an inheritance, although when I was a child his father and mother had lived in the 'Big House of Poyntdale' and had been for me almost legendary figures of power, grandeur and beauty. When I was very small my father had been grieve to the old Sir Torquil, managing the home farm and helping to administer the large estate that lay to the north of us, and Lady Lydia, who was the daughter of an English duke, had had for me an unspeakable glamour, with her 'English' voice, her ash-blonde hair that was so unlike the local dark or red hair and her dainty elegance of dress, especially on summer Sundays at church, when her weekday tweeds gave way to pastel chiffons, large beflowered hats and long white gloves with many small buttons. Those days were gone. This 'young' Sir Torquil had inherited only the cumbersome big house, its gardens and home farm, and was hard-pressed, I had heard, to hold even this together.

As I walked towards the group at the gate, with the flock of lambs rippling between us and them, I had a sudden nostalgia for the simple, well-ordered days of my childhood. I wished that I were eight years old again, and that the old Sir Torquil and Lady Lydia were standing there, for it had all been so natural and so easy to make my small curtsey of deference to rank before going on to answer the questions of my good, kindly neighbours as to my progress at school and the growth of my flock of ducklings.

'Going through with them, George?' Sir Torquil called to my uncle over the white backs of the lambs.

'Aye, Sir Torquil!' he called back and the two young men opened the gate.

'Say, these ain't *lambs*!' said Martha in a disappointed voice. 'I been waiting here at this gate ever since lunch to see lambs come in and all that comes is these darned great *sheep*!'

There was a sudden burst of laughter as George followed the flock down the yard to the gate to the Little Fieldie that my father was holding open.

'They are sheep now, Martha,' I told her.

'Who are you telling? You said *lambs* this morning!'

'They were lambs as long as they stayed at Johnnie Greycairn's, where they were born last spring, but from now on we'll be referring to them as sheep.'

Martha stared at me belligerently. 'Are you trying to tell *me* that these — these animals turned into sheep on the way home?'

'Psychologically, yes.'

'Psychology, phooey! I don't go anywheres on psychology! For *me* psychology is —'

'Strickly for the birds?' Monica put in helpfully.

'You said it!' said Martha, jumping down from her seat on the stile. 'Lambs is lambs and sheep is sheep, that's what. I'm going in to help Auntie with the tea.'

She ran down the yard, and as I shook hands with Sir Torquil and Alasdair I saw Monica walk slowly away down the yard after her. My father came up towards us at the gate.

'Good day, Reachfar,' Sir Torquil said. 'Big doings here these days. Your lights will soon be in, I see.'

'Aye, Sir Torquil, lad. We're moving with the times. Get a shot the-day, Alasdair?'

They patted their game bags. 'A brace or two. We'll come down and leave a few at the house.'

'Kate'll be pleased. Come down to the house for a droppie tea whatever ... You've never met my son-in-law, Sir Torquil?'

The two ends of Scotland seemed to meet when Sir Torquil and Twice shook hands at the barn door, for they are both truly of their country, yet diametrically opposed in physical type. Sir Torquil is tall and rangy, with reddish-fair skin, hazel eyes and dark hair on a long head, although his moustache shows a glint of sandy red. Twice is stocky and compact, with a tanned skin, blue eyes and darkish brown hair on a round head above his thick neck.

At tea the talk ranged round the miracle of 'the lights coming in', which was my family's main interest, and at one point Sir Torquil said wistfully that he hoped to be able to make an installation at his farm the next year.

'What lighting have you now?' Twice asked.

'An old engine that my father installed at the big house about thirty years ago. I moved it to the farm when I closed the house, but it hardly ever works and I've given up spending money on it. There's not much wrong with it except age, but I'm such a fool with engines.'

'Could I have a look?' Twice asked.

'I'd be delighted.'

Twice drove down to Poyntdale the next morning, had his 'look', and the lighting plant, though sadly stricken in years, responded, and Sir Torquil also responded to the explanation he was given of its temperament. This resulted in Sir Torquil and his two children coming back to Reachfar that afternoon to tell us of their miraculous morning. The children had all the charm of their age. Lydia, a skinny hoyden of six years old with untidy pigtails, attached herself to Twice, Matt and Jim as they went on with their wiring job, got thoroughly in their way and talked incessantly, while Torquil, a solemn person aged five, went straight to Monica, laid a hand on her knee and stared up with wonder at her lovely face, speaking no word. As I watched them covertly, I thought that I should have found that silent, round-eyed stare embarrassing and disconcerting, that it would have forced me into speech or action, but not so Monica. Occasionally she would detach her attention from the general conversation to smile at the child, and when she rose to move from one place to another she would cover the hand that lay on her knee with her own hand for a second, but otherwise their communion was a silent one.

'You two get on very well together,' I ventured to say when tea was over.

Monica looked at me without expression and then smiled at the boy.

'The wee master and Monica got on together from the very start,' my aunt said. 'Eh, Torquil?'

'She is my friend,' Torquil said, 'but not sick now.'

'No, she is better now,' my aunt agreed.

'And I can come again to see her?'

'But surely! You can come every day if you like. Isn't that so, Monica?'

'Yes. Every day,' said Monica quietly.

This quietness was new, something which had developed since we came up to Reachfar, and it was something I did not like, something which frightened me, something that I did not understand. It was like the unnatural quiet which precedes a thunderstorm, when even the birds have twittered themselves into an uneasy silence and the trees are still, with only a leaf moving here and there as if flicked by a ghostly, unseen hand. But the fear I felt was only momentary. There was too much going on at Reachfar these days, too strong an ebb and flow of people and events and impressions, so that Monica had too many ways of screening herself for me to get near enough to her to study her. When little Torquil was not attached to her limpet-like, Jim Garvin was taking her for evening walks and drives. When she was not making beds with Martha, she was helping my aunt to make butter or sitting in the barn listening to Tom's and Mattha's yarns of fifty years ago.

I am finding it difficult to reconstruct the happenings of this time in my memory without giving the impression that Monica dominated the scene. Such an impression would be false. It is true that she dominated my own thoughts and I was aware that George was observing her closely, but on the surface she and I were the good friends that we had always been, and among all the coming and going in our small community I think Monica went on her way without anything unusual in her coming to the general notice.

We had all been at Reachfar for four weeks to the day before 'the lights came in'. When I say four weeks, like that, I mean four cycles of from Saturday midnight to Saturday midnight, but this, though the commonly used method of computing time, really means very little. Four of those cycles in the Highlands of Scotland is quite a different thing from four of those cycles in a mass-production factory in the Midlands of England. Time at Reachfar has an Old Testament quality which leads one into phrases like 'and in the fullness of time' or 'at the time of the harvest' or 'in the time of Old Hughie the Molecatcher' or 'at the time when Granda's old Aunt Betsy was a lassie'. Time at Reachfar has the fullness of infinity and

216

is not measured by days, weeks and months, but by events in the lives of the people, and the 'coming in of the lights' was an event which my family was determined to prolong to the utmost and enjoy to the full.

Now that the 'pylon men' were right there within sight of the house, digging their holes, bolting their pylons together and setting them up in their blocks of wet cement, my father, my uncle, Tom and Mattha would walk out each day to 'give them a bit hand with the work'. This consisted mainly in everyone sitting down for a smoke, a yarn and a general exchange of views on everything under the sun. The pylon party consisted of an energetic young foreman who was a native of Perth and four men who had been recruited locally. At first the young foreman did not take easily to the business of sitting down for a smoke, for he could put a cigarette in his mouth and shin up a pylon like a monkey, but after a day or two of the Highland: 'Och, take your ease, lad. What's your hurry?' he fell a victim to the Reachfar concept of time and would pause to discuss football, politics, the weather or the latest gossip about the new people at the shop at Dinchory crossroads with the best of them. At long last, however, the last pylon was up, the last connection was made, the lines and wiring of the house were inspected by a business-like young man who pronounced himself satisfied and went away, having told us that the power would be available at the end of forty-eight hours.

We then got into what Twice and I in private called the 'fiddling with knobs' period. My father, George and Tom now lurked about the house and could not pass a switch without clicking it either up or down, and they turned the main switch on the cooker, twisted the knobs on the cooker itself and pulled in and out the plug of the standard lamp. When my aunt hounded them out of the house they went and fiddled with the switches in the barn and other places, but as soon as they had gone my aunt would push the plug of the electric iron into the socket provided for it, set the iron on the table, turn the switch and stand back and look upon it with pride, her head on one side, as an artist might look upon his canvas. Twice and I seemed to spend most of our time turning switches to the 'off' position.

It had been decided that Tom, as the oldest inhabitant, would switch on the first light, which was to be the main ceiling light in the kitchen. I have already commented on the Reachfar concept of time, and I am now about to comment on the Reachfar concept of space. Yards and miles have nothing to do with distance at Reachfar. If, ten miles away, there lives someone that you like, that person is a 'neighbour' and the distance to his home is 'a wee bittie to the east' — or west, as the case may be. If, a mile away, there lives someone that you do not like, that person is 'that craitur that lives west there Dinchory way' and the distance to his house is 'away west yonder and a devil of a bad road'. As if this were not confusion enough, Reachfar space can be conquered, in time, by a news transmission system which leaves the African bush telegraph — not to mention Reuter or the Post Office system — at a standstill, so it came to be known that 'the lights were coming in' to Reachfar at a certain time on a certain evening, and from three hours before that time and onwards the 'neighbours', in defiance of all normal space and time, began to gather. Long before dusk the whole house and the grass patch in front of the door and most of the farmyard were seething with people, and every flat surface in the kitchen and entrance passage was piled high with baskets of all sorts, containing gifts of food and drink. The neighbours were bent on a party, from Sir Torquil down to Old Hamish the Tinker, who had been made 'respectable by the Government,' and now, instead of roaming the country in a small cart and camping where he could, lived with his wife, Old Cripple Maggie, in a concrete bungalow to which he referred as 'a hoosie wi' a library'. It had taken even the quick-witted Twice a little time to discover that the paper contained in Hamish's library was neither incunabula nor modern books, but a toilet roll ... But that is by the way. What I wished to convey was that the coming in of the lights to Reachfar was like the visit of the coal boat to Achcraggan when I was a child, in that everybody was there.

About an hour before the ceremony was due to take place

Tom was visited by the appalling thought that he might depress the switch and nothing would happen.

'That,' he told Twice quietly in a corner, 'would be making a man look terrible foolish.'

'But I will know whether the light is there or not,' said Twice.

'Will there be a noise or anything?'

'No.'

'All right, lad. I'll trust what you say, but it is a-all very mysterious and is enough to be making a man supersteetious and be believing in witches and MacAbers like the old people would be doing.'

Martha, who is prone to mass suggestion, was almost beside herself, so that she darted about like a small humming-bird, and even the laconic Jim said to me with a quiver in his voice: 'Say, this is the darnedest thing I ever been mixed up in! It's like waiting for a *miracle* to happen!'

It was Monica who replied: 'The thing *is* a miracle, but it takes somebody like Tom to tell you and me, fools that we are, when we are in the presence of a miracle.'

'Gee, you could be right at that,' said Jim.

'I think you should try it now, Tom,' Twice said, coming in from the passage where the fusebox was located.

'Is it there, think ye?' Tom asked, approaching the switch.

'Aye, I think so,' said Twice into the breathless silence that had descended over the crowd of people.

Very slowly and carefully Tom put his fingers on the switch, drew back, looked up at the lamp which hung from the ceiling, took a deep breath and depressed the switch. The room was flooded with light that shone down on the up-turned faces, silent, transfixed, in a wonder that was worship of the truest kind.

'There!' said Tom, looking up at the light, 'isn't that chust beautiful!'

That one phrase seemed to express what everyone felt, and with a sigh of satisfaction the crowd broke into a mass of movement, as people began to go all over the house and steading, switching on lights and switching them off again. Twice and I and one or two of the others were taking no part in this orgy and we went out of the kitchen on to the grass patch by the door for a breath of air in spite of the midges that were dancing in clouds in the dying light. We had been there for some ten minutes when Twice suddenly said: 'Hi, does anybody smell anything?'

'Smell?' we said, and then I looked round and saw clouds of smoke pouring out through the kitchen window.

'Great God!' said Twice and we dashed into the house.

The top of the cooker was a smouldering pyre of sundry scarves, gloves, hats, coats, Flora Mackenzie's shopping-bag, Mrs. Gilchrist's fox fur and Sir Torquil's glengarry bonnet. The fiddlers with knobs had left the cooker with every switch standing at 'Full On'.

'Well,' said Twice, 'there it is. If I've turned off that main switch once today I've turned it off a dozen times.'

'They certainly go the whole hog around here' said Jim. 'They have their miracle and then they go in for a burnt offering.' The words summarised with accurate truth the atmosphere of wonder and gratitude that was abroad that night when the lights came in to Reachfar, making a new bend in the long river of its time.

There had been a tacit, unspoken understanding among us all that the 'coming in of the lights' was to mark the end of our visit, and the next morning at breakfast we visitors gathered in the kitchen to be met with an aspect of my family which was familiar to me and to Twice, although not to the others. My father, my aunt, George and Tom were pursuing a policy of what they called 'taking no notice'. They did not want us to go away, so they were treating the thought of our departure as if it were some childish tantrum, some old man's whim or some latest request on the part of the Government that they should fill in yet another foolish form. Even when Martha, Jim, Matthew and their chauffeur arrived with all their baggage packed in the car, my family ignored the fact that they were booted and spurred for travel and went on with their post-mortem on the party of the evening before.

Mrs. Gilchrist had been extremely angry about the loss of

her fox fur in the cooker conflagration, and my family chose to regard this anger of hers as one last and clinching proof of the basic 'foolishness' of Mrs. Gilchrist. Their attitude, it seemed, was that Mrs. Gilchrist could not in reason expect to be present at the miracle of our lights coming in and at the same time be upset at the loss of a fox fur in the course of the miracle. The fox fur dominated the breakfast table.

'What I canna quite grasp,' said George in his most parliamentary voice, after the Garvins had been more or less forced to sit down and have a cup of tea, 'is why she put *on* the fox fur to come to Reachfar last night. She's never worn it to come here before and it wasn't a cold evening.'

'No, now that ye mention it, George,' my father said weightily, 'that's quite a point that you are making. That's quite right. Always, before, she never wore that fox fur except to the church on a Sunday.'

'Ach!' said my aunt disgustedly. 'She put it on to impress our visitors — what then would she put it on for? The silly craitur! As if Monica and Martha had never seen a fox fur before!'

'And a fine stink it made, too, and it burning,' said Tom thoughtfully. 'Of coorse, they always did tell me that the fox was a terrible beast for the stink.'

At long last, however, the Garvins managed to break through the conversational barrier of the fox fur and announced that they were on their way to John o' Groats.

'Ach, what's your hurry?' — my father.

'You could be waiting for your dinners at least, for Lord knows what the hotels on the road will be giving you!' — my aunt.

'God knows to me why ye should be needing to be going up to that bleak place where there is nothing but a puckle sheep!' — Tom.

'Why not stop here and take a run up on Sunday chust for the day? I might even get a loan of the Laird's kilt and come with you myself' — George.

That almost did it, for Martha, of course, wanted my uncle to come with them right away, not recognising the Highland

221

cunning that did not wish to go anywhere, but merely wished to maintain the *status quo*. Twice broke through this new barrage of discussion and simplified matters for the Garvins by announcing that he, Mattha and I would have to go back to Ballydendran in a day or two, and behind the screen of the resistance set up to this the Garvins and Matthew said their goodbyes and got away, but not before Martha had tears streaming from her bright eyes.

'Och, well,' my father said as the car disappeared as a mere speck on the main road some miles away, 'maybe Monica will stay with us for a whilie.'

Monica looked at him with this strange, new, silent glance of hers and said: 'Maybe, Reachfar.'

There was a lot to do about the house that day, for my aunt is the type of woman who will not rest until the last vestige of an upheaval such as the party of the night before has been cleared away and the house restored to its norm, so all morning Monica and I washed, dried and stacked away the extra glasses, crockery and cutlery that had been in use, while the men, finding the house too busy for comfort, decided they had much to do out of doors and took themselves off with various excuses. In the later afternoon Sir Torquil arrived in the barn with his gun over his arm, and Twice took my uncle's gun from its rack and they both disappeared on to the moor.

'Sir Torquil and Twice get on very well,' I said to Monica over the sink that now held the tea dishes.

'They would, of course,' she said.

'I don't see why,' I countered. 'They've got nothing much in common.'

'Maybe not,' she replied in this new, quiescent way of hers. I hated this passive quiescence which was so foreign to the Monica I had once known.

'Next time I come up here,' I said fiercely as I wrung out the dish-cloth, 'I'm going to bring Loose and Daze to wash the dishes. I'm sick to death of dish-washing, but they don't seem to mind it . . . Come for a walk, Monica!'

'Why?'

'Why not?'

She smiled very faintly. 'Oh, all right.'

We set off north-easterly from the house, over a few arable fields first, and then on to the open slope of the East Moor. I had a tense 'now or never' feeling, as we followed the grass track that was smooth and green from the years of trampling by cattle and sheep, in contrast to the rough brown of the short heather on either side.

'So you are not going to California with Jim Garvin?' I asked bluntly.

'No,' she said.

'He asked you to go, of course?'

'Yes.'

'Poor Jim. I'm sorry.'

'He's young. He'll get over it.'

'He's older than *you*, Monica.'

'Don't pretend to be a fool,' she told me. 'He is an innocent young soul from a raw, young world ... I could be his great-grandmother. Jim Garvin doesn't need *me*.'

I sat down on one of the many boulders that bestrew our infertile Reachfar moors. 'Have a cigarette, my pet, and be taking your ease, as Tom would say ... Monica, why didn't you tell me that you had been ill when you were up here?'

'So they told you?'

'They had to. Don't be foolish. I am *bound* to find out *any*thing that goes on around here.'

'Yes,' she said. 'That's true, I suppose.'

'But *you* should have told me.'

'Why? I didn't think it was of epoch-making interest.'

I do not think that a conversation for any of us consists merely in the words and present thoughts exchanged. I am certain that, for me, conversation is not like this, anyhow, for in my mind no conversation is a straight progression of question and answer, comment and counter-comment, but a jumbled mass of impressions, sidelights, shafts of light and blocks of shadow that come unbidden out of the past to alter and change the significance of the present words that are being spoken. In a nostalgic flash now I thought that there had been a time in Monica's and my life when that word 'epoch' could not have been used between us without evoking a silly but enjoyably companionable giggle.

At one stage during the war a new senior administrative officer was posted to our unit, a long, thin, depressed-looking man who was introduced to Monica and me as 'Wing-Commander Enoch'. When the Commanding Officer had moved away round the mess with him, Monica said: 'Enoch. You would hardly believe it, would you? Why is it that the syllable "och" is so very all right in Scotland and so fantastically wrong in England. It simply isn't in the language, I suppose.'

'It is, you know,' I said. 'Look at "epoch".'

'True — well, this is the epoch of Enoch,' said Monica.

That was the sort of thing that we laughed at.

'I bet you couldn't say that after the fifth whisky,' I said.

'If your mess bill limit will stand the other four each, try me and see!' she challenged, and before the night was out she and I were going around testing the enunciation of the entire mess, including the amazed Enoch of the epoch. I giggled again, now, when she spoke the word 'epoch', but when I said 'The epoch of Enoch' in explanation of the giggle, she merely gave a flickering smile that died away at once into her new, quiescent pensiveness.

'What odd ideas you have!' I said then. 'The fact that you were on the verge of a nervous breakdown like that seems to me to explain a lot that wants explaining.'

'But it doesn't,' she said. 'To say the breakdown explains it would be the easy way, but — it doesn't.'

'Doesn't?'

'No.' Her voice was cold and flat. 'It wasn't a nervous break-down that made me try to break up you and Twice. It was trying to break you up that caused the nervous breakdown.'

'But, Monica — why did you want to — break us up, as you put it?'

'The obvious reason.'

'I don't see it,' I told her. 'You mean, you wanted Twice for yourself?'

'No. Not that.' Her voice was calmly indifferent. 'I wanted

you for myself. He was taking you away from me — as David took Sybbie. I thought that if I could create a situation — before you were married, this was — you would break the thing off. I know how fastidious you are about relationships.'

Without my own volition I had drawn physically apart from her, putting distance between us as much as I could. She looked down at my hand, making me realise that I was pressing my skirt against my thigh. Her mouth twisted a little.

'Don't get me wrong, Janet. Don't pull your skirts aside for the wrong reason. It isn't a Lesbianistic or sexual thing — I am not like that. You ought to know that.' Quietly, she began to cry, slow, painful tears rolling down her cheeks. 'I have it all sorted out in my mind now. But it is all to late. I have destroyed something that I can never rebuild.'

I was suddenly filled with love and pity for her, which seemed to travel in my bloodstream and along my nerves and threatened to burst out through the tips of my fingers.

'Monica, you must tell me. You must tell me all about it, simply, so that I can understand. Tell me right from the beginning. Remember that awful night in late 1939 or early '40 when Garrity and the other one had the fight? And you brought out the Tsar's flask?'

'Yes. That was the beginning. No. The beginning really goes away back before that. Oh, where does anything begin? . . . Janet, do you know something? Something peculiar? I am the wealthiest member of my whole family. Did you know that?'

'No,' I said.

'No. People don't. Naturally they think of Papa being the one.'

She was silent for a little. 'You once told me about your friend Muriel — you said she was "money-funny". I am not like that. At least, I don't think so. But it is easy for people to get money-funny. I'll try to tell you about it. You see, Aunt Harriet, Papa's sister —'

'The one in the painting at Beechwood who is so like you?'

'Yes. That's the one. She was a famous Edwardian beauty — she married an American Jew called Schliemann —'

'Ball-bearings?'

'Yes, and steel and railroads and razor-blades and a million other things. They had no children. I was her favourite niece, because I was so like her in looks. In 1938, when she died, the Schliemann fortune, which had come entirely to her, came to *me*. I was twenty-one. Money really is a funny thing, Janet. Whether it is a little or a lot, it is a funny thing. Funny-peculiar. There is some justification for saying that the love of it is the root of all evil. I don't want to be tedious, but that money spoiled every relationship I had except the one with Mama, and even that was not quite the same. But the worst thing was Sybbie. She and I had been friends — real sister-friends — when we were children — you have no sisters — maybe you don't realise how deep the relationship can go — and Sybbie and I were very close in age. Something happened. I can't explain it. I gave some of the money to Sybbie, but it did no good. The break was there and she simply grew away from me, went off in a different direction — maybe she would have done that, anyway, and I am wrong in saying it was the money. Then she married David, and he is *really* money-funny. I don't think he thinks of anything much else, and Sybbie started getting more and more like him and further and further away from *me*. So the war came and I joined the ranks of the W.A.A.F. Papa had got me some sort of secretaryship or something in one of the ministries, but I quarrelled with the family and went off into the W.A.A.F. I don't think Mama understood it at all, but she wasn't nasty about it. I wanted to get away. I wanted to be in something where everybody was part of a herd, where I would be treated as someone who was no different from anybody else. It worked. The title, even, did not matter — there were lots of titles in the W.A.A.F. — in all the real ways, it did not matter. Then I met *you*.' She paused for a moment, gazing away across the firth at the hump of Ben Wyvis. 'I had the feeling now of being free from the eyes of the family, which was a thing I had wanted, but the life was so *unreal*, so beyond imagination that I could not believe that it was a real way of life or that I was among real people at all. Remember that house where Haggerty and Garrity used to be

226

drunk? The small rooms, the pinched-in-ness of it all? And the lack of solidity? The feeling of instability? If you moved, a hunk of plaster fell down? And there were you, right in the middle of it, solid as a rock, a real person with a mind I could understand and yet as solid as a lump of granite in the middle of all that papier mâché. And you were so kind.'

I? Kind? Kind to Monica Loame? She was going on again.

'And you had your firm, definite standards, and you weren't in the least nervous about applying them, *forcing* them on all these unreal people, with your: "Haggerty, you filthy cow! Don't leave that comb lying there full of hair!" and your "Empty these ashes in the dust-bin — we don't have to make a slum of the place!" and your "Clean that stain off your tunic, Garrity — it's the King's uniform you're wearing, you slattern!" ... Oh, I can remember them all, the things you said. Small things, big things; the standards were there and you fought for them tooth and nail. It made you, for me, the only steady thing in the world. Remember, you know, that my background had cracked on me. I was young enough to have written it all off — family, tradition, Beechwood, everything — as decayed and outworn because it seemed to have let me down. And as you know, I am quite articulate — I told my family in fairly round terms how little use I had for them all ... I came to depend on you more and more, and when the war ended I determined to see where you came from, what had made you what you were. You did not invite me to your home — oh, I know that you thought it had nothing to interest me or to offer me — but I came.' With the tears on her cheeks, she gave a little laugh. 'I had quite an amount of difficulty — especially with Aunt Kate — at first. She couldn't think why I had come to Reachfar and was too polite to ask! But I am not without wit of a sort — I talked about *you* until I had won them round. Before I left, their attitude to *me* was very much like their attitude to you — that I was a member of the younger generation and that maybe they had something they could give me if I wanted it. It gave me a feeling of being loosely protected — that I had a place to run to if things got difficult. It helped me — I went back among my own people, but the feeling of closeness, of being part of a group that would protect me if necessary, wasn't there. They regarded me as an adult, separate entity — and very wealthy, of course — who could dree my ain weird, as Mattha would say. It did not seem to occur to any of them that maybe I was a backward child and not a very good weird-dree-er.' She gave another faint smile at the comical expression and then sighed. 'When I got your letter saying that you were going to be married I had been all round my family — staying with this one and that one — I seemed to be out of touch with all of them — no roots anywhere — you can have no idea of that loneliness, the feeling of being abandoned, cast away, lost. And then I heard that you were marrying, leaving me, dropping out of my world, going to change and go away as Sybbie had done — as if anything on earth or in Heaven could change *you* — just when I had made a plan of you and me doing something together — a business venture of some kind, or some charitable sort of thing that would be worth while, something useful that we could have built up and done together ... I am telling you all this in sequence, as if I were behaving all the time in conformity with some thought-out, complete plan. It wasn't like that. There was no plan. I just had a vague, groping idea that during the war when I was with you, we had been happy together in a healthy, well-met way, and that since the war ended I had missed you and that none of the people I was seeing now could fill the breach and take your place.'

She sighed again, paused for a little and wiped her eyes before she went on: 'I am taking a long time to tell you all this and I am telling it badly, I suppose, but there aren't any words for all the things I want to say. I thought that if I came up here with you this time and told you it all, I could make you understand. Then, when we got here, I became afraid to tell you. I am not trying to apologise — I am only trying to make you understand, that is, as far as I understand it all myself, which isn't very far ... When I came up to Scotland that first time, after I had had your letter telling me that you were going to marry Twice, I came in all good faith — or so I thought — looking forward to seeing the man you were going to marry.

I hadn't seen you for over two years, but during that time, when I was rattling about trying to find my feet, it was as if you had always been with me. At the end of '46, for instance, I got engaged to Sandy Westchester — did you ever meet him at Laura's? — not that it matters — but after a week of it I woke up one morning and thought, "Janet wouldn't do a thing like this. Sandy is a parliamentary bore — Janet would say you were stopping your gap with shabbiness".' She glanced at me, reminding me of the time that I had used that clumsy phrase on an earlier occasion. 'So I broke it off, and there was a fuss with the family and old Ma Westchester cut Papa in Bond Street. The fuss didn't do any good, it only made me think that in the world I had known with *you* these silly fusses never arose, for one never felt like doing the things that led to them ... Anyway, I came up to see Twice and I don't quite know *when* the thing started, but I suddenly got the idea that if I could "shabby up" your relationship with him you would never marry him. So then I got myself into your job at Slaters', and after that I don't know what happened to me, except that Twice would have no part of me at any price and yet I *could* not stop. And I was not in love with him, you know. I *liked* him and I did not want to make him unhappy.' The tears still flowing from the corners of her long eyes, she frowned and shook her head in her effort to comprehend what had motivated her. 'I don't know *what* it was that drove me on. I knew that I would never get him even to touch me, and yet I *had* to go on.' She shuddered suddenly and gripped her hands together. 'It was like a nightmare. All the time, when you were paralysed, one side of me was begging and praying for Twice's sake — as well as for my own — that you would get better and the other side of me was hounding Twice from pillar to post. Then there was the night when you and I were alone in the house and your muscle moved — remember how I lay across your bed and bellowed? And then we sat drinking and yarning? That evening — please, Janet, you've *got* to believe this, anyway — all my thing about Twice fell away. I was clear of it and out into the light for about an hour — and then they all came back and you told Twice about your muscle —'

'I remember. And Twice kissed you —'

'Yes. I cannot explain why, but that is when I went really mad, for it *was* madness, as near as makes no difference. It was because of *you* that he had kissed me — as if — as if — there you were, the two of you, wrapped away and serene and happy in your own world and you had so much between you that you had a kiss to spare even — one for me and one for the dog. I know it is disgusting — but as far as there was any reasoning in it, that was the reasoning. From there I went to what I thought was hatred of both of you and jealousy and a need to take vengeance, to destroy. That is how it was for a long time until it culminated that night at Birmingham . . . It is all a dreary, sordid muddle, Janet. I shouldn't have done any of the things I did, but I did them. It was all wicked and destructive and these things make an outcast of one, but I did them. I went wrong from the first moment when I tried to make a cleavage between you and Twice. There is no point in saying that I am sorry. In the end the destruction turned inwards on myself. From that night when you made the first movement in your leg until I ran away from Birmingham to Reachfar I knew that what I was doing was wicked and wrong, but I would not stop. There is a stage of evil when it gathers its own momentum, like a stone rolling down a hill, and it carries you along with it. I do not remember driving from Birmingham to Reachfar, and I don't know what made me do it . . . It was a bad-taste sort of thing to do — to rush to your home in the circumstances — a sort of final betrayal . . . But I simply woke up one day and found myself here and I did not want to go away. But I'll go now. I wanted to come here with you so that I could try to tell you all this, although it doesn't do any good or undo anything I have done. But I'll go now.'

'No,' I said. 'I don't want you to go. I want you to stay here — for ever, if you like. Why not? Oh, I don't mean literally stay here for ever and ever, but have this place as *yours* because my people regard you as their own.' She had begun to cry again and I let her cry and went on talking. 'You cannot go away from them now and never come back. You have made a place for yourself here and they would miss you if they knew that you were going away for good — and they *would* know, you know. And *you* know what it is like to miss people. You are part of their world now, you and your old power-line! And if you went out of it its foundations would rock . . . That power-line was a magnificent gift, Monica!'

'Magnificent — two hundred pounds!' she sneered.

'Magnificent, I repeat, by Reachfar standards.'

'Oh, of course, the standards,' she said with a faint smile and began to dry her eyes. 'I can never tell you how I feel about what you have said to me — after all that has happened — and I am not going to try, Janet.' She threw the hair back from her face. 'I am all right now. Everything is all right. I have caught up with myself at last.'

She was trembling, and the delicate bones were standing out in her face as they used to do under the harsh arc-lights of the Operations Rooms in the old days of the bombs and rubble, and the greenish shadows were lying now under the long eyes. She looked utterly spent.

'What a hellish fool one can be!' I said suddenly.

'You, as Martha would say, are telling *me?*'

'I don't mean that,' I said. 'I was thinking of Middle Debling and that damnable night they dug us all out in the end.'

'What on earth made you think of that now?'

'Your face reminded me. It's hard to forgive myself. I remember saying: "Loame, take over Collins' sector, she's pooped — to hell with war-weary women!" '

'I don't remember that specifically,' Monica said. 'What happened?'

'Nothing. You took over. We were the only two plotters on our feet when the roof fell in . . . Listen, Monica, you have not been wicked, as you put it, or inhabited by a devil.' I smiled at her. 'You have been very sick and a lot of it is my fault. I was a heller in those Ops. Rooms — I had no imagination . . . I wasn't even human!'

'But you *were* — that was the whole thing of it. You were human, you were a woman and you were completely unafraid. Half the time I was working on *your* strength, not my own.'

'That's what Martha would call a lotta hooey. You can't

231

make a big strong heroine out of me. Bombs were just some- thing that — like My Friend Edna — I preferred not to think about.'

'No. There was more to it than that —'

'Well, I'm not going in for a tissitissint at this stage about it —'

'You mean you are going in for a never-mind-that-now?'

'What's that?'

'What you always say when you are tired of a subject. You used to say it every time anyone —'

'Well, never mind that now,' I said without thinking, and she laughed, the old nonsense laugh from long ago. 'You know what I think.'

'No.'

'I have done a lot of thinking about you this last year or so. So have a lot of other people. They have all done a lot of talking, too, and I've done a lot of listening to them. And now, *you*'ve done a lot of talking and I've done some more listening and I've taken every wit I possess out of my string bag and put them on the table and made them work on you —'

'I,' she interrupted, 'keep my wits in a small roll-top desk I have inside me, in drawers, and when I want to think about money I pull out the one labelled Finance and —'

'Why call it finance and not just money? . . . But never mind that now, we can talk about that another time. What I was saying *was* is that what I think *is* that all the talking and thinking don't get one much forrarder. There are people that you just naturally like and people that you just naturally don't like — like My Friend Muriel, although it took me years to find out that I didn't like her — and once you like a person that person becomes a permanent part of you. It gets built into you, and if the person changes through experience and this and that, you go on trying to understand her, because you like her and the part that's built into you about her just gets bigger and bigger, that's all.'

'*Plus ça change, plus c'est la même chose?*' she suggested.

'I would have said it myself except that you are so rude about my accent,' I said. 'You know what I think?'

'No. And don't keep on saying that and making me feel like a comedian's feed!'

'All right. I think you ought to get married.'

'What a very banal idea! Why?'

'It's this business of being a mere magnet. In every situation you react into sex. Where I would bare my teeth, give a few eldritch yells and fight, you become slumberous and sinuous and dangerous — largely to yourself. That is bound to get you into trouble, and the older you get, the more magnetic you seem to get ... For the kind of person you are, you've been born into the wrong era. For your Aunt Harriet things were simple. She was led to Court, then round the ballrooms and without a low, vulgar word being spoken, she knew what was expected of her and did it. But you, in your era, were allowed to run loose round a world that you didn't begin to understand and you fetch up on a Highland moor crying salt tears. Now me, if I hadn't married, I'd probably have turned into a spirited spinster going round bullying everybody. But not you. You are really a delicate sort of plant that needs a nice, warm greenhouse. *You* are an anachronism — listen, why are all the words that relate to something to do with time either almost impossible to say or so damn-silly-sounding when one says them? Like anachronism and epoch?'

'And aeon and era — and, of course, chronological. Remember how Sergeant Mitchell was always telling us that he couldn't understand 'ow the orficers just seemed to 'ave no idear of puttin' the files back in chron*i*cological order —'

'— so that the perishin' chaos was somethink chronic!' I finished for her, with which we both had a rousing fit of the giggles.

'Listen,' I said, after we had caught our breath, 'let's go back to the house and have a drink!'

Monica rose and shook some thistledown from her skirt. 'Oh, Janet,' she said then, 'I feel wonderful!'

That story I have told happened several years ago, but about six months after the end of the story Monica married Torquil Daviot. He was a widower, and I think she married him, in the

233

first place, more out of love for his small son than for himself, but they are very happy. We see them about once or twice a year, but we have to go to *them*, for they have a houseful of children and seldom leave Poyntdale. But the man who thought out and first said that thing '*Plus ca change, plus c'est la même chose*' was what My Friend Martha would call 'one smart guy' and I will tell you why I say this. We had an unsigned telegram the other day which Twice opened and read aloud: 'Please go Edinburgh urgent send up complete outfit twins this time both boys am very well but flabber hyphen gasted feel am merely mere magnet.'

All I could say was: 'That's from My Friend Monica!'

THE END

MY FRIENDS THE MISS BOYDS
By Jane Duncan

The My Friend books tell the story of Janet Sandison, of her Highland family, and of the fascinating and varied friends who shaped her life.

MY FRIENDS THE MISS BOYDS is the story of her family home, Reachfar, a Ross-shire farm run by her stern grandparents. It tells of life in a Highland Village before the first World War and of the shocked consternation caused when the Miss Boyds, frivolous, men-mad old maids, bring their scandalous behaviour into the community.

This is the first of the My Friend books.

"An enchanting novel. It is a full, rich life that Miss Duncan describes, and her characterisations are sharp and sometimes poignant.'

THE TIMES

'It grows on you uncannily. This is only the first of the happy saga.'

MANCHESTER GUARDIAN

0 552 128740   £2.50

MY FRIEND MURIEL
by Jane Duncan

The My Friend books tell the story of Janet Sandison, of her Highland family, and of the fascinating and varied friends who shaped her life.

Janet Sandison first met My Friend Muriel when, as a brash determined young woman of 20, with a degree from Glasgow University in her pocket, she went South in search of a job. As well as a job she found Muriel, ordinary to the point of oblivion, but who was to prove a catalyst in Janet's life. For it was Muriel — and her slightly shady husband — who suggested Janet should come back to Scotland and work at 'Slaters', and it was at Slaters that Janet met Alexander Alexander, a Scot in whom she had met her match.

This is the second of the My Friend books

'It is beautifully written, full of moving and funny incidents, and highly entertaining.'

JOHN O'LONDON'S

0 552 12875 9   £2.50

THE SUMMER OF THE BARSHINSKEYS
by Diane Pearson

'Although the story of the Barshinskeys, which became our story too, stretched over many summers and winters, that golden time of 1902 was when our strange involved relationship began, when our youthful longing for the exotic took a solid and restless hold upon us . . .'

It is at this enchanted moment that *The Summer of the Barshinskeys* begins. A beautifully told, compelling story that moves from a small Kentish village to London, and from war-torn St Petersburg to a Quaker relief unit in the Volga provinces. It is the unforgettable story of two families, one English, the other Russian, who form a lifetime pattern of friendship, passion, hatred, and love.

'An engrossing saga . . . she evokes rural England at the turn of the century with her sure and skilful touch'
Barbara Taylor Bradford

'The Russian section is reimiscent of Pasternak's *Doctor Zhivago*, horrifying yet hauntingly beautiful'
New York Tribune

0552 12641 1   £2.95

A SCATTERING OF DAISIES
by Susan Sallis

Will Rising had dragged himself from humble beginnings
to his own small tailoring business in Gloucester — and on
the way he'd fallen violently in love with Florence, refined,
delicate, and wanting something better for her children.

March was the eldest girl, the least loved, the plain
unattractive one who, as the family grew, became more and
more the household drudge. But March, a strange,
intelligent, unhappy child, had inherited some of her
mother's dreams. March Rising was determined to break
out of the round of poverty and hard work, to find wealth,
and love, and happiness.

0 552 12375 7   £2.50

HARNESSING PEACOCKS
by Mary Wesley

'Delightful, intelligent entertainment'
Thomas Hinde, Sunday Telegraph

Hebe listens in the darkness of the hall to a family
conference. The stern hypocrisy of her grandfather is
winning the day. He has summoned her three horsey
sisters' successful husbands and they are discussing Hebe's
unexpected pregnancy. The decision, unanimous, is that it
be terminated. Hebe, dissenting, flees into the night.

Twelve summers later she is living happily alone with her
son in a seaside town in Cornwall. He is receiving an
expensive education. Hebe has organised her life oddly but
well. She has two chief talents in life — cooking and
making love — and these she has exercised with dignity, in
privacy and for profit.

It is when the separate strands of the web of Hebe's life
become entangled that the even tenor of her days is
threatened, and her life is changed.

HARNESSING PEACOCKS, Mary Wesley's third novel,
is suffused with freshness, warmth and wit. The author's
delightful literary skills are here fully engaged in a story of
independence, honesty and sensual charm.

'Mary Wesley goes from strength to strength ... She has a
great zest for life ... The book is tremendously lively,
very funny, touching, spirited'
Susan Hill, Good Housekeeping

0 552 99210 0   £3.95

A SELECTED LIST OF FINE NOVELS
AVAILABLE FROM CORGI BOOKS

THE PRICES SHOWN BELOW WERE CORRECT AT THE TIME OF GOING TO PRESS. HOWEVER TRANSWORLD PUBLISHERS RESERVE THE RIGHT TO SHOW NEW RETAIL PRICES ON COVERS WHICH MAY DIFFER FROM THOSE PREVIOUSLY ADVERTISED IN THE TEXT OR ELSEWHERE.

☐ 10757 3	WITCH'S BLOOD	*WILLIAM BLAIN*	£2.50
☐ 12458 3	DANCING IN THE STREET	*CLIFFORD HANLEY*	£2.50
☐ 12455 9	ANOTHER STREET, ANOTHER DANCE		
		CLIFFORD HANLEY	£2.50
☐ 12677 2	THE DEAR GREEN PLACE	*ARCHIE HIND*	£2.50
☐ 07583 3	NO MEAN CITY	*A. McARTHUR & H. KINGSLEY LONG*	£1.95
☐ 08335 6	CUT AND RUN	*BILL McGHEE*	£1.95
☐ 12641 1	THE SUMMER OF THE BARSHINSKEYS		
		DIANE PEARSON	£2.95
☐ 10375 6	CSARDAS	*DIANE PEARSON*	£2.95
☐ 09140 5	SARAH WHITMAN	*DIANE PEARSON*	£2.50
☐ 10271 7	THE MARIGOLD FIELD	*DIANE PEARSON*	£2.50
☐ 10249 0	BRIDE OF TANCRED	*DIANE PEARSON*	£1.75
☐ 12579 2	THE DAFFODILS OF NEWENT	*SUSAN SALLIS*	£1.75
☐ 12375 7	A SCATTERING OF DAISIES	*SUSAN SALLIS*	£2.50
☐ 12880 5	BLUEBELL WINDOWS	*SUSAN SALLIS*	£2.50
☐ 12700 0	LIGHT AND DARK	*MARGARET THOMPSON DAVIS*	£2.95
☐ 99130 9	NOAH'S ARK	*BARBARA TRAPIDO*	£2.95
☐ 99056 6	BROTHER OF THE MORE FAMOUS JACK		
		BARBARA TRAPIDO	£2.50
☐ 99126 0	THE CAMOMILE LAWN	*MARY WESLEY*	£3.50
☐ 99082 5	JUMPING THE QUEUE	*MARY WESLEY*	£1.95
☐ 99210 0	HARNESSING PEACOCKS	*MARY WESLEY*	£3.95

All these books are available at your book shop or newsagent, or can be ordered direct from the publisher. Just tick the titles you want and fill in the form below.

ORDER FORM

TRANSWORLD READER'S SERVICE, 61–63 Uxbridge Road, Ealing, London, W5 5SA.

Please send cheque or postal order, not cash. All cheques and postal orders must be in £ sterling and made payable to Transworld Publishers Ltd.

Please allow cost of book(s) plus the following for postage and packing:

U.K./Republic of Ireland Customers:
Orders in excess of £5: no charge
Orders under £5: add 50p

Overseas Customers:
All orders: add £1.50

NAME (Block Letters) ....

ADDRESS...

....